A Guide to Fake Dating Your Enemy

Nikki Bright

A Guide to Fake Dating Your Enemy

Copyright © 2024 by Nikki Bright

Editing: Main Woods Editing and Happy Ever Author

Cover: Lunatic Covers

All rights reserved.

No part of this book may be reproduced in any form or by any electronic or mechanical means, including information storage and retrieval systems, without written permission from the author, except for the use of brief quotations in a book review.

This is a work of fiction. Names, characters, places, and incidents are either the product of the author's imagination or are used fictitiously. Any resemblance to actual persons, living or dead, or historic events is entirely coincidental.

www.nikkibrightbooks.com

ISBN: 9798306266633

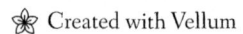

❀ Created with Vellum

Chapter 1

Natalie

Tip #1 for fake dating your enemy: *Hit your enemy/fake romantic partner with a smile. Preferably one that doesn't look like it's causing you physical pain.*

"Before we move on to our next agenda item," I began, trying to keep my tone even, "I'd like to extend our sincerest thanks to Samuel Warner for Warner Print's generous donation to our organization."

I stood at the head of the table, my palms sweating as I addressed the small group of Friends of the Library members. The musty scent of old books permeated the meeting room we occupied, and the faint hum of the ancient heater provided a constant background noise. The worn carpeting beneath my feet had seen better days, and the once-white walls had yellowed with age, but all of it was familiar and soothing. And I needed every source of comfort considering whom I was about to deal with.

I forced a smile in Samuel's direction, though every fiber of my being screamed in protest. (Sure, I didn't like the guy, but I couldn't deny that his company's donation was going to make a real difference for our little library.)

"Thank you, Natalie." Samuel leaned back in his chair, hands clasped behind his head, looking far too casual for an official meeting. "Warner Print is happy to support the Fox Creek Public Library."

Samuel was shockingly out of place among the elderly members of my organization. His tailored suit perfectly fit his athletic body, and his styled dark brown hair managed to walk the line between professional and fashionable—something he needed since he was the CEO of his family's business despite only being a few months away from thirty years old.

"Of course," I continued, gritting my teeth, "Warner Print is welcome to specify how they'd like us to use the funds."

Samuel's eyebrows rose, feigning surprise. "Oh, right. I completely forgot about that part." His gray eyes twinkled as he looked at me, and that charming smile of his made it all too easy to forget what a jerk he could be.

"Really?" I tapped my fingers on the top of the table before giving up and plopping down in my metal folding chair. "You've donated quarterly for the past few years, yet you always seem to forget this little detail." The scents of moldy carpet and stale coffee filled my nostrils as I set my elbows down on the table.

"I apologize for my shortcomings," Samuel said. "I might be the CEO of a company that makes over a billion dollars in revenue every year, and we might be the largest employer in the county, but that's no excuse for not remembering standard protocol for charitable donations."

Humility was not Samuel's strong suit.

"If you're so busy, why are you even here?" I asked. "Isn't this the kind of thing one of your employees-slash-minions could handle?"

"Let's see. Where *would* Warner Print like to see the money used inside the library?" Samuel ignored my question so he could pretend to ponder the issue. "Hmm ... how about we discuss the library's most urgent needs over coffee at a later date, Natalie?" He flashed me another one of his infuriatingly charming smiles.

"Nice try," I drawled. "But I'm way ahead of you. I've already prepared a list of suggestions."

I whipped my phone out. My fingers flew across the screen as I emailed the list to Samuel without missing a beat.

Samuel's expression shifted from surprise to amusement. "Look at you, Miss Efficiency. You even know my email address. I didn't know I was that important to you."

Samuel liked to flirt with me just to upset me. He'd discovered back when we were teenagers that it was the fastest way to annoy me. (Long histories were one of the few drawbacks of living in a small town like Fox Creek.)

"Of course I have your email." I tucked a strand of my wavy ash-brown hair behind my ear and mentally added destressing via yoga to the list of things I'd have to do tonight. "I had to record it so I could have your emails sorted straight into my trash folder."

"OK, OK, we get it already," said Marjorie Mallhoney, the vice president of the Friends of the Library and a force to be reckoned with despite being well into her eighties. "Nat dislikes Samuel, Samuel dislikes Nat, and your families have hated each other and will continue to hate each other until both of your lines die out or you get a *Romeo and Juliet* situation to cry over. Can we move on? I'm missing bingo night at Saint Christopher's for this!" She smacked the table with her giant, ever-present handbag for emphasis.

"I'm sorry, Marjorie, did you feel left out of my flirting?" Samuel asked. "I'll make it up to you now: That dress suits you perfectly. You're the epitome of elegance and grace."

"Save your pretty boy ways for someone who'll appreciate it, Samuel Warner," Marjorie snapped. "And put a sock in it. I don't want to hear another word out of you until you look at the list of possible causes Nat emailed you and decide where Warner Print wants their donation to go."

"Thank you, Marjorie," I said, grateful for her intervention.

She waved her hand dismissively. "You can thank me by hurrying this meeting along. I have a bingo jackpot with my name on it."

I chuckled and glanced at Samuel to see if he was ready to call a temporary truce. He shrugged as if conceding the fight, then pulled out his cell phone, hopefully to start looking at my list.

I sat up straighter in my chair, gathered the paper agenda, and announced, "All right, while Samuel considers the possibilities, let's move on. Our next item is picking the date for the annual winter book sale. Let's get this done so Marjorie can still make it to her bingo night."

Chapter 2

Samuel

Tip #2: *Display memorabilia of you together to the public. (Patience might be a virtue, but passive-aggressive wall art is an art form.)*

I leaned back in my chair, rubbing my temples as I tried to chase away the last remnants of a headache. Outside, fat snowflakes floated through the dark night sky and occasionally spattered the floor-to-ceiling windows of my office.

My Warner Print office was comfortably furnished, if not a little sterile. It had everything I needed to get my work done, which seemed to be all I did lately.

The only decorative piece in my office that gave it any kind of personality was the giant canvas-printed photograph that hung on the wall. It was of Natalie and me shaking hands in front of the new furniture Warner Print had purchased for the Fox Creek Public Library with the first donation my family's company made.

Natalie, with her long, wavy brown hair and expressive green eyes that were easy to get lost in, was a dead ringer for the beautiful girl-next-door type. However, in this photograph she looked like she was ready to eat glass. (When I'd carted the blown-up image to a Friends of the Library meeting and informed her I was hanging it in my office, she'd turned scarlet with anger.)

"Such fun memories," I mused.

I looked over the stack of completed project folders on my desk that I had plowed through that workday. The Warners were notorious workaholics, and I was no exception. I glanced at the clock and rolled my shoulders, shaking off some of my stiffness.

There wouldn't be more than a couple cars left in the underground parking lot by this late hour, and I'd bet they all belonged to members of my family.

"Maybe I should just move in here," I muttered.

It would certainly save me some time commuting, but the idea of never leaving the office didn't exactly thrill me.

A knock on the door interrupted my thoughts. "Come in," I called.

Isaac, my twin brother and the financial genius behind Warner Print's success, entered the room first, with Miguel, my excellent but somewhat bossy executive assistant, right behind him.

Miguel smoothed his meticulously groomed goatee as he eyed me and the stack of folders on my desk. His coat was draped over one arm, signaling he was about to leave for the night.

"Samuel, since you seem to have made it your goal to die

from overwork," Miguel started, "I brought Isaac along to play the angel of death for you."

"Nice of you to join me in purgatory." I raised an eyebrow at Isaac. "But surely you have better things to do?"

"Unfortunately, no." Isaac adjusted his glasses, which gave him a distinguished air that suited his role as chief financial officer. "My evening is just as thrilling as yours."

Although Isaac and I were identical twins and although we both were almost always stuffed into suits tailored to our matching heights and builds, Isaac exuded an intelligence I couldn't have copied no matter how hard I tried.

"You both need hobbies," Miguel said, his voice sharp. "Something to pry you away from this place at a decent hour."

"Your advice is noted." I mock saluted him. "Now go home to your husband and let us workaholics continue our descent into madness."

"Fine, but don't say I didn't warn you." Miguel gave us a knowing look before leaving, closing the door behind him.

Isaac sat down in the comfy armchair positioned in front of my desk. "Speaking of work, I've identified some new risks that will require changes to next quarter's cash flow management."

I groaned. "Seriously? I thought we'd finished all the financial talk for today."

"Apparently not," Isaac said, a hint of amusement in his voice. "But we can discuss it tomorrow if you prefer."

"Tomorrow it is," I agreed, relieved. Then, noticing the slight frown on Isaac's face, I asked, "What's wrong?"

"Nothing." Isaac narrowed his eyes—gray, just like mine. "I was merely wondering how the meeting with the Fox Creek Friends of the Library went last night."

"Ah, yes." I sighed, recalling the tense atmosphere at the meeting. "It went about as well as I could hope for, given the circumstances."

"Meaning?"

"Meaning"—I leaned back in my chair and crossed my legs at the ankles—"despite publicly thanking Warner Print, any progress made was purely superficial."

"Sounds delightful," Isaac deadpanned.

"Natalie Mann's dislike of me continues." I drummed my fingers on my desk. "It is annoyingly inconvenient."

"Obviously," Isaac said. "Expanding Warner Print and increasing development in Fox Creek would be a walk in the park if the Manns weren't so determined to preserve Fox Creek, historically speaking. Instead, we've been at odds since moving here."

The Manns, entrenched in Fox Creek's history and community, were stubbornly opposed to the industrial growth and development we Warners would like to see. The families butted heads on everything from deciding which historic buildings should be saved to deciding how the city needed to expand. Our families had never gotten along, and things had heated up as my generation joined the fight.

"Apparently, a quarter century isn't long enough for Fox Creek residents to consider us locals," I joked.

"Changing their minds might require another twenty-five years," Isaac said, clearly not amused.

I sighed and ran a hand through my dark brown hair. "Regardless. Natalie is still just as closed off as she was before we started donating to the library, which means my plan is failing."

"And?" Isaac asked.

"Do you have any advice or clever ideas to offer?" I tapped my fingers on the top of my wooden desk, some of my aggravation surfacing.

Isaac scoffed. "Sam, I'm the CFO because I like numbers,

not people. I leave interpersonal matters and emotional scheming to you."

"It's not scheming. Or at least it's not *good* scheming or it would have worked by now." I groaned.

Natalie was a notorious champion of the Fox Creek Public Library. I'd thought the donations would be sure to win her over, or at least make her less suspicious of my actions.

"Don't worry too much about it," Isaac said, his tone more sympathetic. He knew the years of effort I'd expended on Natalie and her stubbornness.

"Easy for you to say." I reluctantly stood, pushing my desk chair back. "But if I want to make any progress on my plans, I need the opportunity to act. Natalie, unfortunately, won't give me an opening."

"Then wait for the right time," Isaac said. "She'll have a moment of weakness. It's inevitable. That will be when you strike."

"I hope so." I glanced at the canvas print of my triumphant grin and Natalie's poorly disguised grimace. "But patience hasn't done much for me over all these years."

"You could take a class," Isaac wryly offered. "The internet is a wonderful place. Surely someone has a seminar or online masterclass on learning how to efficiently communicate with and win over your lifelong rival."

I rolled my eyes. "You better stick to numbers, Isaac. You're terrible at life advice."

Isaac stood up with a smirk. "You were the one who asked me. I'm just telling you what I think."

"Yeah, that was my mistake. Don't worry, it won't happen again," I said. "Come on, let's finally call it a night and head home."

Chapter 3

Natalie

Tip #3: *Before fake dating your enemy, confirm they're your least-worst option. You want to avoid hitting rock bottom unless absolutely necessary.*

The air was thick with the scent of buttery popcorn and enthusiasm as I stepped into the bustling high school gymnasium. The Fox Creek Players had just wrapped up their performance of *Romeo and Juliet*, and the small reception afterward was in full swing.

Laughter mingled with animated conversations as the attendees milled around, sipping orange soda from paper cups and munching on pretzels and popcorn. The worn wooden floorboards creaked beneath my feet, a nostalgic reminder of my own school days.

I stood on my tiptoes, struggling to see through the crowd.

Some of the guests were chatting with the actors, who still wore their elaborate period costumes, but it wasn't long before I spotted my brother Owen, still in his hospital scrubs, manning the raffle table. (The raffle proceeds would be going to our local hospital, where he worked as a nurse.)

"Owen!" I wove my way through the crowd and almost rammed the table. "Sorry I'm late!"

"Ah, there's the city's henchman," he teased, offering me a warm smile that reached his tired eyes.

"You joke about that, but one of the Fox Creek town board members cornered me in the auditorium to discuss the agenda for this month's meeting. He didn't like some of the abbreviations I'd used." I wrinkled my nose.

Owen, understanding all too well how intense my role as town clerk could get, chuckled. "That sounds about right. How do you cope with being at everyone's beck and call?"

"Years of practice and a healthy dose of sarcasm." I grinned. "Now, how's this raffle going? Are we raking in the big bucks for the hospital, or what?"

"It's going better than I could've hoped." Owen lifted up a plastic bin that once held cheesy puffs but was now halfway filled with red paper tickets. "I had to upgrade from the glass pickle jar to this just to hold all the tickets!"

"Wow! That's fantastic!" I said, proud of our town's support.

As we chatted, a cute, blond-haired man approached the table, his friendly smile lighting up his face. "Natalie, Owen, good to see you both!"

"Jordan! It's good to see you." I waved to him. "How's your wife doing?"

"Melissa's great, thanks for asking. She's pregnant with our first child!" Jordan beamed with pride. "Expect an invitation to the baby shower in the mail soon."

"Congratulations, Jordan! That's wonderful news," I said.

"Thanks, Nat." He turned his attention to the raffle table and pulled out his wallet. "Now, let me get in on this action. Two raffle tickets, please."

"You got it." Owen tore off two tickets and handed them to Jordan.

Jordan scribbled his name on the tickets before dropping them into the makeshift container.

"Thanks for participating in the raffle, Jordan," Owen said. "It means a lot to the hospital and the community."

Jordan adjusted the brim of his baseball cap. "Of course. Happy to help."

"Tell Melissa I said hi, and I can't wait for the baby shower!" I said as he turned to go.

"Will do, Nat!" He threw me a friendly wave before disappearing into the sea of smiling faces.

As the gym buzzed with conversation, Owen leaned into me. "Didn't you and Jordan have a thing back in the day?"

"Jordan? Yeah, but that was ages ago. We dated briefly when we were in our early twenties," I said. "I'm really happy for him and Melissa. They're such a great couple, and I love them both to death."

I waved at a few familiar faces passing by, and Owen played with one of the raffle tickets. "You know, it's pretty amazing that you've managed to stay friends with all your exes, Nat."

"Ah, well." I shrugged. "It's a necessary skill when you live in a small town like Fox Creek. You never know when you might need a favor—or a raffle ticket—from someone." I playfully elbowed him. "You know that as well as I do."

Some people would say the necessity of playing nice when you lived in a small town was one of the downsides. Personally, I loved it. Needing to get along to make the town thrive was what made Fox Creek so special.

Owen laughed, his green eyes crinkling at the corners. "I suppose I do. Neighborly love is important ..." He trailed off as he stared into the crowd.

I sold four tickets to a mom herding her four kids, who looked like they were on the verge of a sugar rush. (It was probably from the orange soda they'd been guzzling if the spatters of orange on their clothes were anything to go by.)

Owen still seemed distracted, so I craned my neck, trying to see where he was looking. Following his gaze, I realized he was watching Jenna Warner, the cousin of the despised Samuel Warner.

Like Owen, Jenna was also dressed in her scrubs. She must have rushed to the performance straight from work. Her blond hair was tucked back in a neat bun, and she was talking animatedly with one of her friends.

"Jenna looks beautiful tonight, doesn't she?" I asked casually, trying to gauge Owen's reaction. He'd never approached her with anything other than general friendliness birthed between coworkers. However ...

"Yes. She does." Owen immediately turned his attention to sorting the raffle tickets, but I knew my brother too well.

"Do you work directly with Jenna?" I asked, pretending to be only mildly curious.

Owen shook his head. "No, we're in different departments in the hospital. But I run into her pretty frequently."

"Is she nice? She seems really sweet."

"Jenna is very nice," Owen confirmed, smiling softly. "She's always kind and friendly to everyone. It's hard to believe she's a Warner."

"Right?" I agreed. "If I didn't know better, I'd say she was adopted or something." I narrowed my eyes as I pondered this strange juxtaposition in the Warner family tree.

"Street rats," Marjorie called out to us. The beehive her silver hair was fashioned into tilted as she waddled up to our table.

"Hi, Marjorie!" I said. "Are you having fun tonight?"

Marjorie harrumphed. "Can't say I enjoy dramatic romances about silly, sniveling teenagers, but I did think it was funny when Romeo almost fell into the coffin right on top of Juliet." Marjorie hefted her enormous black handbag. "I need two tickets. One for me and one for your grandmother."

"You've got it," Owen said.

"You and Grandma Mann better not go too wild tonight," I warned her, only half joking. (Grandma Mann was a wild card, and Marjorie was a force of nature.) "The Fox Creek Players don't need a couple of rowdy seniors wreaking havoc on their reception."

Marjorie sniffed. "I can't make any promises. I wouldn't want to, anyway. Your grandmother is a hoot when she's outraged."

As Owen handed Marjorie her tickets, he stole another wistful glance at Jenna, who was still chatting with her friend.

I'd suspected for a while now—probably about two years—that Owen had a thing for Jenna, but they hadn't made any progress. Admittedly, the pesky family feud probably hadn't made things easy.

"Thank you for supporting the hospital," Owen said.

"Naturally. You have fun, kids." Marjorie tossed the tickets with her name written on them into the growing pile in the bin. She waggled her handbag at us, then shuffled off into the crowd.

"Owen." I shifted my weight from foot to foot and hoped I was coming off as casually curious. "Would you ever consider asking Jenna out?"

Owen blinked. "Where is this coming from?"

"You seem to get along with her," I said. "So I was just wondering."

Owen's expression didn't change, but his shoulders slumped ever so slightly. "She's lovely, Nat, and I'm sure she'd be fun to date. But it wouldn't be a good idea."

"Really?" I asked, trying to keep my tone light despite the heaviness of the topic. "Why not?"

"Living in a small town ... it's complicated," Owen said. "Like you said before, small-town life makes certain things necessary."

"Like?"

"Like dating people who like your family," Owen said bluntly. "Our families don't exactly get along, and with how important family life is to both of us, it would make things difficult."

I frowned.

Don't get me wrong, I didn't like the Warners—in fact I just about *hated* Samuel Warner—but it seemed ridiculous that something like an old feud could stand in the way of my brother's happiness.

"Maybe we Manns could get over it for your sake," I suggested.

"Maybe our family would." Owen gave me a half-hearted shrug. "But probably not. And even if they did, I wouldn't want Jenna to be subjected to the years of gossip, drama, and potential hurt it would take to finally get through to our families." He turned away from me and called out to a neighbor passing by. "Hey, Mr. Felton! Care to buy some raffle tickets? The proceeds go to the hospital."

As Owen busied himself with selling tickets, I chewed on my lip, lost in thought.

I adored my older brother more than anything. We were

partners in crime for life—why else would I be selling raffle tickets to benefit the hospital on a Wednesday night?

It made me sad that he'd pined after Jenna for so long, but I understood why he was reluctant to make a move. He cared too much to risk causing her any pain.

Still. If you had the right attitude (shameless) it would be possible to convince (threaten) the families to bury the hatchet. But, yeah, I couldn't really see sweet Jenna and my too-caring brother managing it as well as someone with my more outgoing (pushy) personality.

The reception continued for an hour, and the number of tickets in the plastic bin grew. By most accounts the night would have been considered a hit, but every time I caught Owen glancing at Jenna, something twisted in my chest.

It wasn't until half of the play attendees had left the reception that I finally had a moment to think some more about Owen and Jenna.

I half listened to Owen chat with his neighbor Mrs. Thompson as I scanned the crowd, looking for Jenna.

I spotted her chatting with the actress who'd played Juliet. Her smile was as infectious as her laughter. It was no wonder Owen had fallen for her. But was there really no way to help the pair? Probably not when the mere thought of Jenna's cousin—who didn't need to be named—made me want to crumple the dollar bills Owen handed me.

"Here you go, Mrs. Thompson." Owen passed her the purchased raffle tickets. "Thanks for supporting the hospital. Your daughter did a wonderful job as Juliet."

"Yes, she did," I echoed, the dutiful sidekick. "She was a great Juliet."

"Thank you." Mrs. Thompson beamed. "I'll be sure to pass your praise along. She always gets so squirrely before opening night! This time that worked in her favor since *Romeo and Juliet* is such a dramatic love story."

Owen laughed and said something in response, but I didn't hear it as I stared down at the folding table, Mrs. Thompson's words ringing in my brain.

Romeo and Juliet was a dramatic love story.

Owen wouldn't ask Jenna out because of our families. Marjorie had said at the Friends of the Library meeting that only death or a romance like Romeo and Juliet's would ever get the Manns and the Warners to be civil. What if I could manufacture a love story like that?

Owen himself had said that our families would probably get over our disagreements if faced with a Mann-Warner romance. It just would be a bumpy and likely unpleasant ride to get there.

I, however, wouldn't care if I was subjected to gossip and drama. I already dealt with that as the Fox Creek town clerk. The family spats wouldn't be fun, and the thought of having to get along with the Warners made me grit my teeth, but if it was for Owen, I could do it.

Besides, the romance didn't have to be real. It just had to last long enough for Owen to ask Jenna out. Once they were established, I could say farewell to my fake Warner beau with zero regrets and pretend to still be on good terms with him so the families wouldn't restart the fight.

Actually, that would be the easiest part to carry out. I'd done it with all my previous boyfriends, so despite their hatred of the Warners, my family wouldn't have any reason to suspect I hadn't managed to end the fake relationship amicably.

"Who, though, would be my pretend Romeo?" I muttered.

The Warner family tree had a few options, most notably the heirs apparent: Isaac Warner, the company CFO; Logan Warner, Jenna's older brother, who also led Warner Print's legal team; and last and certainly least, Samuel Warner.

But I'd exchanged maybe ten sentences with Isaac since attending high school with him, and he was about as emotional as a rock. And Logan terrified me. (Unlike Samuel, Logan knew when to keep his mouth shut, but with his broad shoulders and the dark, brooding look he always wore, there was something intimidating about him.)

That left me with Samuel.

Ick.

No.

There were two other Warner relatives—Connor and Max, the sons of the only Warner daughter. But they'd left Fox Creek for college and hadn't come back since except for the occasional visit.

"Hey Owen, do you know if Connor and Max Warner have any plans to move back to Fox Creek?" I asked.

Owen blinked in surprise. "Yeah. Jenna told me they're working with other companies to get experience and are planning to eventually transfer back here. But I don't think that'll be for another year or two. Why?"

"No reason." I folded my arms across my chest as I thought some more.

Connor and Max were obviously out. So, within the available options, Samuel was the only real choice.

He and I interacted regularly enough to make it believable that we'd somehow fallen in love. He also had the charm we'd need to convince everyone we were madly in love despite frequently being at each other's throats.

But no matter how much I wanted to fool everyone, I doubted my acting skills were up to pretending to be in love with Samuel, the Warner who had been nothing but a pain in my ass for years.

"I think we can probably start cleaning up," Owen said.

"Looks like they're out of soda and putting away the snacks, so everyone will clear out soon."

"When will you draw for the raffle?" I asked.

"I'll do that tomorrow," Owen said. "Mr. Patel—he directed the play—is coming over to my house to help draw the tickets and contact the winners."

"Sounds good to me. Do you have the lid for the cheesy puffs container?" I asked.

"I think I left it out in my car." Owen ducked around the table and started to walk backward toward a set of double doors. "I'll go run and get it."

"Great! No rush." I grabbed the giant roll of red tickets we'd been using for the raffle and moved to put them in the cardboard box Owen had brought in.

When I looked up, Owen was talking to Jenna, his bright smile washing away all the signs of fatigue he'd previously shown.

He *really* liked Jenna.

And I *really* wanted my brother to be happy.

I sighed, dragging it out so long it ended in a hiss.

I'd have to do some more thinking to see if I could come up with any other idea, but I couldn't see any way around it: I'd be proposing a fake relationship to Samuel. Chances were he'd laugh in my face and publicly tease me for secretly crushing on him. I'd have to form a good argument before I approached him and come up with a bribe to make him interested.

Samuel didn't strike me as the loyal type, except to his precious Warner Print and family. I'd have to go in from that angle. Somehow.

I grimaced as I took the lockbox of money Owen and I had gathered and placed it on top of the tickets. "If I can convince him, these next few months are going to be ugly," I grumbled.

"Not to mention that it's going to kill every ounce of my self-respect!"

Chapter 4

Natalie

Tip #4: *Attempt to explain the how/why of your fake dating plan to your enemy without sounding completely unhinged.*

I nervously clutched my matcha latte and wondered if meeting Samuel at his office would have been a better choice. But then again, that would mean stepping into enemy territory.

Instead, I'd chosen to meet Samuel in the private back room of Literum, a cozy café/bookstore located in one of the handful of historic buildings in downtown Fox Creek.

The giant picture window offered a view of the snow-dusted side street, and the mismatched furniture gave it a sense of charm. A few chairs, a tufted love seat, and a worn coffee table filled the space, while bookshelves lined the walls.

It was private enough for our meeting, but as I sat there, it occurred to me that this might not be the most neutral ground. (The Warners had tried to buy the building over a decade ago with plans to knock it down, a move my family had successfully campaigned against.)

"I never expected you, of all people, to invite me for coffee," drawled an aggravatingly charming voice, drawing me out of my thoughts.

My nemesis entered the room, a few snowflakes dotting the shoulders of his black wool coat and his dark hair slightly mussed from the frigid wind outside. "When Miguel told me, I thought he'd lost it." He shrugged off his coat, revealing a stylish suit that was probably from a fashionable European brand I would never be able to pronounce, much less afford.

"Trust me, Miguel was just as shocked as you when I asked him to pass along the message." I set my latte down on the coffee table in front of my armchair, afraid that if I held it while talking to Samuel, I'd spill it.

The sound of him flopping down onto the faded velvet love seat across from my overstuffed armchair snapped me out of my anxious thoughts. He sat with a casual air, his dark eyes unreadable.

"Did you finally decide to take me up on my offer to discuss donations to the Friends of the Library over coffee?" he asked in that charming tone of his he used to get whatever he wanted, but I could sense an underlying curiosity.

"No," I said. "I want to propose an idea to you."

"An idea?" Samuel raised an eyebrow, surprise flickering across his handsome features. "That's certainly new. Usually when a Mann approaches a Warner, it's with an argument, not an idea. Go on, then. Tell me what you have in mind."

Gathering my courage, I took a deep breath. "I think we—I mean you and I—should ... fake date." The words sounded even more ridiculous aloud than they had in my head, but I pushed forward. "With the goal that it would ease tensions between our families."

Silence. Samuel stared blankly at me, saying nothing. The café background noises filled the void—the clink of cups and saucers and the faint hum of the espresso machine.

I plunged on. "I believe it's time for the Manns and the Warners to overcome their differences. Don't get me wrong, this would be for the sake of Fox Creek," I fibbed. (I'd decided earlier there was no way I was going to reveal Owen's feelings for Jenna. Not only did it feel disloyal, but who knew what Samuel would do with the information?)

Samuel's expression didn't change, his eyes remaining unreadable. It was unnerving—like trying to read a book with half the pages missing. But I refused to let him rattle me.

"It would be temporary," I continued. "Just a couple of months. Long enough for our families to cooperate and see how great things could be when we aren't at odds. Then we can end the fake relationship—amicably."

Samuel's face stayed blank. I nervously twisted a lock of my ash-brown hair around my finger. (I knew I should have put it up today. It was wavy on a good day, but whenever I was stressed out, I swear it frizzed up out of spite.) "You're probably thinking a breakup might reignite the fight between our families, but it doesn't have to. I mean, I've managed to end all my romantic relationships on friendly terms."

My ability to end relationships well aside, it wouldn't be too hard to keep the peace between the Manns and Warners. Hopefully, once Jenna and Owen started dating, they'd seamlessly transition to being the new rallying point for our families.

Samuel shifted in his seat, his eyes never leaving me as he kept his silence. The scent of freshly brewed coffee and the faint smell of books filled the air, mingling in the back of my throat with my growing anxiety.

I racked my brain for the points I'd rehearsed before the meeting. "I think it'll be better for the community if our families get along," I blurted out. "Our petty fights have made Fox Creek settle for stalemates when if we'd worked together the outcome would have been better for everyone. And while I want to do this out of love for our town, I don't expect you to do this for nothing. I can help the Warners ingratiate themselves with the Fox Creek residents. We can improve Warner Print's reputation."

Despite the avalanche of words I'd unleashed, Samuel was *still* silent, his gaze fixed on me as if he could see right through my desperate attempt at subterfuge.

The longer his silence stretched, the more my stress level rose, and I found myself clutching at the arms of my armchair, my fingers pressing into the scratched wood.

"Look," I said. "If you have any other ideas for mending the rift between our families, I'm all ears."

Samuel moved, breaking his stare. He leaned back in the love seat, his face thoughtful for a moment before that teasing smile of his appeared. "Well, Miss Mann," he drawled, "I believe you've presented a creative solution to our admittedly inconvenient war. No need to consider alternatives." His gaze locked on mine again, his eyes full of mischief. "I'm in. Let's fake date."

My jaw dropped. That was it? No arguments, no questions, no conditions? He just agreed?

That was way too easy. I'd prepared for at least fifteen minutes of criticism followed by an hour of strenuous arguing and deal striking.

A seed of suspicion wormed its way into my mind. What ulterior motives could he be hiding?

"Really?" I asked. "Just like that? You're agreeing to this? What's the catch?"

"Would you prefer if I refused your offer?" Samuel smirked, as if he had the upper hand in this. (Which, I suppose he did.) "There's no catch. We both want our families to get along and improve relations in Fox Creek, right? If this is what it takes, then I'm game."

"Right," I slowly drew the word out. Although the idea had been mine, facing Samuel and his handsome, crooked grin, I couldn't help but feel I might have made a mistake.

He caught onto my growing reservations. "We're both adults here, Miss Mann. Surely we can handle a fake relationship for the greater good."

"Yes," I agreed. I hadn't come up with any other ideas to help Owen out, so this was my best plan.

Samuel pulled out his cell phone, tapping away at the screen. "If we want to sell our families on this fake relationship, we'll need a believable backstory."

"I've already considered that." I paused, still a little bothered that he'd accepted my idea so easily, then squared my shoulders. I needed to be focused for this part of the deal. "I think keeping our story simple is best. We should say we recently realized our feelings for each other and all of our bickering was flirting."

Samuel broke into a coughing fit, which weirdly ruined the mold of the perfect image he always presented.

Concerned, I started to stand.

"I'm fine," he got out, waving off my worry as he hacked one last time.

I slowly sank back into my seat, settling back into the puffy cushion of my armchair. "Are you sure?"

"Just fine," he repeated. He cleared his throat, shook his head, and then his ever-confident smile/smirk was back. "Does your suggestion mean all those times you called me insufferable and the most arrogant person in Fox Creek, you were actually flirting with me?"

"Sure," I agreed, not rising to his bait. "Just like you were flirting with me when you called me nosy and overly invested in Fox Creek."

Samuel cocked his head as he studied his phone screen—I realized with some surprise he was taking notes. At least he was serious about this crazy plot of mine.

"We certainly are a unique couple," Samuel said.

"Fake couple," I corrected him.

Samuel ignored me. "But while I agree that a recent realization of our feelings makes for a believable explanation for our newfound closeness, what if we say we started dating in secret several months ago instead?"

I narrowed my eyes. "Why?"

Before Samuel could respond, Lauren, Literum's owner, swept into the back room, bringing with her the rich aroma of freshly brewed coffee.

She set a white cup and saucer down in front of Samuel. "Here's that Americano you ordered, Samuel," she said, giving us a once-over. "You two are an unlikely duo I never thought I'd see in my store."

Samuel flashed his dazzling smile. "I've finally worn Natalie down, and she agreed to have coffee with me."

Lauren looked at me skeptically and fluffed her hair—a pretty shade of gold in a pixie cut that she made fashionable when it would have looked stupid on me. "Really?"

I laughed, a sound that came out nervous and stretched. "Yeah, he can be quite persuasive."

Internally, I cringed at my poor acting skills. If I wanted to fool our families and friends, I'd have to step up my game.

"Alright then. Enjoy your drinks." Lauren gave me a

knowing look, then left, her footsteps echoing as she disappeared into the bustling café/bookstore.

"That was eye-opening," I muttered, flexing my fingers against the plush fabric of the armchair.

Samuel leaned forward, his elbows resting on his knees. "See? That's exactly why we should say we've been dating for a while. If we present our fake relationship as a new development, everyone will think we're crazy and our families will focus on convincing us we're nuts instead of making up."

I picked up my paper to-go cup, and the warmth of my matcha latte seeped through the paper. I took a sip, and the creamy green tea and milk flavors danced on my tongue, soothing my nerves as I mulled over Samuel's suggestion.

He was right. Lauren's skepticism had been warranted, as she knew me quite well. It would be worse with my family, and if we wanted to clear the way for Owen and Jenna, we needed to convince the Manns that they had no choice but to get along with the Warners.

An older relationship would achieve that much faster.

I inhaled the steam from my latte for courage. "You're right."

I braced myself for a smug response.

Samuel—who was in the middle of sipping his Americano—set his drink down and immediately moved on, pushing the plan ahead with a suspicious amount of eagerness. "Good. Then, since we've been a couple for months, we'll need to adopt some habits long-term couples have, like pet names. Naturally, we'll also need to be physically expressive."

"For nicknames we can just call each other Nat and Sam, since that's what our families call us," I said.

Samuel idly tapped his phone screen. "You know my family calls me Sam?"

"Of course I do," I said, a little irritated. "We might not get along, but I've seen you almost every week of my life."

"True." Samuel gave me a more thoughtful look that made me shift in my comfy seat. "I guess I just didn't expect you to pay attention to details about me."

"Oh," I said.

I suppose since the two of us rarely did anything besides bicker, I'd never given him a reason to believe I saw him as anything more than a picture I tacked to a dartboard to take out my aggression on.

"Alright, so we've got our pet names down," Samuel said. "Now to address the physical aspect of our relationship."

"Yeah. About that." I took another sip of my latte, then set it back down on the coffee table. "We'll have to stick to hugs and occasional hand-holding."

"What?" Samuel sat on the edge of his love seat. "What kind of serious couple only hugs and holds hands? We should at least be prepared for short kisses."

"Kisses?" I cackled. "I don't think I could believably kiss you without looking like I want to wipe that smug smile off your handsome face."

Samuel playfully tilted his head. "I'm flattered you think I'm handsome, Nat. Don't worry—I promise not to let it go to my head."

"Focus, Samuel. Focus," I said.

Samuel relaxed and once again leaned back against the couch. "Of course, you want to stick to business. Fine, we can *start* with hugs and hand-holding."

"Occasional hand-holding," I corrected.

"If either one of us thinks our act isn't convincing enough, we'll revisit the physical touch aspect." Samuel typed out his notes on his cell phone. "Does that make you happy?"

"Yes," I reluctantly agreed. "We'll probably have to adjust as we go anyway. Could you email me your notes?"

"I'll do you one better and text them," he said. "What's your number?"

I internally weighed the pros and cons of giving him my number. Knowing Samuel, he'd start texting me in the middle of the night, asking me what the process was to submit construction permits, just to be annoying.

"Nat, darling, honey," Samuel cooed. "What kind of serious boyfriend would I be if I didn't have your number?"

Oh yeah. He was definitely going to send me annoying text messages.

I reluctantly gave it to him and retrieved my phone from my canvas backpack. (When I first graduated from college and joined the workforce I'd insisted on getting a handbag to carry my things in since it looked professional. But now, as I was roughly a year away from thirty and forced to visit the chiropractor like she was my best friend since I sat at my desk so long, I was forgoing professionalism for better posture.)

When my phone chirped with his incoming text message, I added him to my contacts. "I'm going to have to tell Owen the truth about us," I said. "He'd never believe it otherwise, even if you went to Juilliard for acting classes."

"That's fine. I'll need to tell Miguel the truth," Samuel said. "Since he's responsible for my work schedule, he'd know our dating timeline couldn't exist."

"Sounds good. I trust Miguel," I agreed.

"Really?" Samuel asked. "Even though he works for Warner Print?"

"Yeah," I said. "His husband, Kyle, is my second cousin."

"Of course he is," he rolled his eyes. "You Manns are related to half the town."

I ignored him and eyed my phone's clock. "We need to plan

a hard launch for our relationship, but can we do that over email? My lunch break ends in ten minutes."

"Sure," Samuel said. "Don't worry, it will be easy."

I stared at him. "Easy? This is going to be anything *but* easy."

He shook his head. "Nonsense, Nat. We're a match made in heaven—or rather, a match made in Fox Creek."

"We have to be convincing," I said.

"Piece of cake." He shrugged, his confidence unshakable. "After all, who wouldn't believe that the charming Samuel Warner has finally won over the heart of the lovely Natalie Mann?"

Instead of being annoyed by his confidence and ridiculous charm, I actually found it comforting. He needed to be confident or my family would eat him alive.

Chapter 5

Samuel

Tip #5: *Keep your plans subtle. If your fake partner finds out you're scheming on the side, they could label you a "villain in a suit."*

A smirk played on my lips as I swirled a glass of bourbon, the ice clinking with each movement. The rich aroma of the liquor wafted up as I leaned back into the comfortable embrace of my ergonomic computer chair and once again looked at the night sky out the giant windows in my office.

This. This is what victory tasted like.

"Still celebrating your victory with Natalie Mann's fake relationship proposal?" Miguel's voice cut through the silence as he sauntered into my office, his terra-cotta–colored skin a healthy tone despite the ghostly lighting of my office.

"You know me too well." I lifted the glass to my lips and took a slow, deliberate sip. The smoky warmth of the bourbon slid down my throat, igniting a fire in my chest. "I do love to savor my successes."

"Years of planning, and now everything is falling into place." Miguel slid his hands into the pockets of his trousers. "She's letting you get closer, which is exactly the chance you've needed."

"Exactly." I set my glass of bourbon down on the polished wooden surface of my desk. The thrill of anticipation coursed through me, mingling with the lingering warmth of the liquor, which felt almost as intoxicating as my growing satisfaction.

"Finally," I said. "I have Natalie exactly where I've wanted her."

Miguel furrowed his brow. "Although are you sure you're not celebrating too early? You've had a breakthrough, and I don't doubt your abilities, but you're dealing with *Natalie Mann*."

"Relax." I stood up and prowled up to my executive assistant. "I know what's at stake here, and I'll do whatever it takes to come out on top."

Miguel clenched his jaw. "Even if it means playing dirty?"

"Especially if it means playing dirty," I said. It wasn't like I hadn't bent the rules before, although never quite like this.

Miguel smoothed out his suit jacket. "Don't say I didn't warn you."

"Wouldn't dream of it." I grinned and clasped his shoulder. "Thanks for having my back."

"Always." Miguel nodded to me before he made his way to the hallway, closing the door to my office behind him.

I wandered back over to my desk and raised my drink. I studied the golden liquid, then raised the glass in a lone toast. "Here's to you, Natalie. May the best man win—no matter what it takes."

Chapter 6

Natalie

Tip #6: *Inform at least one trustworthy outsider of your plan. You might need their testimony should your enemy test your patience one too many times.*

I needed to tell Owen about my plan. He knew me way too well to buy the lie that I could actually stand Samuel Warner, much less date him.

That was how I found myself awake at the butt crack of dawn and very unhappy about it.

I shivered as I climbed out of my hatchback, the frigid January air biting at my exposed skin. Glancing at my watch, I groaned. 6:38 a.m., way too early for any sane person to be tromping around a park. Especially on a Saturday morning.

Grumbling under my breath, I crossed the icy parking lot,

my boots crunching on brittle bits of ice. Our cars were the only ones in the parking lot, which was nice because it meant I wouldn't have to be paranoid about anyone overhearing us on this morning hike through the park—which was almost three hundred acres. (Visiting the park required a county park pass, and there were two dog runs and a few fields that could be used by sport teams in addition to all the different hiking trails.)

The scent of pine trees hung heavy in the air as I approached Owen, who was disgustingly chipper for this ungodly hour.

"Natalie, you made it! Ready to hit the trail?" He grinned, brandishing a large flashlight.

I grunted an acknowledgment, pulling my white pom-pom beanie out of my coat and cramming it over my unruly ash-brown hair.

"We'll go on the yellow path today." Owen started down a hiking trail that went straight into the dark forest of bare deciduous trees and evergreens. "It should give us a great view of the sunrise, but we'll have to use my flashlight until then."

"You know you're a complete psychopath for getting up this early on a weekend, right?" I asked, half teasing, half serious.

Owen chuckled, unfazed. "The early hour helps me keep my sleep schedule on track for my early shifts at the hospital. Normally I'd snowshoe or cross-country ski, but we don't have quite enough snow for either of those right now. But that's alright, there are lots of positives to winter hiking too!"

I rolled my eyes. Figures.

"Did you hear the newest gossip about the old middle school?" Owen asked.

Fox Creek had built a new middle school several years ago on a new property, leaving the old building empty. Now it was mostly used for after-school programs and the occasional adult education class.

"No," I said. "What about it?"

"Supposedly there's an interested buyer," Owen said.

"Oh."

"You don't sound impressed."

"There's been lots of interested buyers before, and yet it's still for sale years later," I said.

"True."

We were quiet for a few moments, but Owen—ever the morning person—apparently couldn't handle the silence.

"So." He purposely bumped his shoulder into mine, making our thick jackets crinkle. "Why'd you really want to come out here with me? And don't say it's just to hang."

I knew this was going to be difficult. He was too smart.

I pushed past my grogginess and innocently batted my eyes. "What, I can't want some quality sibling-bonding time?"

Owen chuckled as we continued down the path. It was so cold the thin layer of snow on the ground had hardened into a crust, which crunched underneath our boots as we trod along in the darkness. "Please," Owen said. "I know you'd rather eat nails than get up before nine on a Saturday. Fess up, Nat."

I huffed out a frosty breath as we emerged into a meadow, the sky just beginning to turn purple. Pretty soon we'd get the first light of the sun. "Fine. You're right. I need to talk to you about something."

"I'm listening," Owen said as the trail took us back into the shadowy woods, plunging us back into darkness.

Here goes nothing. "Samuel Warner and I are going to pretend to date each other."

I could practically hear Owen's eyebrows shoot up. "Come again? You and Samuel Warner? Fake dating?"

"Yes."

"Why?"

Here was the tricky part. I couldn't tell him it was because I wanted to make it easier for him and Jenna to date. He would insist I stop my profitable plan. So I'd have to slowly lead him into it ...

"I think it's time for the Manns and Warners to end our feud. For the good of Fox Creek. If Samuel and I can play nice, maybe the rest of our families can too," I said.

Owen stared at me.

"I know the Warners and the Manns will probably never see eye to eye on town issues," I nervously continued. "But if we actually learned how to compromise, things might get better." I paused, then added jokingly, "Including my job! As the town clerk, it is such a pain to deal with the constant fighting!"

"Cut the crap, Natalie. That fairy-tale story might work on Mom or Dad but not me. Why are you really doing this?"

"It's all true," I argued.

"Part of it is true," Owen countered. "I'll buy that you think it would be better if we got along, but that doesn't explain a fake relationship with Samuel Warner. Our families bicker, but you actively hate Samuel because of all his meddling in your passion projects, whether it's donating money so he can dictate how the Friends of the Library organization can use the funds or the way he bothers you the day after every town board meeting, requesting meeting minutes and finance records that take half the morning to show him and explain."

"Uh," I awkwardly said. There wasn't anything I could say to counter him, as it was all true.

"If you really wanted to mend the fence with the Warners," Owen relentlessly continued, "you'd be better off working with any Warner besides Samuel since he has a tendency to tease you. So why are you fake dating him?"

I blew out a breath, watching it fog in front of me. How was I going to talk my way out of this one? It looked like I would have to mention Jenna after all.

Glancing up at the brightening sky peeking through the barren branches, I slowly forged on. "Well, you have to admit, it would make things a whole lot easier for you and a certain Warner cousin if our families called a truce. No one would bat an eye if you asked Jenna out."

Owen's steps faltered and he shot me a suspicious look. "Wait a minute. Are you doing all this just because ..." He shook his head in disbelief. "Natalie, please tell me you're not fake dating Samuel Warner so I can date Jenna."

I scoffed, feigning offense. "Wow, you really think I'm that selfless? That I'd willingly subject myself to Samuel's company just for your sake?"

"Yes. Yes, I absolutely do."

It was very inconvenient that he knew me so well.

I threw up my hands in mock exasperation as the hiking trail left the forest to ramble across a hilly area that was reclaimed prairie when it wasn't covered in snow. "Fine, believe what you want. I can see there's no getting through to you." Then, sobering, I caught his arm. "But seriously, Owen, I need you in my corner on this. When Samuel and I go public, it's going to be World War III. Grandma and Grandpa Mann will have a conniption. Our aunts and uncles will lose their minds. I'll be disowned by second cousins twice removed that I didn't even know existed. I need you on my side."

Owen groaned and rubbed his mitten-covered hand on his face. "You've officially lost it. This is, hands down, the dumbest idea you've ever had."

"I'm offended. I think fake dating is pretty tame, all things considered." I pulled my scarf tighter to ward off the chill of the air.

"It might be, except you're fake dating *Samuel Warner!*"

I wisely stayed silent and waited for my brother to process

his feelings. Owen was too loyal to leave me floundering on my own. I hoped.

After some more grumbling, Owen heaved a gusty sigh and clicked off his flashlight as the sun crested the horizon, painting the snowy field in glowing pinks and golds.

"Alright, alright," Owen said. "Against my better judgment, I'll back your act. But when Samuel drives you crazy, I reserve the right to say 'I told you so.'"

"You're the best!" I threw my arms around him in a quick hug I could barely feel thanks to our thick winter coats. "And I can't wait for you to ask Jenna out." I waggled my eyebrows suggestively.

"Oh no you don't." Owen scowled at me. "Don't go stirring up more trouble when you've already got a heaping helping on your plate. Do you really think you can pull this off? Convincingly playing the part of Samuel's doting girlfriend?"

I waved away his concerns. "Piece of cake. I'll just stare dreamily at his irritatingly perfect face and tune out the condescending words coming out of his mouth."

Owen eyed me dubiously as we started up the next hill. "And he agreed to this harebrained scheme of yours? How long did it take to convince him?"

I bit my lip. "Actually, it was weirdly easy to get him on board. I'm still not entirely sure he doesn't have an angle."

"You think he's up to something?"

"With Samuel, who knows?" I shrugged. "As far as I can tell, he could use our relationship to boost his reputation, but besides giving him a leg up in future arguments, I don't think Warner Print would profit from it. Still, I'm keeping my guard up."

Owen smiled wryly. "I'm glad you're being careful. Samuel does like to play with you."

"Yeah, he's too crafty for his own good. And mine."

We reached the crest of another small hill. "I'll say this much," I admitted grudgingly, taking in the stunning dawn vista. "You sure know how to pick a hiking spot. But you're still certifiable for doing this voluntarily. On a weekend, no less."

"If I'm certifiable, you're a sociopath," Owen drawled. "Need I remind you, you're the one in a fake relationship with *Samuel Warner*?"

"Touché." I laughed, falling into step beside him. "So, how much farther does this little nature walk of yours go?"

"A lot longer than you want it to."

I yanked my scarf up higher so it covered my nose. "You're really bossy and opinionated."

"I'm your older brother. It comes with the territory."

Chapter 7

Natalie

Tip #7: *If your fake partner attempts unsanctioned PDA, remind yourself it's for the greater good.*

I took a deep breath as Samuel and I stepped into the lobby of Trinity Church. The Winter Craft Fair stretched out in front of us, bathed in pale sunlight that streamed through the enormous glass ceiling. Families, couples, kids, and grandparents bustled about, their laughter and chatter filling the air.

"Ready for this?" Samuel asked, his eyes searching mine.

"Considering your surprising obsession with details, yeah, I think we're ready." I recalled the many, many emails we'd exchanged before Samuel was satisfied with our fake-relationship launch plan.

Samuel grinned, looking more relaxed than I'd ever seen him in a fitted black zip-up sweater. "My attention to detail is but one of my many qualities that you find charming. Remember?"

I rolled up the sleeves of my soft blue-and-green flannel shirt to my elbows. "Yes, of course. But in order to establish that, we have to show the people, so let's get started."

We strolled up the first row of craft tables, pausing to admire a stand of handmade cards next to a counter filled with tubs of homemade fudge. The scent of chocolate would normally have made me drool, but I was too nervous to be distracted.

"Launching our relationship at the Winter Craft Fair instead of directly facing our families first was a smart move," Samuel said. The praise sounded a little odd since it was coming from him, but I could tell it was genuine.

"Thanks," I said. "I knew the crowd would be the perfect audience, and who doesn't love a good craft fair?"

The atmosphere was infectious, and my laughter mingled with the excited voices of everyone around us. I saw one or two people glance our way and do a double take, but it didn't seem like the majority of people had noticed us yet.

An announcement came over the PA system that the bake sale would be starting soon, causing a stampede for one of the side meeting rooms.

I leaned in so Samuel could hear me. "I thought by now we'd start getting text messages and phone calls from our families."

"We're just walking together." Samuel's voice was closer to a smug purr than I would have liked. "That's not even a warm-up. Just wait until we really get going."

I was going to ask Samuel what he was plotting when I spotted a harried dad barreling toward us. He was struggling to push a two-seater stroller with one hand and hold onto his wriggling, red-faced toddler with the other.

Samuel wrapped an arm around my shoulders and pulled me against him, saving me from certain collision.

"Sorry!" the dad called back over his shoulder as he hurried on his way.

"Whoa." I pressed my hands to Samuel's chest to steady myself.

I could feel his pecs through the soft fabric of his sweater. His muscles were a lot more defined than I'd expected, which made my stomach twist in a way I really, really didn't want it to, considering this was Samuel Warner I was touching.

My instinct was to pull away, but we were supposed to be in a fake relationship, and Samuel had admittedly done well to earn us this moment. I needed to do my part.

So I looked up at him, my green eyes meeting his gray ones, and murmured, "Thanks."

"No problem." Samuel smiled at me as he slid his arm all the way around me so he could rest his hand on my hip. I could feel the heat of his fingers through my flannel. It made my traitorous spine tingle, and for the first time I wondered if maybe this was a very bad idea.

I knew Samuel was handsome. Heck, I'd grown up with him and had gotten to see him perfect his annoying smirk firsthand. Not that it mattered—I was immune to his good looks. But apparently I wasn't prepared for the realization that we had some chemistry between us.

Owen. I had to think of Owen and why I was doing this crackpot stunt.

I focused on maintaining a casual expression even as my heart threatened to pound right out of my chest.

"Should we get back to enjoying the craft fair?" I took a step away from Samuel and forced a smile.

"I've always loved getting lost in your eyes, but I suppose we are in public," Samuel agreed, his arm finally leaving my back to drop at his side.

We continued to walk up the rows of tables and displays. I stared at a rack of homemade doll clothes with way more focus than was warranted.

Samuel stood close enough to me that my shoulder bumped his chest. "I think we're getting some traction."

I tried to discreetly look around to see what he meant.

My gaze landed on Lauren. She'd already seen us together at Literum, her café/bookstore, but she must have thought it was a one-off thing, because her eyes were visibly bulging behind her black-framed glasses from two craft stands away.

Lauren grabbed the arm of the woman who was with her. Piper was another friend of mine—she was a fellow member of the Friends of the Library.

Piper turned to Lauren with confusion, and Lauren pointed at Samuel and me. I gave them a little wave. Piper's mouth dropped open, and Lauren ripped her cell phone out of the front pocket of her oversized hoodie.

Samuel casually side hugged me again, pretending to be interested in a woman selling homemade spice mixes. He asked me in a lowered tone, "I know Lauren is your friend; I assume the gawker with her is as well?"

"Yep, that's Piper."

Piper tapped her phone, and her cell phone's flash went off. "Annnd she just took a picture," I said.

Samuel chuckled. "The perfect souvenir. I'll have to request a copy."

"Trust me." I tugged on the bottom of my flannel shirt. "It'll probably get posted on the Fox Creek town Facebook page before the end of the fair."

"One can hope." Samuel placed a hand on my elbow, directing me further down the row of craft stalls.

We browsed our way around a corner and up a new row before Samuel laughed lowly. "Look. They're Warner Print employees." He discreetly nodded at a husband and wife who kept trying to steal glances at us in between herding their elementary school–aged children.

"I imagine that means it won't be long until my family finds out about this," Samuel theorized.

"Mmhmm," I agreed. "No going back."

"Hey, Nat!" a familiar voice called out. I turned my head to see my younger cousin Keely, her wild russet curls unmistakable, standing behind a table displaying an array of homemade candles. Her freckled face lit up with excitement as she waved us over.

"Keely! I didn't know you were planning to sell your candles here," I said.

Samuel and I strolled up to her impressive candle collection, complete with a laminated sign and pretty streamers wrapped around the table legs.

"I wasn't," Keely said. "Great Aunt Bea was going to sell her crochet blankets, but her cat, Meatloaf, who she thought was a boy, unexpectedly had kittens in her project basket, so she gave me her spot last minute."

I picked up a vibrant blue candle that was decorated with glittering swirls. It smelled like a freshly cut spruce tree, with a faint sweetness that, according to the label, was winter berries. "Your candles are amazing, Keely. You've got some serious talent."

"Thanks!" Keely beamed. "But, uh, who's this?" She nodded at Samuel with raised eyebrows.

"Right! Sorry, Keely. This is Samuel Warner. Sam, meet my

cousin, Keely Mann." I took a breath, steeling myself. "Sam is my boyfriend."

Samuel was instantly all charm with his friendly smile. "Hi, Keely. Nice to meet you."

"Hi—wait, what? You're dating a Warner?" Keely's eyes widened in shock, her jaw dropping as she processed the news. "When did this happen? How? Do Grandma and Grandpa Mann know?"

I opened my mouth to respond, but my phone buzzed in my pocket. I dug it out and opened the screen to a flurry of incoming text messages from various family members and friends. They must have seen the photo Piper took.

"Grandma and Grandpa certainly know now," I concluded, seeing their names in the list.

Keely snorted and fiddled with her ear—she was probably adjusting her hearing aid. "And here I thought Meatloaf's gender reveal and indiscretion were going to blow up our family chat."

I smiled, aware my young cousin was trying to comfort me.

Samuel's phone started to ding. He unlocked the screen and showed it to me. "Look at that. I'm getting cross-examined too."

"The whole town will probably know by the time we leave the fair." I put my phone in silent mode, cutting off the endless buzzing.

Samuel and I had just finished the easiest part of our plan. As daunting as it was, convincing our families that we were the real deal and they needed to make up was going to be a full-scale, multimonth quest.

"Don't worry, Nat." Samuel leaned in and kissed the top of my head, which was *not* on the list of approved physical displays of affection we had finalized. "My family is going to love you."

I peered up at him, intending to give him the eye for the

rule-breaking, but blinked in surprise when Samuel winked at me. Not in that overly charming way that always felt like death by strangulation via cloying and smarmy suaveness. It was something almost ... conspiratorial.

I wasn't in this alone. Samuel wasn't my friend, but at least he was a fellow soldier in this war. Right now, that was good enough.

"I wish I could say the same about my family loving you," I said. "But the truth is my grandma might try to take a cast iron skillet to your head. She's still holding a grudge over that diner you knocked down on the edge of town when you expanded the Warner Print campus."

"You should take a football helmet when you have to run the gauntlet," Keely advised. "Maybe get some shoulder pads too. Uncle Mike is built like a sumo wrestler, and he might try something as well."

Samuel studied Keely. "I don't suppose you could be convinced to put in a good word for me with your parents?"

"Sam," I hissed.

Samuel shrugged. "I have to start somewhere with you Manns."

Keely folded her arms across her chest. "Buy a candle and I'll think about it."

"Now I see the family resemblance between you two." Samuel pulled out his wallet. "That's a move straight out of Nat's playbook."

Keely beamed. "Why thank you!"

Samuel picked up the blue candle I'd sniffed earlier. "You still have things to learn from her—she would have pushed for at least three candles."

Keely looked from me to Samuel, her wrinkled nose emphasizing her freckles.

"I would have bargained for hard cash," I admitted.

Samuel chuckled as he gave Keely a couple of folded bills and ignored his cell phone as it continued to buzz. "Natalie, you are going to make this *fun*."

Chapter 8

Natalie

Tip #8: *When introducing your enemy to family, keep explanations simple: "It just happened" is less suspicious than "I'm trying to emotionally manipulate you all into harmony."*

I maneuvered my little hatchback into a spot along the curb in front of my parents' ranch-style house. The front lawn was blanketed in a pristine layer of fresh snow that sparkled under the winter sun. It was cute and idyllic and totally misleading considering the stakes of the visit.

I glanced over at Samuel in the passenger seat, his chiseled features illuminated by the sunlight streaming through the windshield. "Just to warn you, I only called my folks about thirty minutes ago to let them know we were stopping by," I said.

One of his dark eyebrows arched. "They won't find a last-minute drop-in rude?"

"Nah." I waved a dismissive hand. "Mann family members are always popping in and out at all hours. My parents are used to it. Besides, if I'd given them any more notice, half the clan would've heard about it and come over to spy on us. I'm trying to be considerate so you don't have to face the firing squad right off the bat." I flashed him a wry smirk. "Mom and Dad are the safest to start with."

"Thanks for that." A smile played at the corners of Samuel's mouth. "Why are they the easiest place to begin this little charade?"

"They're the only easygoing ones in the whole Mann family. But keep in mind, our definition of *easygoing* is probably very different from yours."

Samuel laughed, a rich sound that did funny things to my insides. "I see. Any last-minute warnings or advice before we head into the lions' den?"

"Let's see ... eat whatever Mom offers you unless you're deathly allergic. Stick to safe topics like sports, hunting, and the weather with Dad. And whatever you do, avoid *any* mention of Warner Print."

"Got it. I can handle a little small talk." Samuel's slight smile bloomed into the charming one he used to convince people to give him whatever he wanted.

I snorted. "We'll see, city boy. Ready?"

"As ready as I'll ever be." Samuel reached for the door handle.

We climbed out of the car into the cold winter air. I carefully picked my way up the shoveled and salted driveway, very aware of Samuel's tall, broad-shouldered form following close behind me. When we reached the front stoop, I rang the doorbell out of courtesy, then pushed the door open and waved Samuel inside ahead of me.

"Mom? Dad? We're here!" I called.

As soon as we stepped into the small entryway, I toed off my snow boots. Samuel gave me a quizzical look but followed suit with his much more expensive shoes. We hung our coats on the overloaded rack and walked into the cozy living room with its plaid couches and knickknack-covered shelves.

Mom sat in her favorite rocking chair next to a kid's play kitchen, pretending to nibble a plastic hamburger. Noah, one of my cousin's kids, stood at the tiny stove, studiously stirring a pot with a wooden spoon and narrating his culinary process. Dad was seated in his ratty plaid recliner reading the sports section of the *Fox Creek Daily Times*.

"Sweetie! You made it!" Mom popped up to wrap me in a hug. The flowery smell of her perfume—the same kind she'd used since I was a kid—instantly calmed my nerves. "And it's nice to officially meet you, Samuel. Welcome!"

"Thank you, Mrs. Mann. It's a pleasure to be here." Samuel's voice was so friendly and *normal* I gave him the side-eye in surprise.

"Oh, call me Patty." Mom beamed and tucked some of her chin-length silvery blond hair behind her ear.

Dad hauled himself out of his chair and lumbered over, sizing up Samuel with an unreadable expression. "Paul," he said gruffly, sticking out a beefy paw.

"Good to meet you, sir." Samuel pumped Dad's hand, holding his gaze.

Dad, a man of few words, nodded.

Samuel released Dad's hand, and Dad scratched his beard while Samuel smoothly moved to stand shoulder to shoulder with me.

I tried to rack my brain for something to say, then Samuel

took my hand in his. The warmth of his fingers radiated reassurance, but Dad's obvious stare at our hands made it hard to think. "Oh. Oh," I stammered.

Mom, always the perfect host, broke the strained moment. "I'm so glad you two stopped in for a visit! We're watching Noah—he's our grandnephew," Mom explained for Samuel's benefit. "He's the son of Natalie's cousin Madison." Mom turned around to beckon. "Noah, come say hi to Cousin Nat and her boyfriend!"

Noah abandoned his toy stove and barreled toward us. After he skidded to a stop, he craned his neck to look up at Samuel. "Why are you tall?"

Samuel smiled. "My entire family is tall."

"Why?" Noah asked.

"It's a family trait."

"Why?"

Samuel's family must not have many kids, because his brow furrowed and he glanced at me.

I unapologetically grinned at him, enjoying his rare moment of discomfort. "Aren't kids great?"

Samuel mock shook his head at me and adjusted his hold on my hand, twining our fingers together. "Of course. I just *love* the idea of having children."

I would have pinched him for the comment, but I was too distracted by our clasped hands.

Before today I would have said that hand-holding was about as low on the scale of signs of physical affection as you could get. But the feel of Sam's fingers sliding against mine and the soft caress as he rubbed the top of my hand with his thumb made my throat tighten.

Because I have great luck, the movement drew Noah's attention from Samuel's height to our hands.

Noah's eyes widened and he pointed an accusing finger at our clasped hands. "Unprotected hand-holding!" he shouted.

"What?" I asked.

"You're breaking the law," Noah declared. "You're holding hands and you're not married! Mommy said that's a *crime*."

Dad erupted into a sudden coughing fit while Mom placed her hands on her plump cheeks. "Oh, dear. Noah, that isn't precisely what she meant, I'm sure."

"It is," Noah insisted. "Mommy said I exist because Daddy held her hand on the beach during a romantic sunset."

"Ahhh," my mom said, wide-eyed and at a loss as to how to follow up that statement.

Samuel grinned at me like the Cheshire Cat. I resisted the urge to face-palm.

This visit was off to a fantastic start.

"Kids are just so hilarious and perceptive." Samuel gave my hand a little squeeze, sending tingles racing up my arm that threatened to short-circuit my brain.

I was starting to understand why so many women in Fox Creek found him so irresistible.

Desperate to change the subject before Noah could traumatize us further with his interesting takes on my cousin's romantic life, I blurted out the first thing that came to mind.

"Hey, Noah, what happened to your hair? Last time I saw you, it was a lot longer." I reached out and playfully ran my hand over his stubbly hair.

Noah scrunched up his mouth. "Me and Anna were playing hair salon, but like a real hair salon, so Anna cut my hair. Mommy didn't like it, so she shaved the rest off."

"Well, I think it looks very cool," I assured him. "You're totally rocking the buzz cut, my dude."

"Thank you." Noah barely acknowledged my compliment,

as he was back to eyeing up Samuel. "Are you going to show off your magic?"

"Why do you think I have magic?" Samuel asked.

"Mommy said the only reason Natalie would date a no-good Warner was because his face was magic. Why is your face magic?"

I choked on air, and I felt my face heat up. I was going to have some choice words for Madison about what she said in front of her very impressionable six-year-old son.

"I'm not sure. Maybe we should ask Nat," Samuel suggested, the traitor.

Noah turned his gaze to me. "Cousin Nat, why is his face magic? And what's a Warner?"

Mom cleared her throat. "Who wants cookies? Noah, honey, why don't you go wash your hands so we can all have a snack?"

Noah's eyes lit up at the mention of cookies, the Warners forgotten. "OK!" He scampered off to the bathroom, and Mom turned to Samuel with an apologetic smile.

"Samuel, would you like a cookie? They're chocolate chip, fresh out of the oven. Noah and I made them this morning."

"That would be wonderful, thank you." Samuel was all polite charm.

Mom beamed at him and bustled off to the kitchen.

Dad looked from me to Samuel, then to our still-joined hands. He grunted, then trailed after Mom.

I exhaled and nodded to Samuel. "At least the introductions are over. Remember, Green Bay Packers, hunting, and weather!"

"That's a breeze compared to fielding questions that veer toward the realm of sex ed." Samuel tugged on my hand, and together we left the living room for the kitchen.

The kitchen was just as cozy and inviting as the rest of the house, with yellow gingham curtains, sunflower-patterned dishes, and the mouthwatering aroma of chocolate permeating the air.

"Did you catch the Packers game last week?" Samuel asked Dad.

Dad stared at Samuel for a moment, resembling a suspicious bear, then nodded. "Good game," he said in his deep, rumbly voice.

"It was a nail-biter," Samuel said. "I didn't know if they'd make it, but they brought it back around in the last quarter with that interception."

Dad's expression turned thoughtful, and the furrow between his eyebrows softened. "Yeah."

Mom placed a plate full of chocolate chip cookies on the island in front of Samuel. "Here you go, dear. And Natalie, I put some aside for you to take home later." Mom pointed to a plastic, gallon-size ice cream tub. (Mom, as a good Midwesterner, always found alternative uses for plastic food containers.)

"Thanks, Mom." I stole a cookie from Samuel's plate.

Samuel made an appreciative noise as he bit into his first cookie. "Wow, these are incredible, Patty. You'll have to give me the recipe." He somehow managed to sound completely sincere instead of chokingly fake like he usually sounded with me.

I watched, so surprised I didn't even taste the chocolatey goodness of my cookie, as he charmed my parents, praising my mom's baking and somehow casually conversing with Dad even though Dad stuck to his usual single-sentence replies. It was like a switch had flipped. Gone was the smug, smarmy Samuel I was used to, replaced by this genuine, likable version.

Maybe this whole fake dating thing wouldn't be a complete disaster or a torture-palooza if he was hiding this kind of personality behind his insufferable attitude—

HONK! HONK!

I froze, my blood running cold at the sound of a horn blaring from the driveway. Oh no. It couldn't be ...

I yanked my hand from Samuel's and raced to the living room window. My stomach plummeted at the sight of the ancient maroon monstrosity idling outside, complete with tacky wooden panels.

"Mom!" I yelled. "You Judas! You betrayed us!"

Mom and Samuel crowded behind me to peer out at the unwelcome arrivals.

"Oh my. I have no idea how they found out!" Mom said. "I only told Owen and Madison and Uncle Mike that you were coming!"

"How could you tell that many people when I only gave you thirty minutes' notice?" I couldn't believe it. She'd practically sent out a Natalie's-bringing-a-Warner-boy-home bat signal.

The van honked again, long and impatient. I groaned.

There was no escaping now.

I reluctantly dragged myself to the front door and yanked on my boots. "Samuel, grab your shoes. We're being summoned. Leave your jacket; we'll be back soon."

To his credit, Samuel looked more entertained by my dread than alarmed as he obediently put his shoes on.

Bracing myself, I opened the front door. Samuel was on my heels as we stepped out into the biting winter air and straight into the tornado of love and sarcasm that was my grandparents.

The van's sliding door whooshed open with a screech of rusted metal. Grandma Mann's wrinkled face, framed by wispy white curls and comically magnified by her thick glasses, poked out.

"Well? Don't just stand there! Get in, you two! We're going for a drive!" she hollered.

I smothered a groan, muttering under my breath, "Steel yourself."

"For a car ride?" Samuel asked. "How bad could it be?"

I shot him a look. "You have no idea. Grandma and Grandpa Mann? They're like the final boss of the family. I was hoping to ease you in before throwing you to the wolves."

Samuel chuckled, unperturbed.

He'd learn.

Pasting on a bright smile, I approached the van. "Grandma! What a surprise!"

"Less yapping, more getting in," Grandma ordered.

I reached the front passenger door, opening it to reveal Grandpa Mann in the driver's seat, his weathered hands resting on the cracked leather steering wheel.

"Hiya, pumpkin," he greeted, eyes crinkling with love. Then his gaze slid to Samuel and all the warmth left his voice. "Warner."

"Grandpa, Grandma, this is Sam—Samuel Warner, my boyfriend." I looked up at Samuel and smiled, doing my best to look lovesick.

Samuel returned my look, then attentively turned to my grandparents. "Ma'am. Sir."

Grandma harrumphed. "This close up, his mug is even prettier than I thought, I'll give him that."

"We've been mighty curious 'bout this fella of yours. Hop in." Grandpa jerked his chin toward the seats.

I pointed Samuel toward the front seat, upholstered in musty maroon velvet.

Samuel balked. "Oh no, I couldn't possibly when your grandmother—"

"Nat and I don't ever sit up front," Grandma Mann interrupted. "We know better. Now park that Warner keister of yours."

Samuel ducked into the passenger seat without further

protest. I clambered into the full-size van's middle row of seats, scooting past Grandma to sit behind Grandpa.

As Grandpa put the van in gear, I leaned forward to tap Samuel on the shoulder while he buckled his seat belt. "Keep your feet off the ground," I said.

"What?"

"Feet. Off the ground." I pointed to the way I held my booted feet off the ground. It made my thighs burn, but it was absolutely necessary in Grandpa's van.

Grandpa Mann revved the van and we were off, rolling down the driveway in reverse to back into the street.

Grandpa's way of driving provided for a ... unique passenger experience. Instead of using one foot and switching back and forth between the gas pedal and the brake, Grandpa used both: his right foot for the accelerator, his left foot for the brake.

This meant there was a lot of lurching in his driving and some drastic changes in speed in very short amounts of time.

I adjusted the way the seat belt was positioned on my chest, kept my feet off the flooring, and leaned back into my seat before Grandpa Mann pressed the accelerator and the van rocketed forward.

"Samuel Warner," Grandpa Mann drawled, drawing out the name. "Never thought the day'd come that a Warner would grow some sense, recognize a good thing, and seize it."

I saw Samuel's shoulders shake in a silent chuckle. "Oh, I've always known Natalie was a good thing. It just took a while to convince her I was one, too, before she'd date me."

My eyebrows shot up in surprise. That was a new addition to our fake love story. We'd agreed to say it was mutual admiration from the start, not Samuel wearing me down. I never thought he'd be willing to paint himself as falling for me first. It didn't match his endless confidence. (Or maybe his endless confidence made his ego incredibly secure?)

The maroon pleather dashboard gleamed in the sun, its cracked surface only adding to the retro vibe. A rolled-up newspaper caught Samuel's eye, and I saw him pause, considering it in blessed, blessed ignorance.

Grandpa Mann took the next curve at a speed that had me white-knuckling the sides of my seat.

"Forget the boy!" Grandma Mann jabbed a bony finger at me. "Are you suffering a brain injury, girlie? How could you lose all your dignity and fall for a Warner?" Her shrewd eyes darted to Samuel. "Even if he is as rich as a king."

"Why thank you, ma'am," Samuel said. "I'm flattered you—"

"Don't you try buttering me up," Grandma Mann said. "I'm wise to you Warners and your silver tongues." She fixed me with a piercing look. "Well? Out with it! What's a smart girl like you doing with this rascal?"

I took a deep breath, mentally preparing myself. "It was a process of elimination. I realized Samuel was my best choice for a serious relationship."

Grandma looked aghast. "Process of elimination?! How could he possibly come out on top?"

"Easily." I ticked the points off on my fingers. "He's got the cleverness and ambition to keep up with me. He shares my passion for community involvement, and we both know our families bring on the crazy. It takes a special kind of guy to handle all of that."

Even as I said it, a sense of unease prickled down my spine. Because it was true. All my past relationships had ended amicably because, deep down, I'd known my exes couldn't handle my over-the-top love of Fox Creek and my bonkers family.

But Samuel ... I glanced up to find him twisting in his seat so he could look back at me, curiosity burning in his dark eyes.

"I respect his work ethic," I said, the words tumbling out in a rush. "And he is active in Fox Creek, just like me. He already donates a lot of money to things I'm passionate about, like the library."

Samuel smiled at me. It was barely more than a twitch of his lips, but it was accompanied by a look of understanding that made me feel like he saw so much of me it was uncomfortable.

"Of course, we disagree on how to keep on improving things for Fox Creek," I continued, trying to lighten the suddenly charged atmosphere. "But that just keeps things interesting—"

"Land's sake," Grandma Mann muttered. "This is gettin' disgustingly sweet."

Grandpa Mann chuckled. "I suppose your reasoning is sound enough," he allowed begrudgingly. "A man oughta match his woman in wits and gumption. But that doesn't mean we like him!"

I exhaled, relieved to have cleared that hurdle. It was too much to hope for my grandparents to like Samuel. As long as they didn't object to our dating, no one in my nosy family would try to pull us apart, and we could clear the runway for Jenna and Owen as I intended.

"Now you." Grandpa Mann scowled at Samuel. "What've the esteemed Warners had to say 'bout you courting a Mann?"

The van's blinker started ticking as Grandpa Mann took a sharp right. A flash of gray fur burst out of the cassette deck, and I yelped, slamming back against the seat.

A rotund mouse scampered up the radio, beady eyes bright and its long tail whipping behind it.

"Cheese and crackers!" Grandpa Mann bellowed. His hand shot out, snagging the newspaper. Driving one-handed, he started whacking at the mouse with the rolled-up newspaper as it climbed onto the dashboard.

The mouse zigzagged between his wild wallops, the newspaper thwapping the dash with dull thunks.

"I've told you before, Francis!" Grandma Mann started. "You need to put traps in this vehicle. Those mice have been freeloaders for too long!"

Through it all, Samuel didn't even flinch. He just calmly raised his legs, now understanding why I didn't put my feet on the ground, and continued, "My family just wants to see me happy, sir."

The mouse ran toward the windshield. Grandpa Mann took aim, tongue between his teeth ...

"And Natalie makes me happy," Samuel said.

... and swung a home-run-worthy smack.

The mouse dove through a crack in the dash, disappearing to safety just before the newspaper connected with the glass in an almighty *THWAP*.

Samuel slowly twisted in his seat to look at me. "Was that ... a real mouse?"

As the van rocketed onward and my grandparents descended into cackling laughter, I could only hope Samuel wouldn't have a psychotic break in the front seat from the Mann chaos.

"It was a real mouse." I reached forward, straining against my seat belt so I could pat Samuel's shoulder in a comforting gesture. "One made a home in Grandpa's van a couple autumns ago. He hasn't been able to evict the little squatter and its ever-expanding family."

Grandma Mann hooted. "They're his tenants now! No amount of newspaper whackin' will convince them to leave."

Grandpa snickered as he swung the van around another

sharp curve. "Now, you were saying about Nat and your family?"

Samuel's expression softened, and my heart stumbled over itself. How could he look so genuinely in love when this was all an act? "My family is thrilled for me," he said, his voice as sweet as honey. "They know how long I've cared for Natalie, and they'll welcome her with open arms."

Grandma Mann scoffed. "Really now? Last time I saw your mother, she called me a nosy old hag."

"Grandma!" I choked out, mortified.

"Trust me, my family's love for me far outweighs any grudge," Samuel said. "They know how important Natalie is to me, and that's all they need to know to be willing to accept her."

I shifted in my seat, my stomach a mosh pit of butterflies. Even though none of this was real, he sounded so sincere and so utterly smitten that it was weirdly disconcerting.

Grandpa Mann harrumphed. "Can't say we find you all that trustworthy. But it will do for now. However, we need to know: What are your intentions with regard to my granddaughter?"

"Grandpa, seriously? I'm twenty-eight, not a teenager going to prom."

Before Samuel could answer, the glove box burst open, belching out a flurry of ancient maps and paper napkins across his lap. And there, perched on top of the van's manual like a fuzzy gray king, was the mouse.

Samuel reached for the window crank, cool as a cucumber, and started winding it down. "I assure you, sir, and ma'am"—he grabbed the newspaper—"that my intentions are entirely honorable."

The mouse skittered up onto the dash. In one smooth motion, Samuel scooped it up with the newspaper and flung it out the window.

We rolled up to a stop sign just as the mouse sailed into an evergreen shrub and disappeared.

"So long, freeloading vermin!" Grandpa Mann called after it. "And good riddance!"

Samuel cranked the window back up, then turned to fix my grandpa with a solemn look. "I'm not dating Natalie for fun, sir. She's the love of my life. I intend to marry her and build a future with her here in Fox Creek because she loves this place so much. She's my forever."

I stared at the back of Grandpa's headrest and reminded myself that it was just a few months ago Samuel had requested that the Fox Creek town clerk (a.k.a. me) attend all the community development committee meetings, which of course he served on as a citizen adviser. (His request had been accepted, and he made sure to sit next to me at *every meeting* ever since and frequently kept the committee members talking late—I was pretty sure just out of spite.)

Grandma Mann watched me, her eyes enlarged by her glasses. "Natalie"—she used my full name so I knew it was serious—"are you happy with him?"

I felt Samuel's gaze on me, and when I glanced at him, he was watching me intently, his gray eyes soft and serious.

"I am, Grandma. I'm having a lot of fun with Sam," I said, surprised to discover this was true.

Somehow, Samuel was a surprisingly good partner in crime. I never would have guessed it, but the rich business guy could roll with the Manns.

Grandpa Mann harrumphed from the driver's seat. "Well, I suppose that counts for something."

"If Nat's happy, we had best let you two be. At least until this Warner boy of yours trips up," Grandma Mann allowed.

I let myself finally breathe normally. We'd passed the test.

They didn't like our dating, but that was more than I could have reasonably hoped for anyway. It was enough that they wouldn't interfere. I could work with this.

Sadly Grandma Mann wasn't finished yet. "But I'm a tad disappointed in you, missy. I thought you had more sense than to go for this star-crossed-lovers shtick."

I raised my hands in mock surrender. "It's Samuel's fault. He's very persuasive."

Samuel chuckled and turned to look out the front windshield again. "We're not star-crossed. You're too stubborn to let anyone tell you what to do, least of all the universe."

Grandma Mann snorted. "At least you already know the worst about him after all these years of fighting. That's more than most couples can say!"

"I agree," Samuel said. "It's Natalie's angry face that made me fall in love with her."

"OK," I said, loudly. "Show and tell is over. Neither of you need to hear these kinds of details. Grandpa, take us home."

Samuel sighed dejectedly, his usual charm back. "It's difficult being the romantic one in the relationship."

"You better be, because she deserves it," Grandpa Mann sharply said. He paused, then added gruffly, "But don't mind her. She's just self-conscious about these things."

"Yeah," I said. "That happens when your grandparents keep asking you about your love life."

Samuel twisted in his seat again and gave me a forlorn look that signaled that whatever came out of his mouth next was going to inspire me to commit homicide. "But now we can actually tell them, honey buns. We can share *all* the details, like how you think my abs are my best feature—"

"SAM!"

Grandpa Mann cackled, but Grandma Mann folded her arms across her narrow chest. "I still don't like this, so be warned, Warner. One wrong move and you'll have the wrath of the whole family coming down on you!"

Samuel dropped the sappy look. "I understand, but you don't need to worry." His dark eyes flicked to me one last time. "I'll never hurt Natalie, and I'm never going to let her go."

Chapter 9

Natalie

Tip #9: *When meeting your fake boyfriend's family, be polite. They might surprise you with their friendliness despite being related to your enemy—genetics are a wonder.*

I sat in the passenger seat of Samuel's Porsche, my fingers tracing the buttery soft leather interior. The new car smell mixed with his expensive cologne was a heady combination that had me distracted. I'd never ridden in a Porsche before, and the ultramodern dashboard glowed with more technology than a space shuttle.

"Thanks for going to visit my family." I studied Samuel's chiseled profile. "I appreciate you putting in the effort to sell our act."

"Of course. What's the family consensus?" Samuel asked.

Outside, the full moon illuminated the snowy landscape, turning the narrow, winding road and dense evergreen trees into a winter wonderland. The Porsche navigated the curves like a dream.

"Successful, I'd say. Well, except for my cousin Madison. She learned she probably shouldn't discuss anything romance-related in front of Noah."

He arched an eyebrow. "Does that mean they like me?"

I snorted. "No, definitely not. A few relatives are questioning my sanity for dating you. But they believe that our fake relationship is real, and they aren't going to interfere with us, which is more than I had dared to hope for."

Samuel's brow furrowed and he seemed less pleased than I expected. Before I could analyze that, he spoke again.

"Meeting my family will be both better and worse, I'm afraid." The Porsche flew around another curve, the engine growling.

I straightened my shoulders. "I'm prepared for the worst. As town clerk, I'm used to dealing with insults from the public with a smile on my face."

Samuel shook his head. "That won't be necessary. They definitely won't be hostile. There's a possibility they might be overly welcoming, actually." He sounded as if that sentence physically pained him.

"Overly welcoming? Why?"

"The usual reasons," he grumbled. "My mom, aunt, and uncle were beginning to despair that any of us kids would get married and have babies. They're thrilled for me that I'm in a committed relationship. It will be a miracle if they don't start asking me if I've thought about proposing after tonight."

There was something off about his explanation. It was like he was holding something back, but I couldn't imagine what.

He didn't say anything more, so it appeared he was setting a boundary. That was fine as long as he wasn't hiding a secret intention to take over the city or something.

"So they're happy for you, that's the better part. What's the worse part then?" I asked.

Samuel shrugged, unbothered. "They'll expect more physical affection between us. More than your family did, I mean."

Just then, he turned the Porsche into a long driveway cutting through the forest. Towering pines heavy with snow stretched out on either side of the pavement.

I frowned so deeply my forehead furrowed. "Why would they expect more PDAs?"

"They won't believe we're really dating without them."

I mashed my lips together. "Fine. You can kiss the top of my head or whatever if needed. You already went that far, anyway, even though we specifically did *not* agree to it."

The corner of Samuel's mouth twitched. "Thank you so much for your gracious and enthusiastic suggestion. However, we might need to step it up more than that. We can play it by ear based on their reactions, I suppose."

I opened my mouth to ask why on earth they'd expect us to be all over each other, but then the trees parted and revealed his mother's house.

A sprawling, classy lake house stood before us, huge windows glowing with warm interior lighting. It was clearly large and luxurious but in an elegant and understated way—not gaudy or ostentatious.

The frozen lake glimmered behind it, the icy surface reflecting the bright moonlight and star-studded sky. It was breathtaking.

"Wow, what a gorgeous home," I said as Samuel parked alongside several other expensive vehicles.

Samuel killed the engine. "Isaac and I each have a place on

this lake, just a few houses over. Actually, everyone but my cousin Jenna lives on the lake."

I suddenly felt underdressed in my nicest black cocktail dress and blue cardigan under my wool coat. At least Samuel looked as handsome as ever in his work suit.

"Does your mom live here alone?" I softly asked. The cold night air bit at my exposed skin. "And I'm so sorry again about your dad. Cancer is ... terrible."

Samuel came around the car and took my gloved hand in his, then closed my door for me. "It's been four years since he passed, but thank you. I remember how respectful you were at his funeral. It meant a lot."

I awkwardly cleared my throat. "Of course," I said.

My parents, grandparents, and I had gone to the funeral together. Samuel's father had been instrumental in building Warner Print into the successful business it was today and had done a lot for the town as the largest employer. He'd deserved our respect no matter how our families got along.

But I was surprised Samuel remembered I had attended the funeral. I vaguely recalled briefly talking to him in the receiving line, but I didn't think he'd remember me on such a terrible day.

Hand in hand, we walked across the driveway, which was salted and meticulously shoveled. The utter stillness of the windless night and the sparkling snow-covered grounds reflecting the moonbeams made for a magical atmosphere despite the frigid temperature.

"To answer you, yes, my mother lives here alone now." Samuel's breath was visible in the air. "Although we Warners are almost as bad as you Manns about constantly dropping in on each other, so she gets plenty of company even when she doesn't come by the office. And she has made it her personal mission to keep tabs on my paternal grandfather, so she's rarely without company. Are you ready?"

I took a deep breath, steeling myself as we reached the sidewalk that led to the front door. "Yep. I brushed up on my manners and etiquette with a library book so I can hopefully make a good impression. And I memorized the guest list you gave me: your brother Isaac, your cousins Logan and Jenna, your mom, and your Aunt Jamie and Uncle Charles."

"Yes, good." He paused with his hand on the ornate door handle. "My grandfather couldn't make it tonight, but you'll meet him eventually. You won't be lucky enough to avoid him for long."

The apprehension in his voice made my nerves jangle.

Samuel started to push the door open, then paused. "Crap. I forgot to tell you about Chuck."

"Chuck? Who's Chuck?"

But before he could answer, the door was pulled open, and a very excited female voice called out: "Natalie! I'm so happy to officially meet you in a personal circumstance instead of something involving Fox Creek. Welcome."

I plastered on my best smile instead of turning around and sprinting back to the car like I wanted to. (I was literally walking into my enemy's family home, and I was supposed to be dating that enemy. It would be a miracle if I didn't get indigestion over dinner.)

I stepped into the foyer, momentarily stunned by the soaring ceilings, gleaming hardwood floors, and an elegant crystal chandelier casting a warm glow on us. Samuel's mother, a stunning woman with steel-blond hair combed back into a stylish chignon, clasped my hands as she continued her greeting.

"Thank you for agreeing to come, Natalie." Her small smile turned her sophisticated but icy beauty into something much softer. "I hope the drive here was pleasant?"

"Yes. Thank you so much for having me, Mrs. Warner. You have a beautiful house," I said, trying to mind my manners.

"Please, call me Estelle. I am so thrilled Samuel finally has you, and I hope you quickly become comfortable with our family." She laughed melodically.

My cheeks heated as I glanced at Samuel. He avoided my gaze as he removed my wool coat for me and hung it in the closet.

Samuel finally has me? What did that mean? Or was she referring to the idea that he has a girlfriend in general?

"Natalie, you remember my brother, Isaac," Samuel said, smoothly changing the subject as he gestured to his twin, standing a few feet behind their mother.

"Of course, nice to see you again, Isaac." I smiled, noting with amazement that his typically cool expression was molded into something almost resembling a welcoming smile.

"Yes, hello," Isaac said. "Thank you for coming."

I blinked at him in shock. I didn't consider Isaac my personal enemy as I did Samuel, but when we were in high school, Isaac and I had had a couple of colorful clashes. I guess it said a lot about him that he was able to be welcoming despite our history.

The relatives parade continued as Jenna glided into the foyer. "Natalie, hello!" she called out to me. She was out of her hospital scrubs and was quite the gorgeous vision in a beautiful blue dress that complimented her blond hair.

I'd have to finagle a picture with her so I could show Owen.

Jenna's brother, Logan—the Warner heir who scared the jibblies out of me—trailed behind her, tall, dark, and as intimidating as ever. He had a kind of Grim Reaper vibe. I wasn't sure if it was because he looked pale next to all his relatives and had dark circles under his eyes or if it was just the way he silently moved around like a shadow.

"Logan, Jenna, you both know my girlfriend, Natalie." Samuel slipped a casual arm around my waist.

I fought the urge to jump. Right, gotta sell this.

"We've met." Logan gave me an acknowledging nod, which I returned.

"Yep, and I know Jenna through my brother, Owen. They work together at the hospital." I watched Jenna closely for her reaction.

"Owen is just the best! You'll have to bring him next time." Jenna beamed at me. "Now come on in. Mom and Dad are waiting to meet you!"

"I look forward to meeting them." I reached down and laced my fingers through Samuel's. He glanced down at me in surprise.

I guess I didn't usually take the initiative. I'd have to work on that, especially in front of his family.

Samuel recovered quickly, squeezing my hand and smiling as if I'd hung the moon in the sky. The slight crinkle to his eyes and slant of his smile made my gut flop.

Geez, no wonder his family was so eager to welcome me. He could really act the part.

"If you two don't stop looking at each other like that, dinner is going to be late," Isaac dryly called, breaking our little moment.

"Isaac, stop that." Estelle's tone was only a little scolding. "Sam, Natalie, please follow Jenna and Logan to the dining room. I will check on dinner. Isaac, you're coming with me."

Isaac gave a mocking half bow that looked like he'd borrowed it from his twin and followed after his mother.

Still hand in hand, we walked into the dining room. It was breathtaking, with a brightly colored Turkish rug and fancy lights that cast a cozy glow over the long mahogany table. Delicate china place settings and sparkling silverware twinkled on the sage-green table runner.

A distinguished older couple rose from their seats as we

entered. The man had a head of silver hair and was so quiet he reminded me of Logan. His wife's blond bob and earnest smile reminded me of Jenna, which meant they were likely Samuel's aunt and uncle.

"Uncle Charles, Aunt Jamie, I'd like you to meet Natalie, my girlfriend." Samuel rubbed the top of my hand with his thumb in a caress that almost made me jump even though he'd done it before.

(I was starting to understand why his mother was willing to invite me into her house and accept me even though I was a Mann. The guy clearly had romantic abilities by the boatload, but he'd never put them to use. I certainly hadn't heard of Samuel having any type of serious relationship since he returned to Fox Creek after college. I knew he was busy, having become the CEO of Warner Print after his father died, but maybe I'd underestimated his workaholism.)

"Welcome, Natalie." Jamie held out her hand, and I was forced to let go of Samuel's. Jamie clasped my palm with a grip that would have made Grandpa Mann proud. "We're so pleased Samuel finally brought you around."

Charles offered a much more sedate nod of his head matched with a slight but genuine smile. "Congratulations, both of you."

"Thank you. It's wonderful to be here." I smiled at them and tried to judge their expressions, but as best I could tell, they really meant their welcomes, which oddly made me feel a little bad.

Not about the lying—heck no. Owen and Jenna all the way!

But. Even if the Warners were concerned for Samuel, they were acting abundantly more welcoming than my family had.

"You work at city hall—as the Fox Creek town clerk, right? How do you like it?" Jamie asked.

"I love my job," I said. "I'm very passionate about Fox Creek, so I love being a part of the city support staff."

Jamie cocked her head. "Don't you have to deal with a lot of angry and peevish residents?"

"If a resident has a problem, I usually end up hearing about it because they bring it to me so I can direct them where to take their issue, but I don't mind. I love it when I can help a Fox Creek resident resolve an issue that's been troubling them," I said, giving them the scrubbed description I gave to most people.

(It was the edition that didn't include me ranting about how much I hated trees on property lines. The number of residents who stopped in to complain about their neighbors' trees dropping leaves on their lawn was almost enough to make me dread autumn.)

Jamie made a clicking noise with her tongue. "You have more patience than I do. I would want to tell off the first silly nob who threw a fit. I can only imagine what those fussy Manns complain about." She shivered theatrically, then froze, her eyes widening as she remembered who she was talking to.

Jenna's small *eep* was audible, and Charles gaped at his wife, clearly horrified by the shade she'd thrown on my family.

I wasn't bothered. Jamie's obvious dismay meant she hadn't purposely slipped up to act petty—as I'd noted earlier, the whole family seemed genuine in their welcome. Besides, I'd come prepared to be insulted. It wasn't like the Manns had pulled any punches with Samuel until he'd satisfied their concerns.

But the Warners' mortification at the accidental affront was unexpected. Unless ... was their welcome just them being polite?

"I am *so* sorry!" Jamie's face was ashen and her forehead wrinkled like a twisted towel. "That was unbelievably rude of me. I'm such a wretch. Please forgive me my thoughtlessness to you and your family. The Manns are ..."

"Very dutiful people," Charles helpfully chimed in.

"Yes! Yes. Very dutiful indeed! It is merely ... It's just that ..." Jamie grimaced. "Please don't think poorly of Samuel for this."

Ahh, that's what was going on! They were being nice to me —a Mann—for Samuel's sake, because they thought we were madly in love and cared about him and his feelings. That was quite sweet.

"Don't worry about it. I know our families have a heated history." I smiled up at Samuel, feeling better now that I understood the Warners' attitude and actions. "Thankfully, despite our disagreements, we can agree that our parents raised great kids."

Samuel dutifully gave me a sappy smile and moved in to wrap his arms around me—he really was following up on his warning in his car about upping our PDAs. "Give your family some credit. After meeting them on a more personal level and not at a community verbal brawl, I think they're a hoot."

I wrinkled my nose at him. "You can say that because you think they're funny and you don't have to live with them."

Jamie patted her left hand over her heart. "Ahh, young love."

Charles nodded, Logan remained quiet and still, as he'd been for the entire exchange, and Jenna looked like she might be ... tearing up?

Wow, the Warners were more of a romantic crew than I would have given them credit for given their workaholic ways.

Estelle breezed into the room, breaking up our conversation. "Dinner is served! Everyone, please take your seats." She clapped her hands.

Isaac, his expression reserved but resigned, followed his

mother into the room, pushing an honest-to-goodness butler's cart that was filled with platters of steaming food.

Samuel pulled a chair out for me. It was the same mahogany as the table, and to my horror it had white cushions that I was going to live in terror of for the entire night lest I spill something. Once I was seated, he pushed my chair in for me and then slapped his brother on the shoulder as Isaac wheeled the cart past us. "Thanks for helping Mother."

Isaac shrugged. "Always happy to be your butler."

Samuel snorted as he sat down next to me. "If you're the butler, I'm the bellhop."

Isaac wheeled the cart on. "What does that make Logan? The security guard?"

"Nah," Jenna said with the decisiveness only older siblings could muster. "He'd be the silent but mysterious gardener, and I'd be the chambermaid."

"So you can nose around through other people's business to your heart's content without getting into trouble?" Samuel guessed.

"Exactly!" Jenna said.

Isaac rolled his eyes as he parked the cart. "Logan, surely as our mysterious gardener you'd be able to find a creative way to dispose of the chambermaid. Be a chap, would you?"

"Ha, ha, very funny," Jenna said. "I'll remember this next time you want me to explain your blood labs to you."

I tugged the sleeves of my blue cardigan up to my elbows and smiled at the exchange. After admiring the fine china with a green fir tree pattern and delicate crystal champagne flute at my place setting, I peered down the table, where Jenna and Logan had already sat down across from their parents. I froze when I spotted something hairy at the far end of the table. "Samuel," I whispered.

"Hmm?" He leaned in so our arms brushed. The fabric of his suit was silky against my exposed forearm.

"What is that?" I kept my voice quiet so no one else would hear me and tipped my head toward the end of the table.

Samuel ruefully shook his head. "Ah. That is Chuck."

Chuck was a small dog of decidedly mixed heritage. He had the slightly bulging eyes of a pug, the wiry white hair and folded brown ears of a wire-haired Jack Russell terrier, and an underbite that showed off his snaggletooth. He was simultaneously homely and adorable, particularly because he sat on top of a yellow plastic booster seat and had a pastel blue bow tie fixed to his collar.

"Mother adopted him after Dad passed," Samuel said in a low tone. "He's basically her third son and unofficially her favorite child."

I bit my lip to hide a smile. Chuck tilted his head, tongue lolling out to the side around his snaggletooth in a way that resembled an adorable grin.

Samuel sighed good-naturedly. "Mother insists on taking him everywhere. Don't worry; he's well behaved. Mother is the problem: She spoils him rotten."

Estelle must have overheard us, because she called down the table as she sat down next to Chuck and his booster seat at the end of the table. "Doesn't Chuck look handsome, Natalie? I wanted him to look as dashing as possible so as to make a good impression on you."

"He's very dapper," I said.

Estelle beamed at me, which melted her elegantly icy looks to make her seem a little more human. The little dog let out a soft snort of agreement and wildly wagged his stubby tail as Estelle affectionately patted his head.

He wasn't the kind of dog I would have pictured with any of

the Warners, especially Estelle, but it was obvious she loved the little canine.

(Wow. Forget how my fake relationship would force my family to mend the fence—fake dating Samuel was making me face a lot of false personal assumptions I'd made about the Warners over the years.)

As Isaac started placing trays on the table, Estelle cleared her throat and announced the menu. "Tonight we will be dining on brown sugar-glazed salmon, wild mushroom risotto, parmesan roasted asparagus, crisped brussels sprouts, and New York-style cheesecake for dessert, served with decaf coffee and tea, of course."

My mouth watered. "That all sounds incredible. You didn't have to go through so much effort, though. I'm just honored to meet you all."

"Don't mind it." Isaac placed the platter of risotto—which smelled amazing—in front of me. "Mother ordered it all from catering earlier in the day."

"Everything needed to be perfect," Estelle tartly said as Isaac added more steaming platters to the table. "To welcome Natalie to our fold, yes, but also because I can never get this bunch to sit down for a proper meal. They work altogether too much."

"Guilty as charged, Mother." Samuel reached over to clasp my hand on top of the tablecloth. "But I have a feeling things will be different now that I have Natalie to pull me away from the office."

He brought our joined hands up and brushed a lingering kiss on my knuckles, his five-o'clock shadow scraping gently against my skin. I sucked in a breath.

Samuel's eyes flicked up to meet mine, his lips still touching my hand. The look he gave me was downright smoldering. I felt that kiss reverberate through every nerve ending in my fingers.

What? I mean ... what? This was supposed to be an act! Just because his gaze made my insides melt like butter on a hot roll didn't mean I could mentally fall apart!

Luckily, Jamie saved me from completely short-circuiting by pushing back her chair and standing. She made a jaunty figure as she slipped one hand into the pocket of her tailored slacks and raised her delicate champagne flute with the other. "A toast! To Natalie, who braved meeting us all for Sam. We're so happy you're here, dear."

"Hear! Hear!" Charles echoed quietly, a smile crinkling his eyes.

I clinked my glass against everyone else's, hoping my flushed cheeks could be blamed on the champagne. "Thank you. I'm truly grateful to be so warmly welcomed tonight."

Chapter 10

Samuel

Tip #10: *Be slow when enacting any private plans inside your fake relationship. Chances like this are once in a lifetime.*

"It was a pleasure meeting with you, Mr. Reeves. I look forward to our next discussion." I shook the client's hand at the entrance of the upscale Milwaukee restaurant we'd met at for dinner. The savory aroma of grilled steak and seared scallops lingered in the air.

"Likewise, Mr. Warner. Thank you for showing my team the print samples. We'll be in touch soon to let you know which design we decide on." Mr. Reeves nodded curtly and turned to leave, his Italian leather shoes clicking on the polished marble floor.

Satisfaction hummed through me as I watched him leave.

Another pleased client. Warner Print wasn't worth so much merely because we had an expansive business designing and printing marketing materials; it was because we retained clients. We still had clients Grandfather Warner had onboarded before my dad even started working with him.

"Sam?" Miguel's efficient voice pulled me from my thoughts. "The valet just brought your Porsche around."

"Thanks, Miguel," I said. "You have all the print samples we brought? The new cardstock options and foil-embossed mock-ups?"

"All accounted for." Miguel patted the sleek black suitcase he wheeled alongside him. "We're good to go."

"Perfect." I clapped him on the shoulder. "Then let's hit the road."

We strode out into the bitter night air. It wasn't snowing, but the wind was awful. I tipped the valet as Miguel stowed the suitcase in the back seat. By the time I slid into the driver's seat, Miguel was hopping into the passenger seat.

The purr of the engine filled the air as we buckled in, and I drove out of the parking lot.

"Thanks for your help tonight," I said as the car smoothly rolled down the street. "The meeting went off without a hitch, and Mr. Reeves is one of our pickier clients."

"Of course. It was the office support staff who prepped everything, though." Miguel pulled out his phone, his thumbs flying over the screen. The blue glow illuminated his face in the dimness of the car. I merged onto the highway, the city lights blurring into streaks of neon color.

As we cruised along, I recalled what I'd heard Miguel tell Charlotte, Isaac's executive assistant, this morning. "Didn't you say Kyle was sick this morning? Is he doing any better?"

Miguel glanced up from his phone, his brow furrowing slightly at the mention of his husband. "Actually, I was just checking in with him. He said he's feeling a little better. Hopefully it was just a short flu and he'll sleep through the night."

"I'm glad to hear that."

"Me too." Miguel tucked his phone away and shifted to face me. "But now that the dinner is over and we have no pressing business matters to discuss, it's high time you tell me how the family dinner went with Natalie."

I kept my eyes on the road, grateful for the excuse not to meet his probing gaze.

Miguel was the only one on my side who knew Natalie and I were fake dating; it was unavoidable since he was privy to my schedule. But he also knew of my additional ... aspirations.

I schooled my features into a mask of nonchalance. "It went as expected, with smiles all around. I poured on the charm, Natalie played her part. Mother and the others were thoroughly fooled into thinking our relationship was genuine."

"Mmhmm." Miguel leaned back in his seat. "And I'm sure you hated every minute of it?"

My mind flashed back to last night—Natalie's melodic laugh, the way that black dress hugged her curves, the spark in her eyes when she smiled ...

"It's all part of the plan, Miguel." I kept my voice light, belying the tension thrumming through me. "Natalie doesn't suspect a thing. As far as she's concerned, this is just business."

"Sure," Miguel agreed. "But you said Natalie did well?"

"Yes. She was perfectly pleasant. She didn't even blink when Isaac slipped up and mentioned it was a shame so much of downtown Fox Creek was protected from being knocked down by historic preservation codes."

"You sound bothered she didn't mind."

"No," I said. "It's just that if I had been the one to say that, she would have probably arranged for my car to be towed by claiming I broke some obscure parking law."

"She must really want your families to get along after all. The poor dear," Miguel said. "She has no idea what's coming, and your insistence on all this subterfuge is going to make your little plan blow up in your face."

"You were congratulating me when I first announced Natalie's proposal."

"I was," Miguel agreed. "Because I thought you would make your move faster than turtle speed."

I tightened my grip on the steering wheel. "I've got this handled."

Even as the words left my lips, a flicker of doubt crept in. I was good at my job. Warner Print was my family's legacy, and I intended to live up to it. But this deal with Natalie ... it did strike me that it was perhaps a little cruel to have her working so hard for our families when I had an ulterior motive.

"I suppose you haven't bungled anything yet," Miguel said, breaking into my thoughts. "I thought for sure Natalie would see right through you, but you've been fine so far."

I chuckled. "Ye of little faith. She hasn't caught on despite all these years."

"Are you so sure about that?" Miguel asked. "You really think she doesn't suspect anything? She's dangerously smart."

"I'm positive." I thought of the way she'd bristled in this very car on the way to my mother's house. "And by the time she realizes the truth, it'll be too late."

Miguel cleared his throat. "Fine, great, but once again I urge you to consider moving *faster*. Since secrecy is required for this, I haven't even told Kyle. He is going to be upset when he finds out about it."

"I know, I know," I grumbled, navigating the Porsche through the downtown traffic with practiced ease. "But I can't afford to rush this. One wrong move and it all falls apart, and I won't get a second chance."

Miguel gave me a look of pity. "I understand."

A moment of silence stretched between us, the hum of the engine and the muted sounds of the city filtering through the car's soundproofing. Then Miguel spoke again, his voice taking on a more businesslike cadence.

"With that fun topic over, shall we discuss tomorrow's schedule? You have back-to-back meetings in the morning to discuss finances with Isaac before you make your presentation to the company board, followed by a luncheon with them."

"Sounds thrilling," I deadpanned. "No wonder Isaac stuck me with the CEO role. He wanted to get out of the endless meetings."

"He knew you were better for this job, but you're also not wrong," Miguel said. "Charlotte told me Isaac took the CFO role because he wanted to see people only when absolutely necessary."

"How giving of him."

"Indeed. So after the luncheon you're scheduled to walk the printer floor …"

Chapter 11

Natalie

Tip #11: *Use nicknames to convince others your relationship is real, and ideally to embarrass/irritate your coconspirator.*

The freezing wind whipped around Owen and me as we huddled together in a grocery store parking lot, standing in line for Javier's food truck. I glanced over at Owen, his nurse scrubs peeking out from beneath his heavy winter coat, and tried my best to ignore the chattering of my teeth. My business casual attire and wool coat were no match for the cold.

"Remind me again, why are we waiting outside in this Arctic tundra for lunch?" I shivered.

"Because in the winter months, Javier's is only open every other Tuesday, and you're addicted to his tacos," Owen said.

"Right, priorities," I grumbled just as my phone rang. Fishing it out of my coat pocket, I saw that it was Samuel. That was surprising, since he preferred texting, not to mention it was the middle of a workday. I answered, tentative. "Hello?"

"Hey, Natalie. Am I interrupting you at work?" Samuel asked.

"No, I'm on lunch break. I'm grabbing tacos from Javier's."

"The food truck? You're standing outside in the freezing cold by yourself?" He sounded incredulous.

"Uh, well, I'm not alone. Owen's here too."

"Ah, well that makes the freezing temperatures and terrible windchill OK then," Samuel teased sarcastically. "Anyway. I called you, Miss Abominable Snowman, because I wanted to review our performance at the Warner family dinner."

"Why?" I asked. "Did I screw up?"

"Not at all," he said. "But you still need to be prepared for meeting my grandfather, and I want to make certain you are satisfied with how things went."

"Aw, wow. You're such a dutiful fa—fabulous boyfriend." As I recovered from almost publicly calling Samuel my fake boyfriend, I glanced at Owen, and he pointedly looked at the other frozen Fox Creek residents standing in line with us.

Samuel chuckled, and the sound caressed my ears even though I was hearing it through a phone. "That's right, I forgot you've got an audience. What other shameless things should I say while you can't retaliate?"

"Watch it, snuggle-boo," I shot back playfully. "If you go too far I'll repay you next time we meet."

"Good point. Speaking of which, we're due for another public appearance around town."

"Why?" I asked, confused.

"Because we're supposedly dating, honey bear." Samuel sounded half amused, half irritated.

"Oh, yeah we are. I would totally love to go on a date with you," I replied, impressing myself that I'd said it without gritting my teeth.

Owen nudged me and whispered, "Invite him to the sledding party tomorrow."

I hesitated, unsure if the smaller group setting was the best way to sell our fake relationship. It wouldn't have as big of an impact. But on the plus side, everyone in the group would gossip about Samuel's presence.

"Hey, would you like to come to a sledding party with Owen and me tomorrow?" I asked, expecting him to decline.

"Sure, sounds fun," he replied, shocking me. "Are you hoping I'll get a face full of snow?"

"Darling, you know me too well."

"Naturally," Samuel said. "Text me the details when you have a moment."

"Sounds great," I agreed. "But, unfortunately, I should go. We're almost at the front of the line. Only one person is left between us and the mouthwatering promise of Javier's tacos."

"Enjoy your lunch, Natalie," Samuel said before hanging up. As I slipped my phone back into my coat pocket, it dawned on me that we'd just had a civil, even friendly conversation. Maybe ending the family feud was actually worth pursuing after all.

"Do you know what you're getting?" Owen asked as the scent of sizzling carne asada and fresh cilantro tickled my frozen nostrils.

"Of course." My stomach rumbled in anticipation. "I assumed we were getting our usuals."

"If it ain't broke, don't fix it." Owen nodded with approval.

While the person in front of us continued ordering, I crowded closer to my older brother. "Thanks for the idea about inviting Sam to the sledding party."

"No problem," Owen replied, accepting my gratitude with a shrug.

"But, you know, as a good girlfriend," I began sweetly, batting my eyelashes, "I'm concerned about making Sam feel welcome. So, if you happen to run into Jenna this afternoon, maybe you could invite her? I'm sure he'd feel so much better if his cousin went sledding with us too."

Owen's expression instantly shifted from warmth to irritation, and he glared at me. But before he could respond, the person ahead of us finished ordering, leaving the window open for us.

"Our turn!" I chirped, brightly bounding up to the truck and making my escape. "Javier! My man! I am dying for your tacos!"

Chapter 12

Natalie

Tip #12: *Snow is an excellent mood setter for both a romantic aesthetic and to throw in your enemy's face while "playing".*

"One more block and we're there," I said.

Samuel and I were walking down the sidewalk, heading for Fox Creek's best sledding hill. (Correction, Samuel was walking, as he was wearing snowboarding pants and a snowboarding jacket, which were easier to move around in. I was waddling in my thick snow pants.)

"Great," Samuel said as we passed another streetlight that cast a cheerful glow on us. It was only six in the evening, but the sun set early in January in Wisconsin. "And you're certain this thing will hold an adult without falling to pieces?" Samuel gestured with my beloved plastic orange sled, which he was carrying for me.

"Rude," I said. "The Flying Carrot is practically a family heirloom."

"Yeah, because it's probably older than either of us." Samuel dubiously studied the sled, which admittedly had seen better days. "Why do you call it the Flying Carrot, anyway?"

"Childhood nickname," I said. "You'll see. It might be old, but its edge is stronger than the ones on the wimpy plastic sleds they make today. It really flies!"

"I see," Samuel said, unconvinced.

"I don't like your attitude, but we have arrived!" I pointed to the snow-covered hill ahead of us.

"How picturesque." Samuel watched as a dozen or so sledders zoomed down the hill with glee.

The popular sledding spot had a shorter slant that swooped down to a chain-link fence that surrounded the tennis court and a steeper section that dumped off into a small swampy retaining pond filled with cattails and some tenacious burdock.

"I haven't been sledding since I was a kid," Samuel said.

"Then you're in for a night of fun." I would have folded my arms across my chest, but my coat was too puffy to manage it, so I settled for planting my glove-covered hands on my hips. "But, fair warning, you might want to pop some painkillers later tonight because bruises are pretty much guaranteed."

"Are you two just going to stand there and watch, or are you actually going to join the fun?" a snarky voice called out.

Marjorie and Grandma Mann were sitting together on a wooden bench on the same side of the street as the sledding hill. They were bundled up in their winter coats and had a wool blanket spread over their laps. They also held steaming to-go cups adorned with the unmistakable Kwik Trip logo, which they'd probably procured from the Kwik Trip gas station across the street.

"Hey!" I waved at them as we walked closer. "What brings you two out here in the cold?"

"Laughing at the sledders and calling EMTs when needed," Marjorie replied dryly.

"Brenda from my bridge club told me about your little sledding date. Naturally, I just had to be here," Grandma Mann chimed in. She used two fingers to point to her eyes and then jabbed her pointer finger at Samuel. "I'm watching you, Warner!"

"Of course," Samuel shouted back to her. "Did you bring any mouse hitchhikers with you tonight?"

Marjorie cackled, and Grandma Mann gave a big, "Harrumph!" But I could see the smile that threatened to take over her mouth.

Samuel was slowly ... well ... maybe not winning her over just yet, but ingratiating himself?

I glanced up the hill. "We'll get a few rounds of sledding in, and then we'll come report in," I told the ladies.

Grandma Mann waved me off. "Have fun!"

"Don't break anything," Marjorie added.

I waved again, then led Samuel up the hill. At the top, we were greeted by Piper, my cousin Madison, and her husband Ryan, who was helping his kids, Noah and Anna, into their watermelon-green sled.

"Hey, guys! We made it! You all know Sam, my boyfriend, right?" I introduced him just as Noah and Anna went flying down the hill, barely missing the tennis court fence.

"We might have seen him around Fox Creek before," Ryan drawled before giving me a friendly wink.

Madison scowled. "Yeah. I've learned more about him than

I ever wanted to know about any Warner." She suspiciously eyed him.

"How appropriate." Samuel grinned. "Because I've learned more about your romance with Ryan than I ever wanted to thanks to Noah's tendency to share overheard details. Shall we call it even?"

Madison studied Samuel with narrowed eyes, so I was guessing it was time to change the subject.

"Where's Owen?" I asked.

Piper pointed down the hill.

The cold air nipped at my cheeks as I turned to see Owen, bundled up like a bear in his winter gear, trudging up the hill. He was dragging a purple plastic toboggan behind him and laughing with none other than Jenna Warner.

I wanted to cackle at the sight. It seemed that our fake relationship really was providing the opening the pair needed. With some luck, things would keep on progressing between them!

"Hey, you two!" I called out, waving them over. "Fancy seeing you here!"

"Hey, Natalie, Samuel," Owen greeted us, a mischievous glint in his eye.

Jenna followed behind him, her cheeks red from the cold and a big smile on her face as she tucked her scarf into her coat. "Hi, Natalie. Hey, Sam!"

"I didn't expect to see you here, Jenna," Samuel said.

"Owen invited me since you were coming." Jenna rushed up to the top of the hill. "This is so much fun!"

"Isn't it?" I agreed, taking the orange sled from Samuel. "Come on, boo-bear. I'll show you how it's done."

"Wait," Owen called after me, too smugly for my liking. "You can't just leave Samuel behind. The Flying Carrot isn't big enough for both of you."

"Thank you, Captain Obvious," I said. "I figured you would be kind enough to lend him a sled."

"That won't be necessary," Owen said. "I thought you two would want to snuggle up, so I brought Uncle Jeff's toboggan." He handed over the rope attached to the front of the purple sled. "Enjoy the close quarters." His smirk was so big it took over his face.

Oh yeah. This was definitely payback for cornering him into inviting Jenna.

I grumbled under my breath about Owen being a twerp as I dragged the toboggan toward the edge of the hill. "Come on, Sam."

Samuel followed after me. "Right behind you, honey buns."

I scowled at him before plopping down on the toboggan. "Alright. Get in ..." I realized there was no way Samuel could scrunch up behind me like Madison or Piper would have. "New plan." I rolled off the toboggan, then patted it like it was a horse. "Since you're so tall, you'll have to sit down first. Stretch your legs out in front of you and push them to the sides of the toboggan."

"Where will you sit?" Samuel asked.

"Between your legs," I dryly said while wishing I could curse Owen for putting me in this position—literally.

"Got it," Samuel breezily said, unbothered. He settled into the toboggan, then I climbed on, sitting between his legs. As I tried to ignore my rapidly growing sense of awkwardness, I told myself that this didn't matter. We were both bundled up like marshmallows—I couldn't even feel how firm his chest was through all the layers.

Samuel rested his chin on my shoulder and wrapped his arms around my waist. "Isn't this cozy?"

"Shut up," I muttered.

"Why, sweet pea, are you maybe feeling our deep and powerful chemistry?" Samuel asked in a mocking voice.

Thankfully, I was spared from answering when Piper called out to us. "Do you want me to push you?"

"That would be great, thank you!" I said.

Piper crunched her way across the snow, then knelt down behind the toboggan. "Ready?"

"Yes," Samuel said.

Piper pushed against Samuel's back, giving us the shove we needed to start our wild ride.

I whooped as we started to rapidly pick up momentum.

The toboggan shot down the hill at breakneck speed—much faster than I'd ever gone with Piper or Madison. I tightened my grip on the rope, and my heart raced as the toboggan wobbled from side to side.

Snow sprayed my bare face when the edge of the toboggan clipped a drift, and I shrieked at the stinging sensation.

Samuel laughed as I tried to shake some of the snow free.

Our toboggan veered dangerously in the direction of the tennis courts—we were going to smash into the chain-link fence if we didn't make defensive maneuvers.

It was time to bail out.

Samuel was still laughing at me for getting a face full of snow, so with no small amount of vindication, I decided to position my fall so as to use him as my landing pad.

I let go of the rope—I could barely see now anyway. We were going so fast the stinging cold air was making my eyes water.

Lurching backward, I crashed into Samuel, knocking us both out of the toboggan. As planned, I landed squarely on top of him, hoping with a flame of satisfaction that I'd knocked the wind out of him.

"Should we call an ambulance?" Marjorie hollered from the bench, sounding almost hopeful.

"Thanks, but we're good!" I yelled back, struggling to peel myself off Samuel.

Before I could move away, Samuel wrapped his arms around me and rolled to the side, pinning me beneath him. I let out a high-pitched shriek, which made him laugh. We tumbled together in the snow, our laughter echoing through the crisp winter air.

"Ugh. Disgusting!" Owen's pretend gag was audible as his voice echoed down the hill from where he stood with Jenna at the top.

Ryan slapped a hand over his heart. "Madison, why don't we frolic and play like Nat and Samuel anymore?"

"Because you have carpal tunnel and bad knees," Madison said.

Samuel and I stopped wrestling in the snow, and our laughter quieted as we locked eyes. Samuel's playful smile faded, but it didn't turn into his usual mask of polite charm. Instead, he looked ... relaxed. And there was something about the way his dark eyes glittered.

Samuel leaned a little closer, and I wondered if he was going to whisper something to me or kiss me when the moment was abruptly shattered.

"No, Marjorie, I think you ought to call an ambulance after all," Grandma Mann drawled. "They are both clearly addled."

"Addled with *love*," Marjorie said.

Up the hill, Owen's gagging noises increased in volume.

I laughed and sat up, brushing snow off my clothes. "Ready for another round?"

"Absolutely," Samuel said.

We got up and fixed our askew winter hats. Samuel grabbed

the toboggan's rope and dragged it behind him as we started up the hill.

Noah and Anna reached the crest of the hill just before us, working together to carry their green sled.

"I want to go as fast as Cousin Nat!" Anna said.

"Yeah!" Noah chimed in.

"That would probably take two adults packed into a sled with you two," Owen said.

"Probably, but how could you fit that many people on the sled?" Ryan asked.

As Ryan and Owen pondered the puzzle, Piper waved Samuel and me over. "You two looked like you were having a blast."

"Oh, yeah, sledding is always fun." I tried to sound normal even though I was winded from climbing the hill in all of my winter clothes.

"It was even more fun than I remember it being as a kid," Samuel said.

I blinked, surprised. "Really?"

"Yes. Because there are new benefits I can appreciate." He wrapped an arm around my shoulders and scooped me close to make his point.

I laughed, and Jenna joined in.

"I never knew you were such a romantic, Sam, but it seems like Natalie brings out the best in you." Jenna turned to me, her eyes bright. "Your family—and friends—are so much fun," she told me breathlessly. "I can't remember the last time I laughed this hard."

"I'm glad to hear that," I said, genuinely pleased. It boded well for Owen's crush, but more importantly, it showed that maybe there was hope for the Warners and the Manns.

Hanging out with Samuel was turning out to be a lot more fun than I'd thought.

Piper called out to Owen, "Do you have a plan for your bullet sled ride, or are you just winging it?"

Owen saluted her. "We've got a plan." He nodded toward Ryan and pumped his arms over his head.

"Two adults will lie in the toboggan," Ryan explained, his breath turning into misty clouds under the golden glow of the nearby streetlights, "one adult stacked on top of the other, and Noah and Anna will sit on top of them like they're riding a pony."

Samuel raised an eyebrow. "And which lucky adults have volunteered for this death-defying stunt?"

Owen clapped him on the shoulder. "I'm so glad you asked, Samuel! We were actually thinking of bestowing that honor upon you and Natalie."

"Absolutely not," I interjected before Samuel could respond. "My survival instincts are way too strong for something like that."

"Oh, come on," Ryan said. "We have two nurses here!"

"Save it, Ryan, I know that mulish look on her face," Owen said. "We'll have to go."

Madison leaned up to give her husband a quick kiss, her voice teasingly sweet. "Have fun, honey. Remember, I have a great life insurance policy on you."

"Thanks for the vote of confidence," Ryan grumbled as Owen retrieved the toboggan from Samuel and set it on the ground.

With a sigh, Ryan lay belly down, his face at the front of the toboggan. Owen followed suit, stacking himself on top of Ryan.

"Enjoy getting a face full of snow," I said as they got into position.

"Bah! A little bit of cold is worth the thrill of adventure," Ryan declared, trying to sound brave.

"For sure." Owen wheezed as Noah and Anna accidentally

kneed him in the side as they climbed onto his back and settled into place.

"Need a push?" Samuel offered, grinning at the precarious tower of people on the sled.

"Please," Ryan said, trying to sound gracious even though he was squashed on the bottom of the pile.

Samuel gave the toboggan a hearty shove, sending them hurtling down the steep portion of the hill.

"Wow, they're going way faster than Samuel and Natalie did," Piper said.

"Definitely," Jenna agreed as the toboggan picked up even more speed.

Madison plucked her beanie off her head, sending her glorious red hair cascading over her shoulders as she shook snow off her hat. "Do you think all that momentum is going to get them into trouble?"

Around then both Ryan and Owen yelled. (It was more of a scream, but I knew my brother and my cousin by marriage would deeply object to that description.)

"Ah, they're getting their faces washed with snow," I said with the wisdom of experience.

They were going so fast now the toboggan was visibly vibrating.

When they reached the bottom of the hill, instead of slowing to a stop as usual, their momentum carried them on, whisking them across the brief flat stretch.

"Uh-oh," Piper said. "I think they're going to go into the swamp."

Noah and Anna must have agreed with this assessment, because both kids bailed out, tipping over so they tumbled into the snow.

Ryan and Owen, however, were lying flat and couldn't get out so easily.

A Guide to Fake Dating Your Enemy

They were still on the toboggan when it went over the lip of the hill. The sled got air, tossing the two men into the sky before tumbling down into the frozen swamp.

Everything was silent, and Grandma Mann even stood up and whipped out her phone, prepared to call 911.

Madison cupped her hands around her mouth. "Ryan, are you dead?"

A pained *"Ow"* echoed up the hill, followed by, "I think I landed on my phone!"

"It's fine." Madison winked and gave us a gloved thumbs-up. "They're alive."

Ryan and Owen climbed out of the swamp, cattail fuzz dotting their clothes, dragging the plastic toboggan behind them.

Marjorie and Grandma Mann cheered—or maybe jeered—at the pair.

"I give their performance a nine." Grandma Mann sat back down on the bench, tugging the wool blanket over her lap as she settled into place now that her moment of grandmotherly concern had ended.

"I give it an early knee replacement," Marjorie yelled for our benefit. "They're going to feel that ride in about four years' time!"

I squinted in the dim light, making out little brown balls that stuck to Owen's and Ryan's hats, scarves, and gloves. "Uh-oh, I think they got tossed into some burdock."

The hooked burrs were a pain in the butt to get out of clothes, and Owen practically had a crown of them.

"Oh no," Jenna said. "I hope they're not hurt!"

Noah and Anna scrambled up the hill, giggling and laughing.

"That was so fun!" Anna said.

"Again, I want to go again!" Noah said.

He must have been loud enough for Ryan and Owen to hear

at the base of the hill, as Ryan desperately shouted, "No! Not again!"

"Aww," Anna said.

"Why?" Noah asked.

I laughed and glanced up at Samuel to see if he was enjoying himself like everyone else. He had a subdued smile, and there was something about the way he watched the scene ... I couldn't tell if it was regretful or wistful.

He must have felt my eyes on him, because he looked down at me, raising his eyebrows.

"So, how does sledding compare to snowboarding?" I asked. "Is it as much fun?"

His subtle smile bloomed back into a full grin, and he somehow managed to wrap both of his arms around me. "Oh, Nat. Anything I do with you is fun!"

Chapter 13

Natalie

Tip #13: *Take time to appreciate the perks of fake dating your enemy—like witnessing their family embarrass them.*

The warm glow of the setting sun streamed through the skylights in Fox Creek City Hall, casting long shadows across the polished floor. I glanced at the clock and saw that it was already five, closing time.

As I helped a middle-aged woman register her dog, my eyes wandered to an older man who had entered just moments before. He looked vaguely familiar, with silver hair neatly combed back, gray eyes, and leathery skin with smile lines that hinted at a lifetime of laughter.

"Here's your dog tag," I said, handing it over to the woman. "Have a great day!"

"Thank you. You've been such a help!" The woman walked away with a smile.

I smiled as the older man approached the front desk, still trying to place him in my mental Rolodex of Fox Creek's residents. "Good evening. Just to let you know, we will be closing soon, but I'll try to help you and get you sent off on your way first."

"Thank you," the man said. "Could you tell me, are you Natalie Mann?"

"Guilty as charged," I joked.

"How wonderful. I'm Walter." He extended his hand over the desk for a firm shake. "I'm here to meet you, actually."

A flicker of recognition sparked inside me. Walter Warner! I'd seen him at various annual town functions but rarely interacted with him. "You're Mr. Warner, Sam's grandfather?"

"Please, call me Walter. Mr. Warner is too formal for my grandson's girlfriend." He flashed me a charming grin reminiscent of Samuel's.

I laughed nervously. "All right, Walter. What can I do for you?"

"Please allow me to take you out to dinner tonight, if you are available. I would love to have a chance to chat with you," Walter politely said.

I hesitated.

I was pretending to be Samuel's girlfriend, and any serious girlfriend would agree to meet her boyfriend's family.

But interacting with one of Sam's family members without him? This could get interesting.

"Thank you for the invite. I'd love to join you tonight," I said. "Where would you like to eat? I can meet you there after helping the rest of the staff lock up."

"I have a reservation at Verona Veranda." Walter's eyes crinkled at the corners as he smiled. "I'll see you soon, Natalie."

Half an hour later I left the howling wind outside and walked into Verona Veranda, a local Italian restaurant. The place smelled of garlic and tomato sauce and had me instantly drooling. The cozy atmosphere was accented by dim lighting, rustic wooden tables draped with red checkered tablecloths, and an array of potted ferns that added a touch of greenery.

Pulling out my phone, I quickly sent Samuel a text. (I realized on my way over I should probably give him a heads-up.)

> Hey, just so you know, I'm having dinner with your grandfather at Verona Veranda.

With that out of the way, a waitress led me to Walter's table, where he sat smiling patiently. I noticed that the round table had four chairs, each set with silverware.

I slid into the chair directly across from him so we'd be facing each other. "Hello! I hope you haven't been waiting too long."

"Not at all," Walter said. "I'm excited to get to know you better. I apologize for not being there when Samuel introduced you to the rest of the family. At the time I thought his revelation of having a secret girlfriend was a ploy to get me to attend a family dinner."

"Ah, family antics. Don't worry about it," I said. "But why would you think Samuel was lying about having a girlfriend?"

Walter studied me for a moment, his dark eyes seemingly searching for something within me. Feeling self-conscious, I took a sip of water from the glass already set in front of my spot.

Walter finally answered cryptically, "Samuel has his heart set on what I believed to be an impossible goal."

My confusion must have shown, because Walter chuckled. Before I could ask what he meant, my phone buzzed with an incoming text from Sam. I hesitated, then apologized to Walter. "I'm so sorry. It's Sam."

Walter's enigmatic smile grew. "Go ahead and read it."

"Thanks." I glanced at my cell phone.

> **Sweetums**
> Don't go into the restaurant!

I quickly texted Sam back.

> Too late, already inside and talking to Walter.

> **Sweetums**
> %$#&@

I stared at his confusing message of symbols. "He must be apoplectic," I muttered. But why was chatting with Walter such a big deal? Since our phone call while I was waiting for tacos, Samuel had briefed me on how to act around his grandfather.

"He's upset?" Walter guessed.

"He's ... something," I said.

"Did he warn you about me?"

"Yes," I hesitantly said.

Walter's smile grew slyer. "And you still decided to meet with me?"

"Yes." I put on my customer service smile and hoped I hadn't made a big mistake.

"Interesting." Walter leaned back in his chair.

I gulped as a waiter appeared beside our table. He carried a basket of steaming breadsticks, their aroma making my mouth water. Setting the basket down on the table between us, the waiter retreated just as quickly as he'd arrived.

"Relax, Natalie." Walter's eyes twinkled with amusement. "Despite any tales Sam might have told you, I promise I'm not some crusty old dragon. In fact, I imagine Sam is racing to the restaurant as we speak."

Walter's guess was likely right but not because Samuel was worried about me. More likely because he was a control freak and was worried our farce would come to light. But I couldn't exactly say that to his grandfather.

"Does it bother you that Samuel and I are dating?" I selected a breadstick and bit into it. It had the perfect balance of crust and soft innards, and the top was dusted with a garlic salt that melted in my mouth.

Walter waved off my concerns with an airy gesture. "Not in the least. I've always been a fan of a good *Romeo and Juliet* remake, and I'm quite happy you're smart enough to think things over instead of making things dramatic." He paused, eyeing me thoughtfully. "Tell me, do you happen to enjoy any particular television shows?"

"Comedies mostly," I said, wondering where this was going.

"That bodes very well for your future," Walter replied cryptically, his gaze shifting to something behind me.

Twisting in my chair, I spotted Samuel speed walking through the restaurant. His necktie was loosened, his suit coat draped over one arm, and the sleeves of his white button-up were rolled up to his elbows.

"Ah. He must have been very upset," Walter said. "He looks quite disheveled."

"That's disheveled?" I asked indignantly.

It wasn't fair! Samuel was still so handsome—he might have even looked more handsome than usual, as the tousled look made him more approachable! Why couldn't perfect Samuel Warner at least turn red or something?

Samuel reached our table, his dark eyes flitting warily between Walter and me. He absently placed his left hand on my shoulder, standing so close I could feel the heat radiating from his body. "Hello, Natalie." He offered me a smile before frowning at Walter. "Why did you kidnap her, Grandfather? I thought we agreed I would arrange a meeting when our schedules allowed for time?"

"Kidnap?" Walter laughed, shaking his head. "I merely lured her here with the promise of food, which she seems to be pleased with." He gestured toward the breadsticks I'd been munching on.

"I am very pleased," I said.

Samuel sighed and took a seat in one of the empty chairs at our round table, although he went through the trouble of scooting his chair closer to mine.

Once settled, he shot an accusing look at his grandfather. "You had a chance to meet Natalie. You chose to pass on it."

"That's hardly fair," Walter countered, his tone light and teasing. "You knew the night Natalie was visiting was the premiere of my favorite detective show. You probably picked that night for that precise reason! And let's not forget how shady you were about the details of your relationship, making the whole thing rather unbelievable."

As they bantered back and forth, I marveled at the similarities between the two Warner men. Similar expressions flashed across their faces, and I could clearly see where Sam got his charm from.

There was a sudden warmth around my shoulders as Samuel slid his arm around me, pulling me closer. With an empathetic pat on his thigh, I locked eyes with him and offered a reassuring smile. "It's OK. I felt the same way when Mom told my grandparents. It's just because he loves you."

Samuel's tense expression softened into a smile. "Sorry for the dramatic entrance, Nat." Leaning in, he brushed his lips against my cheek once, then twice, in a lingering kiss. I even felt his breath fan some of my curls.

I cleared my throat and forced my voice to be normal—I *would* hold steady against this onslaught of chemistry!

"You have nothing to apologize for." I glanced at Walter, who was watching our exchange with an amused smirk.

"Why don't we look at the menus and order dinner, hmm?" Walter asked.

Samuel started to shake his head, but then my stomach growled.

"Fine." Samuel leaned back in his chair. "But if Mother gets upset because we didn't invite her to this little tête-à-tête, I'm throwing you under the bus, Grandfather."

Chapter 14

Natalie

Tip #14: *Be open to befriending your enemy during your fake relationship. Nothing brings people together like trauma bonding.*

The moment I set foot on the snow-dusted grounds of McBride Farm & Greenhouse, the scent of pine and freshly chipped wood had me sighing with nostalgia. The pale morning sun cast a golden glow over the farm, making it feel like a scene straight out of a postcard.

I stood on my tiptoes, struggling to look over the heads of the crowd as I watched for Samuel.

I was bundled up in my winter coat, scarf, and gloves and felt a bit like a woolly mammoth. This feeling was only amplified when I saw Samuel waiting by the charming red barn that served as the entrance to the McBride farm grounds. Samuel's stylish snowboarder coat accentuated his tall, athletic build, and he looked like a clothes model, as he also wore a matching hat and gloves.

"Hey, Nat. You made it." Samuel extended a gloved hand to me.

I took it so we loosely held hands. "Yep! Ready to go in?"

"Yes." Samuel swung our joined hands and tugged me through the barn entrance, passing through so we popped out onto the sprawling grounds on the other side.

The atmosphere was alive with laughter and chatter as people bustled about, enjoying the winter festivities.

"This place is packed," Samuel said.

Around us, families were ice-skating on a frozen pond, building snowmen in a nearby field, and skiing on the flag marked cross-country ski trails. Glass greenhouses filled with concession stands selling hot chocolate, coffee, hot apple cider, fresh doughnuts, and cinnamon waffles tempted us at every turn.

"Yeah, it's always busy during their Winter Weekends," I said.

McBride Farm & Greenhouse changed their offerings with every season. They were open daily in December for Christmas tree sales, but in January and February they limited their time to weekends only and offered an abundance of winter-themed activities. (My personal favorite was the mesmerizing display of ice and snow sculptures. Some of them were the size of small dogs, but the previous year a snow sculptor made a dragon the size of a bus!)

Samuel scanned the farm, his gaze lingering on the area set aside for snow forts—the McBrides had four snow forts in different sizes, with two of them being big enough for adults to walk through.

Going by his expression, Samuel looked like he hadn't seen any of the wintertime fun before.

"When was the last time you came to one of the Winter Weekends?" I asked.

"Never," Samuel said.

"Never? You've never been here before?"

"Correct."

"But coming to McBride for our *date* was your idea," I said.

"My family usually skated on the lake by our house when it froze over," Samuel explained. "Or we went skiing and snowboarding in Colorado. You know, typical Warner things." His tone was light and teasing.

I gave him a flat look. "So sorry, I guess I forgot for a moment I was talking to a rich-kid Warner."

Samuel laughed. "I know it sounds ridiculously extravagant. But my dad loved winter. He was the one that always wanted to go to Colorado, so we Warners haven't done much in the snow since he passed away."

"Oh," I said, my heart aching for him. "I'm sorry."

Samuel smiled a little and swung our joined hands for emphasis. "That's why I'm glad we can do this together. Going sledding with your family and friends made me remember what I've been missing out on."

"Yeah." I cleared my throat and slapped on a smile. "I guess I'll just have to be your guide today. I practically lived here during the Winter Weekends when I was in high school, so I know all the best activities and what to avoid. Starting with the snow forts—don't touch the walls. All the kids like to lick and/or gnaw on them for some reason."

Samuel laughed as he pulled his phone out of his pocket with his free hand. "Sounds perfect." He glanced at his phone for a moment before putting it away. "But first, we have a reservation to get to."

"Reservation?" I frowned, puzzled. "This place doesn't have any activities that require reservations."

"Maybe not normally, but you're with a rich-kid Warner." With a mischievous grin, Samuel tugged on my hand and led me through the crowds, past the bustling sleigh ride station where people waited in line for one of the farm's large sleighs, pulled by a team of draft horses, to arrive.

We slipped away from the crowd, taking an employee path that left the event grounds and wound around a thicket of trees.

"Where are we going?" I asked.

"You'll see."

As we emerged from the trees, I blinked in surprise at the sight of a horse stable with an attached paddock. A stable hand was hooking a magnificent black Shire horse up to a small, elegant sleigh. The horse's glossy black coat gleamed in the pale winter sun, and the sleigh looked like it belonged in a fairy tale, adorned with intricate carvings and painted a beautiful red color.

"Samuel, what is this?" I asked.

"Surprise," he said. "While I've never been here for a Winter Weekend, my family knows the McBrides pretty well. We've arranged for private company events here, and they hold private parties for us when we're entertaining clients. One of the perks is taking them out on sleigh rides."

The stable hand finished checking the horse's hooves, which were covered by white, feathery hair, and beamed at us. "Samuel! Hey! I've got Goose here all ready to go for you!"

"Thanks, Matt," Samuel said. "I appreciate it."

"No problem!" Matt caught me gawking at the horse. "If you want, you can come pet him. Goose is very friendly."

I let go of Samuel's hand so I could approach the large horse. I patted his muscled neck and scratched the white blaze on his massive head when he obligingly lowered it for me. "This is really cool."

"Shall we?" Samuel held out his hand to help me up into the sleigh.

It was a big step up, so I hoisted my right foot up into the sleigh. The cushioned bench we would sit on was smaller than the ones typically used for group sleigh rides, and I didn't think there would be enough room for anyone besides the two of us.

I pushed off the ground, balancing on the one foot I had in the sleigh. "Where's the driver?"

"You're talking to him," Samuel said, his tone confident. "I'll be driving."

I nearly lost my balance trying to turn toward him, but he tucked an arm around my waist, steadying me. "You? You're going to drive the sleigh?" I echoed.

Matt laughed. "Have some trust in your boyfriend! Samuel's been driving horses for about five years now. He learned so he and his brother could take clients out without needing a driver. Warner Print has a special arrangement with us here at McBride."

"Logan worked it out with the McBrides' insurance company, which was quite the battle," Samuel added with a wry smile. "Honestly, driving is not as impressive as it sounds. The horses know the trails by heart and don't spook easily, so I mostly just hold the reins."

Despite my apprehension, I was impressed by this unexpected skill of Samuel's. After he hopped up into the sleigh beside me and tucked a blanket around my lap, I offered him a tentative smile.

Goose nickered and stomped a hoof, eager to be on his way.

"Alright, Goose," Samuel said, picking up the reins. "Walk on."

"Enjoy your date!" Matt gave us a friendly wave as Goose

obediently set off at a walk, the sleigh bells attached to his harness jingling with each step.

I never thought I'd be one to ogle competency, but there was something attractive about the sight of Samuel confidently guiding the massive horse through the picturesque winter landscape. He deftly twitched the reins, steering Goose over to the snowy trail the sleighs used.

The trail wound around the other side of the thicket we'd passed on our way to the stables, popping us out in front of the sleigh loading station.

Goose, his ears pricked forward, pulled the sled along the trail, which cut along the edge of the event grounds, giving us a good view of the crowds and winter fun.

"Hey, Nat! And Warner boy!" a familiar voice called out, accompanied by a sharp whistle. I spotted my Uncle Mike, a short, squat man with a potbelly, holding a tray of steaming drinks. He grinned at us from beneath his thick beard as he strode in our direction.

"Whoa, Goose," Samuel said.

Goose came to a stop, his breath turning into misty puffs in the chilly air.

"Hi, Uncle Mike," I called to my jolly relative. "Good to see you!"

"I could say the same! You two look as pretty as a picture together," Uncle Mike said. "If I didn't have these here drinks, I'd be of the mind to take a picture of you two."

"So you could share it in the family chat?" I wryly guessed.

"You know it!" Uncle Mike laughed, but his expression turned serious when his gaze shifted from me to Samuel. "Now, you better treat my niece right, Warner boy. Nat's a treasure, one I'm not sure you deserve."

"Uncle Mike!" I hissed. I would have shouted, but I didn't want to alarm Goose.

Samuel laughed it off. "I promise, sir. I'll cherish her like the rarest gem."

I worked to keep a pinched expression off my face. It wasn't fair how easily Samuel could respond to my relatives' doubts about our relationship when I had almost sweat through my cardigan the first time I met his family.

Uncle Mike squinted up at us. "Well, Nat seems happy, and I reckon she can take care of herself seeing how there was that time she dumped a bucket of minnows on your head when you two were in college."

"I was in high school then, and I did that to his twin, Isaac," I corrected my uncle. "Isaac told me I was the type of person who wouldn't save for retirement. Even back then he was obsessed with finances."

"I remember that," Samuel said. "Isaac and I were hiking and stumbled on you and Owen fishing at a river." Samuel tilted his head, his voice warm with a fondness I didn't understand. "I'll never forget you hefting the Styrofoam cooler up so you could douse him. You were beautiful."

Uncle Mike and I stared at Samuel.

"You know," Uncle Mike said thoughtfully, "I assumed you were out of your mind, Nat, when I heard you were dating a Warner boy. Maybe it's the other way around and he lost his marbles first."

"Uncle Mike!"

Samuel laughed.

Uncle Mike grinned until he looked away to one of the nearby snow forts. "Better go—my kids are acting like hooligans. Have fun, Nat. And remember, Samuel, the Mann clan is watching!" With that, Uncle Mike hurried off, his belly jiggling as he shouted, "Hey! I told you kids not to start any snowball fights because you'll clip an innocent bystander! You're in high school, you should know better!"

"Walk on, Goose," Samuel instructed, and we resumed our leisurely glide past the lively crowd. I saw a few more friends and family members who I waved to. No one else stopped us like Uncle Mike, but I was pretty sure I saw a few people snapping pictures.

The path veered away from the event grounds, turning into a peaceful lane that cut between rows of towering pine trees. The cacophony of voices faded away, replaced by the gentle rustling of branches, the chirps of birds, and the soft crunch of snow under Goose's hooves. Sunlight filtered through the needles, casting dappled patterns on the glittering snow.

"This was a fun idea, Sam." I tucked my gloved hands under the blanket. "I'm glad you suggested it as a public outing."

Samuel glanced over at me. "I'm happy you're actually enjoying yourself."

"What is that supposed to mean?"

"Just that during our first date at the Winter Craft Fair you looked like you were contemplating murder a few times."

I laughed. "Yeah, but that was then. I think I consider you a friend now." It surprised me how easily the words came out, but that was probably because they were true.

"Friends who kiss and snuggle, right, darling?" he teased, a mischievous glint in his eyes.

"Friends with questionable senses of humor," I sourly said, then added more seriously, "but I've really enjoyed getting to know you and your family better."

Goose continued to pull the sleigh, the runners gliding smoothly over the packed snow.

Samuel was quiet for a moment, his expression turning contemplative. "Do you no longer believe my family is a bunch of villainous Scrooges who are out to ruin Fox Creek?"

I shook my head. "I always knew your family didn't want to

ruin Fox Creek, but I thought you were so focused on economic growth that you'd destroy all its small-town charm."

"Fair enough," Samuel said. "Going around with you ... I see why your family has fought to protect certain landmarks and businesses."

His admission was just another example of the way our agreement had allowed us a glimpse into each other's worlds, and I found that I genuinely liked the person I saw in him.

He adjusted his hold on Goose's reins, guiding the horse and sleigh out of the forest lane. The trail opened up to a field where I remembered the McBrides usually grew strawberries during the summertime.

"I'm glad we're doing this," I confessed as I rubbed my gloved hands together.

"Which part?" Samuel playfully asked. "The sleigh ride or the fake dating to make our families stop feuding?"

"Both," I said. "But I was specifically referring to the fake dating. When I approached you with that crazy idea, I didn't totally believe we'd pull it off. I was surprised you even agreed to it."

Samuel smiled enigmatically. "I have my own reasons for agreeing to this act."

"Are you going to share those reasons?"

"Nope," he replied jokingly. "I need to keep an aura of mystery. I've been told it makes me more attractive."

I laughed as Goose pulled the sleigh across a small bridge that spanned a ditch between two fields and my phone chirped with an incoming text message.

"Who's that?" Samuel asked.

I dug my phone out of a pocket in my jacket. "Owen," I said. I swiped through my phone windows to find his text message.

> **Owen**
> I asked Jenna out on a dinner date.

I frantically typed back.

> And?!

> **Owen**
> She said yes!

I squealed and sent Owen a good half a dozen emojis expressing my excitement, then put my phone away.

"Did something good happen?" Samuel asked.

"Yes!" I said. "Owen just asked Jenna out to dinner, and she said yes!"

"Really?" Samuel asked, surprised.

"Yes!" I clapped my hands in my glee.

"I didn't know Owen liked Jenna."

"Oh yeah. He's been carrying a torch for her for, like, two years now," I said. "So much wistful staring and sighing. It drove me crazy. But I suspected if I cleared the way for Owen and Jenna, they'd end up together!"

"Wait." Samuel looked away from Goose long enough to glance down at me. "Is that the real reason why you proposed we fake date? For Owen and Jenna?"

I sucked in a big breath of air, making my entire chest puff up. "It was a major factor," I said, feeling a little guilty. "Maybe even my main goal …"

"And you purposely hid that from me?"

"... Yeah."

I hadn't expected my plan to work so well, and now that I knew Samuel as well as I did, I recognized that in hiding my real goal, I'd taken advantage of Samuel's goodwill. The thought made me feel a little scummy.

Samuel was quiet, his expression unreadable.

I nervously shifted on the bench, watching Goose toss his head as the trail got to the rows of evergreens the McBrides grew to sell as Christmas trees in December.

Finally, Samuel spoke up. "I can't blame you. We've had years of pushing each other's buttons, so it would make sense you'd doubt me." He smiled down at me.

Relieved he didn't seem upset, I smiled back. "Thanks for understanding." I shivered a little despite my blanket, then gave Samuel the side-eye. "Are you warm enough?"

Samuel twitched the reins when Goose got too close to the edge of the trail. "I'm fine."

"Fine isn't warm," I said.

Samuel started to laugh. "Really—"

He cut off when I scooted closer to him, so I threw the blanket over his lap too. We had to sit closer—our sides pressed together, which I was woefully aware of—but I knew I'd made the right choice when Samuel smiled.

"Thanks," he said.

"Of course. You have to be toasty on a sleigh ride. It's part of the aesthetic."

Goose continued pulling us along the snowy path, the sleigh jostling a little when we passed over bumps in the packed snow. Occasionally a bird darted through the growing Christmas trees, its song mingling with the jingle of sleigh bells.

Samuel bumped his foot against mine, and I settled back in

my seat to enjoy the view, still riding the high of triumph from Owen's text.

As I watched the way Goose's thick black mane flopped with his strides, it occurred to me that if Owen and Jenna's relationship blossomed, there would be no need for Samuel and me to continue our charade. From the get-go I'd planned that once they started dating, they could be the new uniting point between our families, and it seemed like that idea would soon be a reality.

That knowledge sent an unexpected pang through my chest, but it wasn't like Samuel and I would have to stop hanging out. We needed to make our families think our relationship had ended mutually and respectfully anyway. So what was there to regret?

"What are you thinking?" Samuel asked.

"Hmm? What?"

"You look thoughtful."

"Oh. Well, it occurred to me that if things work out between Owen and Jenna, I guess that means ... you know ... our fake relationship won't be necessary anymore."

Samuel's stormy gray eyes searched mine for a moment. "Really." The word would normally be a question, but the way he said it, it sounded like a statement.

"Yeah," I said. "I mean, they'd be the real deal and could tie our families together. Right?"

"True." Samuel clenched his jaw, and I wondered if the thought bothered him like it did me.

"I mean, we're still at least a month or two away from when we could break up," I rushed to add. "We shouldn't stage it until both families know Owen and Jenna are together, assuming they really do end up seriously dating, and Owen is slug slow when it comes to romance ..."

Samuel still held his jaw clenched.

I didn't know how to take that. Was I wrong and he was upset that we had to keep dating? "Uh ... unless you want to break it off sooner?" I asked.

"No."

I awkwardly nodded.

"I still have personal ... goals I need to see to," Samuel slowly continued.

"Got it," I said, a little confused. What kind of personal goals could he have that would involve a fake relationship with me?

"I don't think my mother would take it well if we suddenly broke up," Samuel said.

"That's right. You said she's worried about never getting any daughters-in-law or grandkids," I said. "That makes sense."

"Precisely." Samuel gently tugged on the reins. "Whoa, Goose," he called to the horse.

Goose slowed to a stop.

"Is something wrong?"

"No." Samuel flashed me a brief smile as he held the reins in one hand and pulled out his cell phone with the other. "It just occurred to me we should take some pictures to put on social media."

"That's a great point," I said. "I never thought about making our cover that complete."

Samuel scoffed. "That's because you're too honest and good."

"What, and you're secretly a white-collar criminal?"

He shrugged as he opened his camera app. "No, but I'm certainly not past manipulation to get what I want."

"Is that a threat?" I took his phone from him and held it up so we could take a selfie.

"Not at all. I'm just being honest. Although as your

Grandma Mann said, I suppose you already know all of my worst points."

"Totally. Now, smile!" I leaned in close to Samuel so we were both in the frame and grinning for the camera.

Just before I snapped the picture, Samuel moved. He slid his free hand under my chin to angle my face upward before pressing his lips to my temple, moving quickly so I didn't have time to react before his phone took the picture.

Samuel settled back into place as I tapped the photo, enlarging it. Samuel's eyes glittered enigmatically in the shot, so while I was beaming like an idiot, he somehow looked almost ... intense.

"We can't post this," I said. "Grandma and Grandpa Mann follow me! They would die of heart attacks!"

"That's why you took the picture with my phone. I can post it." Samuel was already fixing his hold on the reins so he could hold them with both hands. "Goose, walk on."

I glanced at the picture again before locking the phone's screen for Samuel. "After we finish with our sleigh ride, do you want to head to the concession area to get something hot to drink?"

Samuel glanced at me out of the corner of his eye. "You want a waffle, don't you?"

"Absolutely!"

Chapter 15

Samuel

Tip #15: *If your coconspirator's timeline doesn't match yours, don't be afraid to force their hand.*

I waited in the parking lot of McBride Farm & Greenhouse for Natalie to leave. She rolled down her window to wave to me, and I returned the gesture, watching as she drove her car out of the parking lot and turned onto the road.

Once I'd seen her off, I slipped into my Porsche, started the engine, and speed-dialed Miguel via Bluetooth.

"Samuel, it's the weekend. This better be important." Miguel's voice crackled through the speakers of my car, his tone dripping with annoyance.

"It's an emergency," I said, backing out of my parking spot.

"What's wrong?" Miguel asked.

I watched for pedestrians as I rolled through the parking lot, pausing at the farm's exit before pulling onto the road. "Things have changed with Natalie. Our dating act might not last much longer. I need to move up the plan deadline."

"Are you sure that's necessary? You know how much Natalie hates being manipulated," Miguel warned. I could almost see him shaking his head in disapproval.

"There's no other option that I can think of."

"Have you considered, oh, I don't know, talking to her about it?" Miguel suggested dryly. "You two have been getting along quite well. She might be willing to hear you out."

Getting along wasn't enough. Not when Natalie had mentioned breaking up since Jenna and Owen seemed to be heading toward a serious relationship. That would make our charade unnecessary, and I couldn't let that happen.

"Things are more complicated than they seem." I tightened my grip on the steering wheel.

Miguel let out a resigned sigh. "Fine. How long do you think we have until Natalie wants to start planning your breakup?"

"She said maybe a month or two, but I'm not risking it," I said, my voice cold and determined. "I'm moving up the timeline and dealing with Natalie immediately."

"If you say so," Miguel said reluctantly. "It's your call, but be careful, Samuel. Don't rush into things you might regret."

"I've gone too far to worry about that." The sun dipped lower in the sky, casting golden hues across the windshield as I navigated the winding rural roads. "I'm going to see Grandfather. I think Natalie unintentionally charmed him enough for me to get what I need."

"Good luck," Miguel offered, his tone a mixture of concern

and resignation. "I'll be ready to shift your schedule as necessary come Monday morning."

"Thanks, Miguel." With that, I hung up, my thoughts racing as fast as my heart.

This had to work. I'd been working toward this for years.

Chapter 16

Natalie

Tip #16: *If your fake significant other decides to increase the PDA, match them. Losing isn't an option, even if you aren't certain what the game is.*

"Why is it so hard to find a bowling ball that fits my fingers? I know I have a big thumb, but it's not like I'm the Cinderella of bowlers." I rummaged through the collection of worn bowling balls, then glanced over my shoulder to check on Samuel.

He stood behind me holding his plain black bowling ball.

"You can go join Owen at our reserved lanes," I said. "You don't have to wait for me."

Samuel stared at me, plaintive. "These rented shoes are crusted with a substance I probably don't want to identify."

"Have you never been to a bowling alley before?" I asked him, bemused.

"Of course I have," Samuel said. "I just don't remember the possibility of getting infected with a foot fungus being part of the experience."

I laughed. "Don't worry. Cosmic Bowl sprays returned shoes with disinfectant spray every time."

"I'm sure," Samuel deadpanned. "That teenager behind the shoe rental counter looks like a paragon of hygiene and medical awareness."

Cosmic Bowl was Fox Creek's local—and only—bowling alley. It was a collision of retro and galaxy aesthetics, and it smelled like popcorn and greasy food with the faint odor of sweaty socks lurking in the background. The cinderblock walls were painted to resemble the night sky, while the flooring was a worn, neon-colored starry carpet that had seen better days.

I finally found a neon purple ball that fit my fingers *and* thumb. Picking it up, I led Samuel to our two lanes at the far end of the room, where Owen, Jenna, Isaac, and Logan were already seated.

Jenna entered our team into the ancient, clunky computer system so our names popped up on the TV display screens.

"The teams are Isaac, Sam, and Nat versus Owen, Logan, and me," Jenna said.

"As long as I'm not bowling with Owen, that sounds great—he tries to give me pointers," I said.

"That's because you *need* pointers," Owen said.

"I'd be willing to take advice from someone who bowls better than me, but we usually end up within a few points of each other, so you're no pro," I said.

Samuel and I added our bowling balls to the lineup, while Owen theatrically rolled his eyes.

"Younger siblings," he said to Jenna. "You know how it is."

Jenna—being the older sibling between her and Logan—giggled.

Owen cleared his throat, then glanced at me. "Thanks again, Nat, for inviting everyone out to bowl."

I was tempted to smirk knowingly, but I was too happy for my brother to rub it in. He was thrilled to have this extra time to spend with Jenna. It had only been three days since my date to McBride Farm & Greenhouse with Sam, and Owen and Jenna's date wasn't until next weekend.

"I'm happy everyone could make it to our first official Mann-Warner outing." I sank into one of the curved bowling sofas with its saggy cushion.

Samuel sat down right next to me, draping his arm across the tops of my shoulders. He was so close I was practically snuggled up to his side.

I tried to casually peer up at him to divine what he was thinking. He, of course, ignored me.

"Isaac, you're up first," Samuel said.

Isaac looked up from his phone. "Understood." He grabbed his forest-green bowling ball from the rack and strolled up to our lane.

"Who were you texting, Isaac?" Jenna asked.

Isaac casually tossed his ball down the lane with zero form or cares. "My executive assistant."

Samuel casually rubbed my shoulder with his fingers, sending a bolt of electricity up my arm. "Maybe we should have invited Charlotte, Isaac's assistant, to join us tonight," he said, oblivious to my reaction.

(For real. Was I the only one doomed to experience our crazy chemistry? He had to feel it too, right?)

Samuel continued, "She's been with Isaac for so long I know her almost as well as a family member."

Having thrown his bowling ball, Isaac had apparently

decided his turn was over. He turned away before his ball even reached the end of the lane. To everyone's surprise, his ball hit dead center and knocked down all ten pins. A burst of retro music played from the clunky computer system, accompanied by a pixelated animation of a dancing bowling pin on our display screen.

"Wow, that was unexpected." Owen whistled, impressed by Isaac's performance. "Looks like the competition might be tougher than I thought."

"Nice strike, Isaac," I said as he returned to the group.

Isaac blinked at me. "What's a strike?"

"Are you kidding me?" I looked up at Samuel. "Didn't you say you went bowling in college?"

He leaned down and planted a gentle kiss on my forehead, catching me off guard.

"*I* went bowling in college. I never said Isaac went with me."

Isaac plopped down on the other side of Samuel, content with his performance. "Your turn, Sam."

Samuel squeezed my shoulder. "Wish me luck." He winked before he got up and picked up his plain black bowling ball.

I watched Samuel walk away, rattled by his sudden increase in public displays of affection. Was he up to something?

"Let's see what you've got, cuz!" Jenna called out from the other lane, breaking my train of thought. She and Samuel bowled simultaneously. Jenna knocked down five pins, while Samuel left just two pins standing.

Jenna pumped her fist in the air. "No gutter ball this time! I'll take it!"

"Great job, Sam! Way to go, Jenna!" I cheered as she and Samuel waited for their balls to return.

Samuel turned to me, giving me a smile that was so warm it

threatened to melt me … until that twerp opened his mouth. "Sugarplum, are you hungry? Want me to grab us some snacks? I saw they have pretzel bites. I'd be happy to feed them to you—it might up the romance factor of the place."

The whole group—except for Jenna—stared at us, taken aback by Samuel's sudden cutesiness. My heart twisted, caught halfway between embarrassment at the open affection and mortification that I was even embarrassed about it, until I saw the sparkle of humor in his eyes and realized what he was doing.

I'd known Samuel pretty much my entire life. The guy *loved* pushing my buttons, so what were the chances he was doing this on purpose to rattle me?

After all, since we'd called a truce, he could no longer troll me at work. Most likely, he was getting creative and using our fake relationship as a substitute.

Well. If he wanted a war, I would be happy to oblige him.

"Thanks for the offer, cuddle bug. You're always so thoughtful." I laid it on thick, making my voice sweet and batting my eyes at him. "But I think I want to wait a little before we get some food, OK?"

Owen made a noise of disgust, but the rest of the Warners—not knowing better—turned their attention back to the game.

Samuel gave me a knowing look—apparently I hadn't upped the ante enough yet—before he grabbed his returned ball. He approached his lane and tossed the ball, expertly knocking down the remaining pins.

Time to pounce before Samuel had a chance to make a move!

"Way to go, babe!" I hopped off the sofa and trotted up to Samuel. When I reached him, I wrapped my arms around his neck and threw myself at him.

Samuel managed to catch me in his arms, which was pretty

impressive as far as reflexes go. Clinging to him gave me the perfect view of his face, so I saw the flicker of shock flash across it and felt the muscles in his shoulders stiffen.

Aw, yeah! Victory. Sweet, sweet victory!

Samuel recovered quickly and wrapped his arms around my waist before slowly turning in a circle so we spun like one of those ridiculously in love couples in a TV commercial.

"Thanks, darling." Samuel set me down and then kissed my left temple. "It's your turn to bowl."

I wriggled out of Samuel's arms. "Great! Don't get your hopes up—I'm just an average bowler." I grabbed my ball from the return and mentally prepped myself for my turn. As I approached the lane, I got closer to Logan, who was already standing in front of his lane.

The quiet Warner cousin unceremoniously whipped his ball down the lane, chucking it with an almost Grim Reaper–like intensity. I watched in shock as the pins violently toppled, leaving only three standing. It made me wonder if Logan's aggressive approach to bowling was a reflection of his true nature or just another aspect of his intimidating facade.

Shaking off my thoughts, I focused on my own throw, lining it up before tossing my ball. It careened down the lane and managed to knock down six pins.

Samuel cheered for me from where he sat on the sofa with Isaac. "You did great, Nat!"

"Thanks!"

I had some time before my bowling ball would return, so I walked up to Samuel and Isaac, who were talking in lowered tones.

"Did you finalize the numbers for the proposal?" Samuel asked his twin.

Isaac nodded. "Everything should be in your inbox."

"Proposal?" I asked. "You two are thinking about work."

Isaac glanced warily at Samuel, but Samuel, ever the charmer, winked. "It's fine, Isaac. She'll find out soon enough anyway since we have to bring the proposal to the town board. That means adding it to a town meeting agenda—which is practically her job description."

Isaac shrugged. "It's your relationship."

Feeling a little more worried—none of this sounded good—I kept a smile in place. "What's up?"

"We," Samuel started, "and by we I mean the Warners, not Warner Print, are making an offer on the old middle school building."

Ahh, yes. Owen had mentioned there was a potential buyer, but I hadn't thought the Warners would be interested.

Samuel was right—this was definitely going to be a thing.

"And do what with it?" I asked.

"We'd renovate the building and turn it into a luxury condo complex," Samuel said.

"Luxury condos?" I repeated. "Even though right now it's used for community events and adult education classes?"

"Those are important things," Samuel agreed. "But Fox Creek needs additional housing."

"It does," I agreed. "But *luxury* condos?"

"There's a demand. The condo building we built on Pine Lake completely sold out shortly after we finished construction," Isaac said, naming the high-rise building—or what passed for a high-rise building in a city as small as Fox Creek—the Warners had built several years ago.

Isaac shifted uncomfortably on the sofa. For a guy who was generally unemotional, he was showing a surprising amount of awkwardness over this, which seemed to hint that he cared about my reaction. Or, more likely, he cared about how my feelings would impact my supposed relationship with Samuel.

Both of our families were making an effort for us. It actually made me feel bad that I'd only been thinking of Jenna and Owen when I made the arrangement with Samuel.

Regardless, if the Warners were being polite because they cared about Samuel's happiness, the least I could do was be polite in return.

"Mmhmm, I see," I noncommittally said.

My bowling ball had returned by this point. I grabbed it off the rack and approached my lane again, mulling over the old school and Samuel's explanation.

I wasn't surprised by the Warners' plans—it was very on-brand for them. And even before I started fake dating Samuel there had been noises in the community that the Warners were eyeing up the building, so it was a forgone conclusion they had a plan.

Although I opposed the idea due to the lack of alternative facilities in Fox Creek that could handle all the adult education classes, I realized I wasn't enraged by their proposal like I normally would be.

Was I hanging out too much with Samuel?

Determined to keep my focus on the game, I threw my ball. It rolled down the polished wooden lane, and I nodded in satisfaction when it knocked down two additional pins.

"Great job, sweetheart," Samuel said.

Isaac gave me a swift, businesslike nod of respect before he got up, ready to start his turn.

When I walked back to the cushioned sofa he was sitting on, Samuel held out his hand to me. I reached for it, expecting a simple high five. Instead, he threaded his fingers through mine and yanked me down onto the sofa, half sprawled across his lap.

I yelped in surprise and shot him a bewildered look as I peeled myself off him and sat up properly. "What was that for?"

"The thrill." Samuel slid an arm around my waist and pressed me into his side, pulling me into a cuddle. "So, are you going to break up with me because of my family's plans for the middle school?"

I glanced up at him, expecting to see a smirk on his face. Instead, he looked unusually solemn. It threw me off guard.

"No." I nodded toward Jenna and Owen, who were celebrating their turn with high fives, attempting to hint I was discussing their relationship rather than ours. "When I started dating a Warner, I knew there would be some fundamental disagreements."

"Those disagreements used to be enough to make our families hate each other," Samuel said.

"True," I admitted, "but I think it would be better for Fox Creek if we argued less and had more ... discussions. Without yelling and insults." I paused, then added, "That being said, we Manns will definitely oppose the idea of turning the middle school into luxury condos."

Samuel laughed. "I'd be disappointed if you didn't." He playfully bumped his foot against mine, the light touch bringing back our fake-date mischievousness and leaving the serious talk behind.

I bumped his foot back and relaxed, assuming that would be the end of it.

Samuel instead pushed his foot into mine. The touch was innocent but ... charged.

Still, I was never one to back down. If Sam thought playing footsie in the open for everyone to see was going to embarrass me, he still had a lot to learn.

I playfully put my foot on top of his, tapping the top of his foot.

Samuel responded by snaking his lower leg around mine, capturing my bowling shoe between his feet.

The innocent contact sent tingles up my leg, but I wasn't

sure if I was the only one who noticed the chemistry or if Sam felt it too, so I was too chicken to let myself react.

I tried to think clinically as I stared down at my captured foot and felt every nudge and touch of his foot.

Finally, I managed to speak. "If you get my jeans dirty with those bowling shoes I am not going to be a happy girlfriend."

I figured Samuel would say something flirty back, but to my surprise Samuel stiffened—pressed into his side like I was, I could feel his muscles tense—and he wordlessly stared at me.

I smiled, and he kept on staring.

I didn't get it—what had made him react like this?

I awkwardly cleared my throat. While I was brave enough to publicly flirt with Samuel, apparently eye contact was too much, so I turned to look at the rest of our bowling party and discovered Owen gawking at us in shock.

His obvious shock—he was the only one here who knew Samuel and I were faking everything—made me feel weirdly embarrassed. But, no! We were doing this for his sake, and Samuel and I were friends now. Friends could do stuff like this! Besides, it was all a joke ... right?

Isaac returned from his turn. "You're up, Sam."

"Already?" Samuel asked, raising an eyebrow. I looked up at the TVs displaying the scores and saw that Isaac had scored yet another strike.

"Congratulations on the strike, Isaac," I said.

"Thanks," he said.

"I'll be right back. Think of me fondly in the meantime." Samuel dramatically wrapped his other arm around me in a tight hug, then got off the couch and sauntered off to the ball return, leaving me with his twin.

I smiled at Isaac. "Are you having fun?"

"More than I expected," Isaac said. "It's been enjoyable to

use mathematics to calculate the trajectory and necessary force required for the ball."

These Warners. They're a different breed.

"Cool," I said. "I never thought about bowling being related to numbers, but I guess you're right."

Isaac nodded. "Have you and Owen bowled much?"

I was a little surprised he was continuing the conversation, but I guess this showed how much he cared about his twin.

"We did a lot as teenagers and kids," I said. "Our parents would send us here with our cousins sometimes. It would get us out of their hair, and we'd still be supervised since most of the community knew who we were and had at least one of our relatives' phone numbers."

Isaac thoughtfully nodded. "I imagine it was fun?"

"Oh yeah," I agreed. "But it didn't exactly make us fantastic bowlers since we never picked up the correct form. We mostly got gutter balls."

"Hey, Nat, can I talk to you for a second?" Owen suddenly appeared next to me, wearing a smile that was way too big considering I wasn't Jenna.

"Sure?" I said.

Owen grabbed my hand and yanked me to my feet. "We're going to check out concessions," he announced to our group, dragging me away.

Owen led me up the handful of stairs that separated the shoe rental desk, arcade area, and concession stand from the bowling lanes, stopping when we were just far enough away that we couldn't be heard by the Warners with the hum of conversation and constant banging of falling pins.

"What's up?" I rubbed the hand he'd yanked so abruptly.

"Did it ever occur to you that you might be overdoing it a tad?" Owen grimaced.

"Overdoing what?" I asked, genuinely confused.

"The whole PDA thing," Owen said. "You were never this affectionate with your previous boyfriends."

"The Warners don't know that." I wrinkled my nose. "And it's not my fault. Samuel started it; I'm just matching him in upping the ante."

Owen shook his head. "Only you and Sam could turn PDA into a competition."

"It's all him," I insisted. "I am an innocent party in this."

"Except you take his bait and fight back." Owen awkwardly scratched his side. "Don't you think it's a little odd that Samuel Warner—the guy you've spent your adult life arguing with—is acting like this?"

We both glanced back at Samuel as he took his turn, knocking down eight pins on his first throw.

"Not really," I said. "It's just a new way for him to annoy me."

Owen made a noise of doubt in the back of his throat.

"That's his thing," I insisted. "Warner Print never gave to the Fox Creek Friends of the Library until I joined and Sam realized he could annoy me in my free time in addition to when I was on the clock." I paused. "Right?"

Owen shrugged.

I mashed my lips together as I considered the issue. Historically Samuel only did things to annoy me, so I didn't have any evidence that pointed to a different meaning.

No, I knew Sam. This was just Owen being my older brother and getting in my head.

I shook myself free of the paranoid thoughts. "By the way, you should know that Sam told me about a Warner plan that's sure to make Grandma and Grandpa Mann blow their tops."

"Oh? Why would I care about that?"

I pointedly stared at Jenna Warner, who was eyeing up the lane for her second throw.

"Shut up," Owen said. "What is it?"

"The Warners want to purchase the old middle school and renovate it into luxury condos."

Owen grimaced. "Yeah, that'll definitely complicate things with our families. I'm surprised you can keep calm about it."

"It's probably because Samuel explained the idea to me straight instead of being overly charming, persuasive, and, frankly, manipulative," I mused.

Owen chuckled.

"Owen, you're up!" Jenna called, interrupting our conversation.

Owen gave his ladylove a thumbs-up, then turned back to me. He patted me on the shoulder in that insufferable way all older siblings possess. "Just don't get in over your head, sis."

With that, he walked back to grab his bowling ball.

"Hey, cuddle bunny," Samuel called out to me. "It's your turn too!"

I returned to our lane, finding Samuel waiting for me at the ball return.

"Is everything OK?" he asked with a hint of concern.

"Everything's fine," I assured him. "Owen just called a quick family meeting to question my sanity."

Samuel chuckled as he took my hand and pressed a soft kiss to the top of it. The warmth of his lips and the scrape of his five-o'clock shadow on my skin made the hairs on the back of my neck tingle.

Maybe Owen wasn't talking about the old middle school when he told me not to get in over my head.

"Y'know," I said, needing to push back against Samuel's invasion of my personal space, "I've been throwing a grubby bowling ball. My hand probably isn't much cleaner than those rental shoes you despise."

"I'll take the risk for you," Samuel replied, his voice husky and full of promise. "It's worth it.

"Sam, stop accosting Natalie," Isaac chimed in from the sofa, "or we'll never finish this game."

Samuel let me go with a laugh, and I picked up my bowling ball, determined to concentrate on the game. After all, at the end of this fake relationship, Samuel and I were just going to be friends.

Chapter 17

Natalie

Tip #17: *Be prepared to improvise when necessary.*

The annual winter used book sale at the Fox Creek Public Library was in full swing. I stood behind the wobbly table moonlighting as a checkout counter, volunteering since the Friends of the Library ran the book sale on behalf of the library.

The scents of old paper and ink mingled with the excited chatter of customers, creating a comfy atmosphere in the library's meeting room.

"Here's your change, Keely." I handed my younger cousin a few bills. "Enjoy the books!"

"Thanks, Nat!" Keely said. "I—whoa! Sorry, my phone is connected to my hearing aids by Bluetooth." Keely pulled out her phone, which was vibrating with an incoming call. She silenced it and smiled at me. "Anyway, I found some really great stories this year."

"Yeah, we had more donations than usual this year."

Keely made a noise of surprise.

I looked up in time to see Samuel enter carrying a small picnic basket. I waved hello, beckoning him over.

To my surprise, Isaac and their grandfather Walter followed close behind him. I waved to them as well, receiving a nod from Isaac and a beaming smile from Walter.

Keely raised an eyebrow. "Seems like your boyfriend can't stand to be parted from you for very long these days."

I rolled my eyes. "He's bringing me dinner since I won't be able to leave until the sale ends at 8 p.m."

"Uh-huh," Keely said skeptically. "I guess I'll go see if Grandpa Mann is ready to pay yet." She left, weaving through the tables piled with used books to join Grandpa Mann and Noah, who were engrossed in the used picture books section.

A few readers came up to my table to buy books, and I completed the purchases and sent them off before I could greet Samuel.

He had lingered near my table, waiting for me to finish the transactions. Once there were no more customers, he finally approached me, setting the picnic basket on the table. "Good evening, Nat."

"Hello! And thanks, Sam. I really appreciate you dropping by to bring me dinner." I paused, trying to figure out how I could hint at our fake relationship without saying anything outright. "I know it's above and beyond your role."

Samuel's expression was unreadable as he leaned in close to me. I was used to his affectionate gestures by now and managed not to blush bright red at the touch of his lips against my skin.

When he breathed into my ear, though, that made my heartbeat kick up. "I'm always happy to help you, Natalie," he murmured.

I held in a gulp and made myself smile. "Right. Thanks," I lamely said.

Samuel opened the picnic basket, and the tantalizing aroma of bacon filled the air.

"What did you bring?"

"BLT sandwiches," Samuel said. "I also brought some grapes, crackers, and assorted cheeses. I picked things that wouldn't be too messy since you'll be checking out people."

"That was thoughtful, thank you." I peeked into the basket. "Wow. You brought *a lot* of food. How much do you think I eat?"

Samuel dragged a nearby folding chair up to the table. "I haven't had dinner yet either, so I thought we could eat together."

"Works for me." I sat down, and he handed me a sandwich.

I took a bite, savoring the flavors of the applewood-smoked bacon as more people streamed into the meeting room for the book sale. Grandpa Mann, Noah, and Keely continued to paw through the picture books while Isaac perused the nonfiction section. Walter, however, kept his eyes glued to Samuel and me, a knowing smile on his face.

Something was up with that.

"Did Isaac and Walter eat before coming?" I asked between bites.

"Yep," Samuel said.

Marjorie marched into the meeting room, her platinum-blond beehive bobbing with each step she took. "I'm here to help with the book sale," she drawled. "But first, I need to find some books worth reading—for the slow hours or for when I see someone I don't particularly like."

"Take your time, Marjorie." Samuel winked. "I can back Natalie up if there's a rush."

"Hmm, so you say." Marjorie fixed her gaze on Samuel. "What are you doing here?"

Samuel maintained his charming smile. "I'm bringing date night to Natalie since she has to volunteer—I'm just that attached."

"Ugh. You two are disgustingly romantic." Marjorie rolled her eyes and shuffled off to peruse the books.

I laughed, but Samuel's smile turned taut, and I realized he was clenching his jaw.

I studied him for a few more moments as I finished up my sandwich. "Are you OK?"

"Of course." He abandoned his half-eaten sandwich, tucking it back into the picnic basket, then scanned the meeting room.

I followed his gaze to Isaac and Walter. Isaac was still browsing the books, but Walter gave us a big thumbs-up when he saw we were looking his way.

"Were your grandfather and Isaac interested in the book sale?" I asked, a little confused by their presence. The only Warner I'd ever seen at the biannual used book sale in all my years of volunteering was Samuel.

"Not particularly," Samuel said.

"Then why did they come?"

"Grandfather didn't give me a choice," Samuel wryly said. "He was coming whether I wanted him to or not. Isaac tagged along for moral support."

"Moral support? For what?" I asked.

Samuel ignored my question and reached into the picnic basket to pull out a leather-bound book.

"I brought something for you." He held out the mysterious book.

I brushed my fingers off on my pants before taking it. The leather-bound book was heavy, and the title, which was embossed on the cover in fancy gold letters, was *Our Story*. There was no author name.

"I don't think I've heard of this book," I said, confused. "Did we talk about it before or something?"

"Open it," Sam said, his voice soft.

I flipped the cover open, revealing the book's hollowed out innards. The centers of the pages had been cut out, and the edges were glued together, creating an empty space. There, a beautiful engagement ring dangled on a white ribbon attached to the glued pages and tied in a bow. The ring was exquisite—an intricately woven band of white gold that held a stunning, round-cut diamond surrounded by tiny emeralds, as if they were leaves cradling a flower.

No. No way. He wasn't going to ... he wouldn't.

"Sam ..." I whispered. My fingers turned numb from my shock and confusion. "What are you doing?"

Sam's smile was brilliant as he got down on one knee, sliding his hands beneath mine so we were holding the leather book together.

My heart raced, and thoughts exploded in my mind. Was this really happening? Why? Had something happened? What was going on?

"For years, Nat, I've known I needed you in my life," Samuel began, his gray eyes locked on mine. "You've challenged me, inspired me, and I can't imagine a future without you. It's always been you. So, Natalie Mann, will you do me the honor of becoming my wife?"

The room spun around me, and a high-pitched ringing filled my ears. I glanced around, realizing we were in public with a lot of witnesses. If I said no, the entire town would know, and all the progress between the Manns and the Warners would undoubtedly be lost on a new feud sparked by Sam and me.

Perhaps Samuel had planned it this way, knowing it would force me to accept.

My irritation flared, but I couldn't think of any reason why Samuel would want to be fake engaged to me, especially considering the risks.

"Natalie," Samuel whispered.

I stared into his dark eyes and realized that despite our differences, I trusted him. Our friendship was no longer surface-deep but something much closer. He must have a reason for doing this. So ... I would follow his lead.

(However, I was going to kick him in the shin for springing this on me without warning the moment we were alone.)

"Sam," I said, my voice trembling a little, "yes, I will marry you."

His face lit up, and he took the book from me, placing it on the table with the picnic basket.

I stood there, feeling weirdly happy even though none of this was real. I'd like to blame my confusion as the reason why, when Samuel stood up and tugged me closer, I didn't realize what he intended to do until it was too late, and suddenly we were kissing.

Full, lips-to-lips kissing.

Me. And Sam Warner.

My mind-boggling shock faded fast, however, under the onslaught of Sam's persistent kiss. It was tender and sweet, like the first rays of sunlight on a cold winter morning, sending a shiver through my entire body. Our lips moved together gently, our breath mingling as we shared a moment that felt both surreal and utterly perfect.

The moment Samuel broke our sweet kiss, the room erupted into chaos. Noah's piercing shout filled the air, announcing,

"They're kissing! That means Cousin Nat and Sam are having a baby!"

I groaned. (I could practically see the rumors spreading like wildfire.)

"Your cousin Madison really needs to figure out how to better explain sex ed to that kid," Samuel whispered in my ear, his warm breath tickling my skin.

I laughed, both relieved and amused by the absurdity of the situation.

Everyone in the room clapped for us, their excitement palpable. When I finally peeled myself off Sam and looked around, I spotted Keely recording the whole thing on her cell phone, Marjorie cackling with glee as she had already called someone on her phone, and Grandpa Mann standing there completely shell-shocked.

Samuel picked up the leather book and untied the white ribbon, removing the ring. He took my hand and slid the gorgeous ring onto my finger. "It's beautiful," I murmured.

"It was my Grandmother Warner's wedding ring."

Shock, my BFF of the night it seemed, once again had my ears ringing. "This," I squeaked. "This is your *grandmother's ring?*"

I wanted to grab Samuel by the lapels of his fancy suit and ask if he was insane, but ... there were witnesses.

Hoping for some sign of sanity, I looked from Samuel to Isaac and Walter.

Isaac wore a small smile, while Walter beamed at us, misty-eyed. Samuel had gone above and beyond in his deception, and I decided right then and there that kicking him in the shins wouldn't be enough. Oh, no. As soon as we stepped outside, he'd be getting a face full of snow.

Walter approached us and wrapped me in a hug. "Congratulations, my dear. I can't wait to call you my grandchild."

"Thank you," I managed, tongue-tied from the whirlwind of emotions.

"Thank you, Grandfather, for letting me use Grandmother's ring," Samuel said.

Walter nodded proudly. "Of course. I approve of your bride, and the whole family was for it. We're all thrilled that your persistence finally paid off."

Isaac and Keely congratulated us next, with a huge grin from Keely and a sincere smile from Isaac. But it was Grandpa Mann who truly surprised me, shuffling up to Samuel and me with Noah's hand in his.

"Congrats, Nat." He gruffly gave me a one-armed hug. "He ..." Grandpa Mann narrowed his eyes and stared Samuel down. "He'll take good care of you," Grandpa finished.

"What are we congratulating them for?" Noah looked back and forth between me and Sam, his face scrunching up with his confusion.

"Cousin Nat and Samuel are going to get married," Keely said.

"Why?" Noah asked.

"You'll have to ask your mother that," Grandpa Mann said.

I laughed nervously as Grandpa Mann dragged Noah off, leaving me alone with Samuel again. He hugged me close, and I could feel my heart racing in my chest.

"You better have a good explanation for all of this when we're alone," I whispered into his ear.

"Your reaction is better than I expected," he said into my neck, his breath fanning my skin.

I gave him a falsetto laugh. "Just wait and see how I react when there aren't all these people around."

Chapter 18

Natalie

Tip #18: *Remember, fake dating isn't about convincing everyone you're in love. It's about surviving the awkward moments with your dignity mostly intact.*

"Goodbye, Marjorie," I said. The used book sale had just wrapped up for the night, and after what Samuel put me through, I felt like a dirty dish towel. "I'll see you tomorrow."

"You'll see me and half of Fox Creek," Marjorie said. "Everyone will want to get a look at that ring on your finger!"

I tried to make an intelligent reply, but all I could get out were strangled noises.

Out of words to speak, I stared blankly at the floor. The library lobby was aglow with soft, golden light that balanced out the plain tile floor. I could see the parking lot through the glass doors lining the front of the lobby. At the back of the room was another row of automatic glass doors leading into the library proper, where rows of books beckoned with promises of escaping my complicated thoughts and feelings.

"Good night, Marjorie." Samuel's voice dripped with charm, but I noticed a hint of smugness in his smile that I couldn't quite place.

"Night, lovebirds," Marjorie replied slyly, her hairdo tilting alarmingly as she walked away. "Enjoy your engagement!"

Samuel chuckled as he slipped on his wool coat. I, not as amused, watched Marjorie while I zipped up my puffy black parka, shivering at the thought of stepping outside into the cold. The second the automatic doors closed behind Marjorie, I pounced.

"Samuel," I snapped, my voice livid, though more playful than truly enraged. "Start. Talking."

"About what?" Samuel asked.

"About *proposing* when we're just *pretending* to be dating and about using your *grandmother's ring* to do it!" My voice's pitch went higher and higher as anxiety built in my gut.

We were in so much trouble.

Instead of responding, Samuel's arms snaked around me, pulling me into a hug. My heart raced as my cheek bumped against his chest.

"Wh-what are you doing?"

"Relax." Samuel's breath tickled my ear. "If you want to murder me, you'll have to wait until we're not being watched. There are a few librarians still manning the checkout desk since the library hasn't closed yet, and they can see us."

My back was to the library's inner sanctum, so I'd have to take his word for it.

"Of course there are," I grumbled. "This town is too nosy—

someone is always watching." I cleared my throat and tried to ignore the impulse to melt into his inviting hug. "But seriously, what were you thinking? Proposing like that?"

"Ah, well ..." Samuel began, his voice suddenly sounding less confident. "I didn't exactly think it through."

"Clearly," I said. "So. What's your excuse?"

As we stood there, wrapped up in each other, a flicker of something more than annoyance sparked deep within me. It was something I didn't want to examine too closely as I suspected I wasn't going to like what it was.

"You see, I might have overdone the whole 'I'm in love with my enemy' act," he said. "My family started asking when we'd get engaged." He grinned and looked oddly pleased with himself.

"Are you serious?" I tried to step out of his embrace, but he firmly held onto me, his eyes darting toward the librarians behind me. Sighing, I decided to let it go for now. "Your family's enthusiasm was the sole reason for proposing?"

"Partially," he admitted sheepishly. "My mother had already started telling her friends that we were all but engaged, and—"

"Samuel," I interrupted, my voice flat, "you're a sellout."

"That's harsh," Samuel said, his grip on me tightening just a bit. "Especially since you're partially responsible for this, too, you know."

"Oh, really? Enlighten me as to how your deciding to propose to me—which is going to make it *a lot* harder for us to break up without reigniting the fight between our families—is partially my fault!" I puffed up with my irritation like a hissing cat.

"It's because you did too good of a job winning my family over."

"What?" I snorted in disbelief. "That's ridiculous!"

"Is it, though?" Samuel asked. "My grandfather practically threw my grandmother's ring at me and all but ordered me to propose to you. They're smitten with you, Nat."

I was about to give Samuel a sarcastic response, but he continued. "And why wouldn't they be? You're delightful and lovely—addictive, even."

That was certainly not what I expected him to say, and surprisingly it lacked the usual charismatic charm he used to manipulate others.

I stared up into his eyes, searching for any hint of insincerity. All I saw was genuine affection shining back at me. It touched something deep within me. Knowing our history, these were about the highest compliments Samuel could have given me.

"Fine," I conceded softly, feeling an unexpected warmth spreading through me. "I still don't get why you had to do it, but it obviously makes sense to you. However! Next time you have to do something drastic, *please*. For the love of all things holy. Call me first and warn me!"

"Deal," he agreed.

I smiled up at him, my grin involuntary and impossible to suppress. Samuel's expression shifted, his eyes softening in a way I couldn't quite place. Before I could analyze it further, he leaned down and pressed his lips against mine.

The kiss was spontaneous, natural, and lingering, like the heat of a crackling fire in the fireplace on a wintry night. It felt different from the one after he proposed. It was more genuine, more intense. I didn't understand how it could feel genuine—this was all an act. But as our lips parted, I was suddenly aware of how much longer this kiss had lasted than the first.

"Personal boundaries, Samuel," I chided, eyebrows raised. "Ever heard of them?"

"The librarians are still watching us through the glass doors," he said casually, as if that justified everything.

I narrowed my eyes. "I'm not sure I believe you."

"Does it matter?" he asked with a shrug. "You enjoyed the kiss too, didn't you?"

My cheeks flushed scarlet. I had enjoyed it—more than I should have.

I pulled myself free from his arms and stomped toward the library entrance.

"Wait, my love!" Samuel called dramatically, his voice forlorn and full of fake despair. I refused to look back at him, still embarrassed by my slip in self-control. "Don't leave me. Darling. Babe!"

"Can it, Sam," I ordered with the long-suffering that came hand in hand with being friends with someone as intelligent and wickedly funny as Samuel.

"But you're breaking my heart with every step you take away from me," he lamented theatrically.

I walked faster.

As I neared the lobby doors to the wintry outside, it occurred to me that while our initial goal was to influence our families and stop the Manns and Warners from fighting, something had changed between the two of us.

Before I could make my hasty escape through the library's automatic doors, Samuel caught up to me, his long strides easily closing the gap between us.

"Are you running the book sale tomorrow morning?" he asked. Apparently he'd left the dramatics behind.

"Not first thing in the morning. I'll be here around lunchtime, though, to relieve the morning volunteers," I said. "Why? Are you planning to come and cause trouble?"

"For once, no." Samuel slid his hands into the pockets of his coat. "But I figured I should ask. My family will expect me to know the location of my fiancée at all times." He hesitated. "Are you heading home now?"

"Yep," I said. "Tomorrow is a Saturday, but I'll have to get up early, so I'd better head to bed soon."

"Why the early alarm?" Samuel asked.

"Because I'll have to stop by my parents' now, because *someone* gave me this!" I held my hand up and tapped his grandmother's ring for emphasis.

Samuel laughed. "I see. In that case, I'll walk you to your car."

"Thanks." I double-checked my puffy coat was properly zipped. "What about you? What are you doing for the rest of tonight?"

"I have to return to Warner Print for a final meeting."

"Work?" I replied, scandalized. "But it's after eight! You couldn't possibly have any work that important to do on a Friday night!"

"Ah, but I do." He grinned. "I need to brief Miguel about a very important development."

"Is it about the luxury condos you Warners want to build in the old middle school?" I asked, my voice laced with apprehension and dread. The last thing Fox Creek needed was more drama between our families.

His eyebrows shot up in genuine surprise, and confusion flashed across his face. "No, it has nothing to do with the middle school."

I let out a sigh of relief. "Good," I said firmly. "Don't work too late, though. You should be off already, you know."

"Don't worry about me." He winked. "It'll be a celebration, actually."

Samuel leaned down, moving into my personal space.

I instinctively hunched my shoulders and narrowed my eyes

at him. "If you're going in for another kiss, I swear I'll bite your lip."

He threw his head back and laughed. "I wouldn't dream of it."

He was still laughing as he pressed a gentle kiss to my forehead, the scrape of his scruff against my skin making me overly aware of him.

I automatically hugged him in return. It wasn't until I was stepping back that I realized that two weeks ago a kiss on the forehead would have been enough to make me sputter.

It was unsettling how easily I now accepted these public displays of affection. I had to be careful, or he was going to get me used to kissing him too.

I wasn't in love with Samuel, but between noticing all the great things about him I'd blocked out before because of my previous dislike and being aware of exactly how handsome he was …

No.

No. I wasn't going to go there. We'd achieved peace between our families, and now we were friends. That was more than I ever thought we'd be. I'd leave the Warner-Mann romance to Owen and Jenna.

"Come on." Samuel took my hand in his, pulling me from my thoughts. "Let's get you to your car."

"Thanks."

We stepped through the front doors and out into the cold night. The darkness was interrupted by the occasional pool of light the streetlights were casting, but there thankfully was no howling wind.

Samuel, ever the cheeky one, grinned down at me. "So, how do you feel about making out in public?"

"Absolutely not and if you ever try it, I'll crash the next

Warner Print board meeting and call you sweetums in front of everyone."

"Ouch." Samuel winced, feigning hurt. "You play mean, Nat."

"Yup."

Samuel swung our linked hands. "It's a good thing, then, that I *like* it when you play mean."

"You just don't know when to quit," I said, determined to keep my feelings compartmentalized. For my own sake.

Chapter 19

Samuel

Tip #19: *Celebrate small victories. Today, it's a fake engagement; tomorrow, it's convincing her family you're perfect together.*

I flung open the door to the meeting room and charged in with a grin plastered across my face. Miguel sat at the table, lounging in an office chair like it was a La-Z-Boy recliner. Clad in sweatpants and a sweatshirt, he looked more prepared for a gym session than our late-evening debriefing.

"Natalie said yes!" I said.

Miguel leaped to his feet. "She said yes?"

"She said yes!"

We shared a laugh before exchanging the typical male shoulder pat/hug.

"Samuel Warner," Miguel said, his smile threatening to split his face, "allow me to congratulate you on finally achieving your dream of getting engaged to Natalie Mann."

My mind raced with thoughts and memories.

I had been smitten with Natalie since high school. While I'd tried to forget her while away in college, my feelings for her had instead flattened me. I knew I was head over heels in love with her way before I became Warner Print's CEO.

My infatuation with Nat was a poorly kept secret within the Warner family. Everyone from Logan to my grandfather knew about my long-standing crush. But now, it seemed my dreams were coming true—even if by unconventional means.

"The only negative," I said, some of my elation leaving me, "is she was backed into saying yes to my proposal through public peer pressure. Even though we're engaged, we're technically not dating."

"That's semantics. Who cares? Now you've got her neatly tied to you with the engagement," Miguel pointed out, his voice full of mischief. "That should get rid of the impending deadline of your fake relationship."

"True," I agreed, relieved to have made progress in my pursuit of Natalie's heart. "And just in time. Owen and Jenna look at each other like a pair of sappy teenagers."

Miguel snorted. "As if you have room to judge in that area, Mr. Loyal Till My Last Breath Samuel Warner!"

I laughed, and the edge of intensity that had dogged me for weeks finally started to fade. "Can you believe it took this long to get here?" I said, both tired and ecstatic. "To be in an actual relationship with Natalie?"

"Don't celebrate yourself," Miguel replied tartly. "If Natalie hadn't approached you about the fake romance, who knows how much longer you would've been pining away."

I couldn't argue with that. When Natalie first asked me about this scheme, I thought I was dreaming.

I laughed. "Remember when I frantically called you after she proposed the idea at Literum? You thought I was either hallucinating or having a panic attack."

"Because it sounded too good to be true," Miguel said. "Although in hindsight, it's probably the only way Natalie would have voluntarily stayed around you."

"Yeah." I rubbed my jaw, almost drunk on my elation. "It's been pretty dicey, though. There were so many times my family all but told her I've loved her for years."

"They have been quite the liability," Miguel acknowledged. "Isaac's taking time off to meet Natalie and making the effort to interact pleasantly with her instead of staying holed up in his office crunching numbers should have been a dead giveaway to Natalie that there was more to your little agreement than one would think. Then again, I was surprised you didn't blurt out the whole story to Isaac yourself. He is your twin."

"I've debated telling him several times, but I'm not sure how he would act around Natalie if he knew, and I couldn't risk messing this up." I groaned. "It's a miracle no one besides you knows the relationship is fake."

"And I'm still mad about that. I want to tell my husband, and I can't!" Miguel scolded.

"Sorry about that." I plopped down into one of the office chairs surrounding the meeting room table. The chair creaked under my weight.

Miguel eyed me but must have thought better of continuing his rant, because he clapped his hands once. "So! How do you want to celebrate? This is probably the greatest emotional and relational achievement of your life."

"Is it sad that I still barely believe it happened?" I massaged my temples, trying to wrap my head around the reality.

"Let's have some drinks," Miguel suggested. "I've got about an hour before Kyle expects me home from the 'gym.' We could go out, or if you are feeling inclined to spill your guts about your relief at finally securing your ladylove after a decade of carrying on over her, we could avoid witnesses and stay here to crack open that brandy you keep in your office."

"Are you angling for my best liquor?" I accused him, smirking.

"Of course not." He snorted, feigning innocence. "I'm trying to help you celebrate the monumental achievement of finally getting the girl of your dreams to agree to a fake engagement with you."

"Wow, when you put it like that, it sounds so impressive," I said sarcastically.

"Hey, it's a start," Miguel said. "And I'll have you know I'm almost as happy as you are about Natalie saying yes, because it means my days of being forced to listen to you lament over her and rant about how beautiful she is might finally be coming to an end!"

"I didn't realize I was such a burden." I chuckled. The weight that had been pressing on my chest for years seemed to have lifted at last.

"Of course you were," Miguel joked. "But that's what friends are for, right? Speaking of friends ... friends also share their plans for the future. So what are your plans for making your relationship with Natalie real and not a highly choreographed fake?"

I hesitated, suddenly unsure. "I don't know yet. I just ... need some time to figure it all out."

Miguel slapped me on the shoulder. "Well, for tonight anyway, let's just celebrate. I'll go grab that brandy. You stay put."

"Thanks, Miguel."

Miguel waved me off as he left the room, leaving me alone with my thoughts.

I closed my eyes and leaned back in the chair, savoring the new peace. It had been incredibly hard having Natalie so near and yet so far, with everything about our relationship being a meticulously constructed lie. But now, for the first time, things were finally progressing between us.

I smiled as I recalled the way her cheeks had flushed when I kissed her. I'd recklessly lost control on both occasions, unable to hold back when she'd looked up at me with that achingly warm smile of hers. Her innocent blush and the fact that she'd kissed me back instead of losing it gave me hope that I might be able to win her over after all and make our relationship real.

As I sat there, lost in thought, I knew one thing for certain: I wasn't going to let her go. No matter what it took, I would find a way to win Natalie's heart for real.

Chapter 20

Natalie

Tip #20: *Timing is everything. Announcing your fake engagement before your dad's second cup of coffee is a rookie mistake.*

The early morning sun warmed the frost-covered windows of my parents' house. I hesitantly opened their front door, dreading their reaction to the news I was about to deliver.

I stepped into the house and started to take off my snow boots. "Mom? Dad?"

The scent of fresh coffee filled the air, so I knew they were up.

I tried again. "Mom? Dad?"

I'd wiggled one boot off when Owen slithered from the

living room, where he'd been hiding, into the entryway, his lanky frame filling the doorway.

Crap.

Owen was the one family member I wanted to avoid the most.

I frantically tried to put my boot back on, hoping I could still escape.

"Nuh-uh," Owen said. "Not happening. Take your other boot off. You're not going anywhere."

"Fine." I reluctantly pulled off my other boot under Owen's watchful gaze.

Hanging my winter coat on the overloaded coat rack that was going to bite the dust sooner or later, I meekly hunched my shoulders and scooted past Owen into the cozy living room, where I was calmed by the familiarity of the knickknack-covered shelves that lined the walls and the plaid couches that invited weary souls, like me, to sit.

Dad sat in his worn but comfortable plaid recliner, still in his pajamas, cradling a mug—he was probably working on his morning coffee. Mom was dressed for the day and perched in her favorite rocking chair, but she got up quickly when she saw me, enveloping me in a warm hug that smelled of her floral perfume.

"Hello, sweetheart!" she gushed, squeezing me tightly.

"I'm engaged," I blurted out. The words tumbled out of my mouth before I could stop them.

The room went silent, and I felt Dad's eyes burning my back.

I gulped. "Sam and I are engaged." I braced myself, preparing for their reactions.

The room was so quiet I wondered if I'd killed my parents with shock. I stepped out of my mom's hug—she didn't resist. My hand shook as I raised it to reveal the stunning diamond ring with little emeralds nestled around it that had once belonged to Samuel's grandmother.

The ring seemed to catch every ray of sunlight streaming through the window, casting a kaleidoscope of colors across the living room.

"Engaged?" My mother's voice was barely more than a whisper as she backed away from me. Her eyes were wide and her eyebrows—penciled in with makeup—kept their perfect arch even as they traveled north toward her hairline.

The weighty silence was shattered when my father's coffee cup slipped from his grasp, thudding against the hardwood floor —empty, thankfully.

"OH MY GOODNESS!" Mom screamed, her voice reaching an octave I didn't know was humanly possible.

I panicked—she was angry. She was so angry she was ... clapping her hands together in delight?

"My baby is engaged! This is so exciting! I'm so happy!" My mom teared up as she beamed at me with joy.

For maybe the first time since I started this fake relationship, I felt a stabbing twinge of guilt for deceiving my family.

Mom continued to squeal in joy while Dad stared into space. Owen, on the other hand, glowered at me from across the room, arms crossed and looking as sour as a lemon.

"Sweetie, when did this happen?" Mom caught her breath as she wiped a tear from her eye.

"Last night, at the book sale. I'm surprised nobody texted you to tattle on us. Grandpa Mann was there with Keely and Noah."

"My phone is dead, dear," Mom explained, patting her pocket. "And your father, well, you know he always keeps his phone on silent until after his second cup of coffee."

"Where's Samuel?" Dad's deep voice resonated with authority as he stood from his recliner.

"Um, I, um, asked him not to come with me," I stammered, avoiding Owen's piercing gaze. "Which I know is kind of weird since the news involves both of us. But. I wanted to come by myself in case there were any ... objections."

"Objections?" Mom fanned herself with a hunting magazine she'd swiped from the coffee table. "Why, we never thought our Natalie would end up with a Warner boy, but Samuel is such a nice young man. Quite handsome too, and even Grandma Mann likes him!"

"Nat," Dad said. "Will you be happy with him?" Dad's eyes locked on mine, searching for any hint of doubt or uncertainty.

"Yes," I said immediately.

Dad wrapped me in a bear hug. "Congratulations, pumpkin," he said gruffly.

I started to get teary—touched by my parents' reactions—until I realized I'd told Dad I'd be happy with Samuel without even stopping to ponder the question, which was alarming given that this engagement *wasn't real*!

"Congratulations, sis," Owen muttered through gritted teeth as he threw an arm around my shoulders. "I'm so happy for you, but can we talk for a second?"

"No—" I started.

Owen interrupted me. "Thanks a bunch. Let's go."

He dragged me from the living room.

"Owen, what are you doing?" I hissed, struggling uselessly against his grip.

"Trust me, it'll only take a second." He pulled me into the small guest bathroom, which was decorated in a chicken motif. The wallpaper was covered with plump hens and roosters, and the hand towels had little chicks embroidered on them. I had mixed feelings about the decor, as it felt a little weird with all the chicken knickknacks staring at me with their little black eyes whenever I tried to go to the bathroom, but Mom loved it.

When the door shut behind us, Owen leaned against it and whispered angrily, "What is going on? You told me the plan was to fake date Samuel Warner, not *marry* him!"

"I know, I know," I stammered, feeling cornered by both Owen and the dozens of chickens staring at me from every surface. "I didn't expect it either. Sam just ... he said he cracked under pressure from his family and proposed."

"Really?" Owen asked, disbelief dripping from his words. "You actually believe that story?"

"Of course I do!" I snapped defensively. "Why else would *Samuel Warner* want to marry me?"

Owen rubbed his face. "I don't know."

I fiddled with the engagement ring until I realized what I was doing and slapped my hands against my jeans. "Is there any possibility this is all some big scheme Samuel has? A new way to get back at the Manns?" I asked, finally voicing the tiny doubt that had nagged me ever since I woke up that morning.

"No," Owen said firmly. "He's too at ease and relaxed when you two hang out. Jenna even says she's never seen him this happy, and she wouldn't lie about something like that."

We stood in silence for a moment, letting the absurdity of the situation sink in. Here we were, two grown adults holed up in a chicken-themed bathroom, conspiring about a fake engagement.

I was a minute away from breaking into laughter—apparently I was more prone to hysterics than I'd realized—but Owen stopped me before I totally lost it.

"Maybe you're right." His shoulders slumped in defeat. "We have to trust that Samuel believed he had to propose to you."

I exhaled, relief washing over me. "Thank you, Owen."

"However," Owen raised a finger for emphasis, "this fake engagement will make breaking up without reigniting the family fight a lot harder. And I'm not thrilled about that." He paused, then added, "And I don't like my little sister getting fake engaged. I'm not sure if I'm supposed to be happy for the engagement or relieved it's not real."

"Leave smoothing over our breakup to Sam and me." I tried to sound confident, but my stomach twisted at the thought. "Maybe we'll have to fake our relationship longer than planned to give Jenna and you time to cement your relationship."

Owen sourly muttered, "It's your choice, but be careful. Mom will have you picking out wedding dresses, and Samuel's mother will get you two to book a venue for a wedding that won't be happening. If you don't watch it, you'll be married to Sam before you know it."

I scoffed, folding my arms across my chest. "That's not going to happen. Samuel wouldn't let it happen!"

Owen made a noise of disbelief, and we stood in awkward silence, watched by the chickens. Finally, he reluctantly offered, "Congratulations on your engagement to your lifelong enemy."

"Can it, Owen. Just open the door so I can leave. I need to get to Mom before she calls up her church ladies and starts planning a wedding that isn't happening."

"Hey, you chose this."

"Thanks for the support."

Chapter 21

Natalie

Tip #21: *The best defense against an overly charming grandparent is a well-timed compliment about their TV subscriptions.*

As I stepped into Estelle Warner's opulent mansion, the inviting warmth of the foyer was a welcome contrast to the chilly winter air outside. Carefully, I removed my boots and set them aside, feeling out of place in my fleece leggings and blue-and-green flannel shirt.

"Thank you for coming, Natalie." Estelle patted her steel-blond hair, perfectly styled in an elegant updo. "I'm so pleased to see you again."

"Thank you, Estelle," I said. "I'm sorry I arrived earlier than planned. I gave myself extra driving time in case I got lost, and I shockingly didn't."

"Any and all apologies are quite unnecessary, my dear," Estelle said, her voice as refined as her appearance. "We shall soon be family, after all. Now, come here." To my surprise, she pulled me into a gentle hug. "I simply cannot wait to call you my daughter-in-law. I am elated for you and Samuel."

"Thank you."

Guilt stabbed my gut. This poor woman was so happy, and Sam and I were *lying* to her.

Walter shuffled into the foyer, his silver hair neatly combed back and his thick eyebrows low over his gray eyes. "Good evening, Natalie. Once again, allow me to say welcome to the family. We're happy to have you," he said. "I'm especially happy for Samuel. It seems all that pining has finally paid off."

I paused in the middle of fixing one of my socks. "Pining?" Before I could ask for clarification, my phone chirped with an incoming text message.

"Sorry, just one second." I dug my phone out of my jeans pocket and saw that the message was from Samuel.

> **Dreamboat**
> Leaving the office now. Sorry I'm late. Give me a five-minute head start before you leave so I can get to Mother's before you.

"It's Samuel," I announced for Estelle and Walter. "He says he's leaving the office now."

I tapped out a quick reply.

> **Nikki Bright**
> I'm already at your mom's.

> **Dreamboat**
> DO NOT GO IN THE HOUSE WITHOUT ME

> Too late! I'm inside, chatting with her and Walter.

I waited for a moment, but Samuel didn't reply. I shrugged it off, assuming he was preoccupied with driving. "He's on his way," I informed Estelle and Walter.

"Typical Samuel to leave work late," Estelle mused. "At least he's thoughtful enough to let you know he's running behind. It gives me hope that he'll work less once you two are married. He works too much; it's not healthy. Unfortunately, being a workaholic is a Warner trait." Estelle cast a sidelong glance at Walter, who looked affronted.

"I'll have you know I have plenty of hobbies as a retiree!"

Estelle raised an elegant eyebrow. "You have one hobby, and that is sitting on the couch watching television. You need more variety in your life, Walter."

Before Walter could muster a reply, a small, furry blob scurried into the room. It was Chuck, wearing a tuxedo bandanna complete with a black bow tie. His underbite and snaggletooth combined with his wiry hair made him look a little wild, and I grinned as he trotted up to me, his nails clicking on the tiled floor.

"Hello there, Chuck!" I squatted down to pet the happy dog. He wagged his stubby tail, dancing from side to side.

"Chuck got a bath today so he would look his best to greet

you," Estelle said, her voice dripping with love as she planted her hands over her heart.

Walter squinted at Estelle and looked a little disturbed. He leaned closer to me and spoke in a stage whisper. "If I were you, I'd make it clear real soon that Chuck there will not be your ring bearer. If you wait too long, Estelle will get her heart set on it."

"Nonsense." Estelle frowned at Walter. "I would never presume to direct any aspect of Samuel and Natalie's wedding. It's their special day!"

"Lucky," Walter muttered.

I laughed nervously. "It's a little early to be talking about wedding plans." Anxiety had a stranglehold on my esophagus—I needed to redirect the conversation.

"Don't say that, dear." Estelle gently scooped Chuck up and patted him on his back like a baby. "You'll want to get started planning as quickly as possible or the wait will feel intolerable."

"I'm not so sure about that," I muttered.

Estelle—involved with loudly kissing her little dog on the head—and Walter—expressing disgust over the display of affection—were too distracted to hear me, especially once Estelle handed Chuck off to Walter, who took the dog with a long-suffering look on his face.

"It's amazing that Chuck isn't the shape of a sausage roll, given you are convinced he shouldn't have to walk a step in his life, Estelle," Walter grumbled.

"Chuck gets sad if he isn't included in conversations," Estelle primly said.

I laughed while Walter almost pushed his lips up to his nose in an exaggerated scowl.

"Shall we retire to the den?" Estelle suggested, gesturing down the hallway. "Dinner is still in the oven, and it seems we have some time before Samuel arrives."

"Sounds great." I petted Chuck, who despite Walter's disdain nestled comfortably in the older man's arms.

"If you'll follow me this way." Estelle started down the hallway, her strides long and smooth.

"Who else will be joining us for dinner tonight?" I asked.

"It is just us, Samuel, and Isaac," Estelle replied. "A small affair."

"It sounds great," I said. "I'm looking forward to another amazing meal!"

Walter shifted his hold on Chuck. "I think it's amazing you didn't get indigestion eating here the first time—with the generation-long feud and all."

Estelle shot him a disapproving look. "Really, Walter?"

"What? Natalie is a Mann. Those fearsome hillbillies appreciate being spoken to straight."

Estelle made a strangled noise of despair, but I laughed. "Walter is right. We Manns are very straightforward."

"I knew it!" Walter declared as Estelle led us into the den.

The room had surround-sound speakers, low lighting that cast a golden glow on everything, a gas fireplace that danced with a fire, and wood-paneled walls. The plush leather furniture seemed to beckon for me to sink into its cushiony embrace, and the smart TV that hung on the wall was big and assumedly pricey.

Walter set Chuck down on one of the leather couches. The pooch immediately made himself at home, wagging his fat tail as he settled in. Plopping down next to him, Walter turned on the TV and began scrolling through the various streaming services.

"Netflix, Hulu, Disney+, Discovery+, Hallmark+ ... what's your pleasure, Natalie?" Walter peered up at me. "Or if you'd prefer something British, we've got Acorn TV. And if none of those strike your fancy, I've got plenty more!"

"Wow." I took a seat in one of the leather armchairs as

Estelle gracefully sat on the end of the couch opposite Walter. "I didn't even know there were this many streaming services!"

Estelle gave a small, elegant shrug. "I don't watch much television myself, but my father-in-law here is quite the TV junkie. I keep all these subscriptions to lure Walter out of his condo so he will come spend time with the family."

"Guilty as charged." Walter grinned sheepishly as he absently petted Chuck. "Don't worry, Natalie. I'll let you hide in here with me before and after family meals. We'll have plenty of fun."

My leather armchair squeaked as I shifted in it, and I laughed when Walter winked at me.

I really liked Walter and Estelle. Estelle was gracious and unbelievably welcoming, while Walter, with his sharp sense of humor, was exactly my kind of person. He was the kind of guy Grandpa Mann would love to hang out with.

I was really glad Samuel and I had done this, and I was more than a little ashamed of everything I'd assumed about his family prior to our scheme.

The Warners were nice people. Sure, we were bound to keep on disagreeing over things—the old middle school building was proof of that. But you could be friends and still disagree about things. In fact, it was *better* if you had friendships with all kinds of people, including those who didn't see things the way you did.

Hopefully, Estelle and Walter would still welcome me after Samuel and I broke up. I knew the odds weren't with me, but I would really regret it if I couldn't talk with them so easily anymore.

"Now, Natalie. What would you like to watch?" Walter held two remotes, like a cowboy from an old Western movie holding his pistols.

Grateful for the distraction, I rested my hands atop my

knees. "I'm a fan of comedies and mysteries. Are there any of your favorite shows you'd recommend that combine both?"

Walter craned his neck, trying to see past Chuck, who had planted his front paws on the older man's shoulders so he could try to lick Walter's face. "A woman after my own heart. I love a good laugh, so I've got plenty of options for you."

Walter made a face when Chuck finally managed to lick his chin, wrinkling his nose in disgust. "Estelle, you need to brush Chuck's teeth. His breath smells terrible."

"Thank you for your input, Walter," Estelle tartly said. She then turned to me, her expression softening. "Now, Natalie. Before Samuel arrives, allow me to say we're both so excited to have you here tonight and to welcome you to the family. Samuel made an excellent choice in dating you."

Walter smiled at me. "When Samuel asked for my wife's ring to propose to you, I was unbelievably happy. You two deserve it all."

My heart swelled with gratitude even as another pang of guilt coursed through me. Glancing down at the diamond engagement ring adorned with small emeralds, I nibbled on my lower lip. "Are you sure it's OK for me to be the one to wear this family heirloom?"

I was going to give it back once this was over, obviously, but even just wearing it made me feel bad.

"Of course," Walter said.

Estelle pressed her hand to her cheek and tilted her head, looking like a movie star from the golden age of Hollywood. "Isaac and all of Samuel's cousins weighed in before Samuel even approached the family with the request. They unanimously agreed that Samuel should be the one to have it."

"Really?" I asked, curiosity piqued. "Why?"

Estelle's lips—perfectly shaped with red lipstick—curved in a smile.

Walter, however, snorted. "All of my grandchildren agreed Samuel has suffered and waited long enough. He deserved the ring."

I furrowed my eyebrows, confused by the cryptic explanation. "What do you mean—"

A loud crash echoed in the hallway, cutting me off.

"Good heavens! What was that?" Estelle exclaimed as we all whipped our heads toward the den entrance.

A moment later, Samuel burst into the room, clutching a briefcase and still wearing his work suit and wool winter coat, which made a stark contrast with his stocking feet.

He skidded across the polished floor as he entered, tossing his briefcase to the ground.

"Sam!" Estelle beamed.

Walter snickered. "Who stuck a bee in your trousers?"

Samuel scowled at his grandfather and turned to face me. The look in his eyes made my heart skip a beat, but I quickly laughed off my nerves.

"That was some entrance." I scraped myself off the armchair and crossed the den to greet him.

"I was in a rush. Hello." Samuel's voice was so low and rumbly it unexpectedly made my nerves jitter as he wrapped his arms around my waist.

Taking his cue, I wound my arms around his neck. "Hello yourself." The joke wasn't funny, but it was the best I could do as I tried to ignore his arms on my waist and his proximity.

Samuel didn't seem to mind. "I missed you. I hope my mother and grandfather didn't say anything potentially embarrassing." He leaned in and buried his face in my wavy hair, which thankfully wasn't a frizzy mess today.

"Not at all," I said, casually. (At least I hoped it sounded casual.) "We had fun."

"That's not reassuring. You'd have the time of your life

listening to all the greatest hits of my most embarrassing moments," Samuel said, his face still in my hair.

I laughed and hoped it didn't sound canned. "That's not true, boo."

Samuel chuckled, bending down slightly so his lips grazed my neck. It was a soft, fleeting touch, but it felt like I'd been kissed by fire.

"Samuel, perhaps you could peel yourself off your love long enough to say hello to your grandfather and me?" Estelle suggested.

Embarrassed, I backed away from Samuel, busting out of his hug.

Samuel frowned at his mother in a look-what-you-made-her-do kind of way.

Walter, who'd gone back to petting Chuck, waved Estelle's comment off with a waggle of his fingers. "There's no harm in it, Estelle. They're young, in love, and newly engaged."

Samuel strode across the den to greet her. He bent over and hugged Estelle, who beamed with motherly pride.

"Since this is the first time I've seen you two together since your engagement, congratulations. You are a lovely match, and I'm sure you'll have a happy life together." Estelle's face softened as she looked at us. "Also, I like my new daughter-in-law very much."

"Thank you, Mother," Samuel said, "but remember, I'm marrying Natalie because I'm in love with her, not because you need another friend."

Estelle huffed, but there was a sparkle in her eye that said she wasn't really offended.

I settled back into the leather armchair I'd vacated, and Samuel shook hands with his grandfather.

"Sam," Walter said, "how was work?"

"Good," Samuel said. "And quite productive. Logan looked

into zoning for the old middle school, and it's appropriate for condos."

My smile faltered. The old school had the potential to be another point of conflict between the two families. It would be a new fight if we didn't navigate the issue carefully.

Estelle seemed to notice my mood shift and quickly interjected. "Samuel, let's not discuss work now. You're home, it's time to relax."

Samuel gave in way more easily than I expected, obediently nodding his head. "Yes, Mother."

Samuel sauntered up to my chair and dropped his coat on the floor. "Up," he said.

"Up what?" I asked, confused.

"Stand up for a moment."

I rose from my seat only to have him claim it for himself.

Chuck hopped off Walter's lap and waddled over to Sam's discarded coat, nestling atop it and shedding white hairs everywhere. Samuel rolled his eyes at the dog but didn't shoo him away.

I, on the other hand, was left to scowl down at my fake fiancé. "Is this your assigned chair or something?"

"Nope," Samuel said. "But it was the most convenient spot since this is your chair. Now, sit down." He slapped his thighs in invitation.

"Really, Sam?"

"Really."

"I'm not going to sit on your lap, especially not in front of your family."

"I'm just being thoughtful." Samuel gave me a wounded look. "I know how much you love to cuddle."

"Samuel!" Estelle scolded, her glare withering. She turned to me, a hint of apology in her eyes. "I apologize, Natalie. I thought I raised him with more decorum and respect than that."

"Believe me, I'm used to it," I said, not even joking as I thought of all the annoying games he'd played on me over the years.

"Mother, you can't blame me." Samuel playfully winked at me. "Natalie's so beautiful, she's hard to resist."

"Samuel Warner, I hope Chuck pees on your coat!" Estelle declared.

"Mother!" Samuel gasped, feigning shock. "Such crass language! What kind of manners are you displaying to your future daughter-in-law?"

Estelle turned to Walter for support, but he shrugged and said, "You did want him happy and in love, didn't you?"

"True." Estelle's expression softened, and she patted her hand over her heart.

Samuel's gray eyes were so bright they were almost blue as he smirked up at me from my stolen seat. "Well, Natalie, since my mother has so graciously provided her blessing, won't you please join me?" He patted his lap again, that charming grin of his never leaving his face.

"Nice try, Romeo," I said, "but we're too old for that."

Samuel mockingly raised his eyebrows at me, which made me want to pick up Chuck and put him on Samuel's lap in hopes that the dog would get white hair all over him, ruining his annoyingly perfect image.

Samuel had put me in a pickle. With all our PDAs, I couldn't just sit across the room. But I would die before I sat in Sam's lap.

Not because he was a Warner, but because then he'd *win*!

Win what, I didn't know. But whatever it was, I didn't want him winning.

The moment was stretching on too long. I could feel Walter's thoughtful gaze on my back.

Thinking fast, I plopped down on the armrest of the chair he'd stolen from me.

With my legs tucked on either side of the armrest, my knee was pushed against Samuel's.

He blinked in surprise at my seat choice, then smirked like the Cheshire Cat. "It's not my first choice, but I guess you sitting here will do."

He nudged my leg with his, then slipped his hand up my side, resting it directly above my knee.

The touch left a trail of awareness on my leg, but I still had the smug feeling I'd won whatever it was we were competing over.

"Are we all quite comfortable now?" Estelle acidly asked.

"Yes, Mother, though not quite in the way I'd like," Samuel said.

"Natalie," Estelle continued, ignoring her son, "I'd like to invite you to join us—the Warner family, that is—at a charity gala in Milwaukee next week."

I paused, balancing on the chair's arm. "Oh. Um. I'm honored, but a gala isn't really my scene."

"Mine either," Walter mouthed to me.

"I understand," Estelle said. "They can be quite trying depending on the crowd." She shook her head in dismay.

"She means sometimes attendees can be petty and arrogant," Samuel interpreted for me.

"Quite intolerable." Estelle straightened her already perfect posture. "However. As you are going to become a Warner, I'm afraid you'll have to learn the ins and outs of socializing with boors. You will be called upon to attend more business dinners and functions as Samuel's wife."

Oh boy. We were really going too far with this fake engagement thing. Why did Samuel break under pressure and propose!?

"Don't worry." Walter picked up on my anxiety but mistook its source. "Most of those dinners will be with clients or Warner Print employees, who are much more fun. We only socialize with the snobs of Wisconsin when we can't avoid it."

Estelle rested her fingers on her temples. "The two of you are doing a terrible job of selling this to Natalie. You'll scare her away!"

"Natalie has too much spine for that." Samuel squeezed my thigh. "You'll come, won't you? I'll die of boredom and heartbreak if you don't."

I smiled widely and clenched my teeth. "Honey boo, don't you think you're being a *tad* dramatic?"

Samuel leaned closer, sliding his arm off my thigh and placing it around my waist. "Come on, it'll be fun. I'll buy you a dress, and we can camp out at the open bar."

Whether it was because of everything we'd been through the past few weeks or the fact that I could feel the heat from his hand on my hip, I gave in. "Fine, fine. I'll come."

"Wonderful!" Estelle clapped her hands in glee. "I am so looking forward to this! I have always wanted a daughter-in-law to do these kinds of things with."

Samuel gave Estelle a pained look. "Again. Mother, I'm not marrying Natalie for your convenience."

Walter snorted as he went back to scrolling through streaming services. "Don't worry, Sam. There's not a single Warner who would think that after all of this."

I opened my mouth to ask Walter what he meant by that, but Samuel abruptly stood up, almost knocking me over. "Now that we have that squared away, why don't we go check on dinner? I'm sure Isaac is here by now." Samuel twined his fingers through mine and tugged me along, pulling me behind him.

"You left your briefcase and jacket," I said.

"Forget them," Samuel said. "They're Chuck's now."

Once we left the den Samuel slowed down enough so I could match his stride. "Are you really OK with attending the gala?"

Ahh, that was the reason for the abrupt exit. He wanted to double-check with me, which was kind of touching. A couple months ago I would have laughed myself sick at the idea of Samuel's being concerned if I was bored.

"It'll be fine," I said. "I'll just consider it a life experience."

"Good." Samuel flashed me a smile. "Then when should we go dress shopping?"

"You don't have to come with. I can pay for my own dress."

"Nonsense. This is my family's function, and you'll need a new cocktail dress for it. I'm coming."

"No," I said firmly.

Samuel raised his eyebrows.

"Not happening," I said.

Silly, silly me.

Chapter 22

Natalie

Tip #22: *Stay on your toes. If your fake fiancé is wealthy, they'll use any opportunity to spoil you, which will make your inevitable breakup awkward.*

The heavy scent of a musky perfume clouded the air as I stood in front of the ornately framed mirror, cringing at my reflection. The blue satin hugged my figure in all the right places, and the black lace overlay was gorgeous ... but the *price*!

Samuel lounged on a vintage sofa nearby, four other dresses draped beside him. "You look perfect. Absolutely stunning and beautiful."

I propped my hands up on my hips. "You've said that about every dress I've tried on."

"I can't help it if you look beautiful in everything." Samuel rubbed his jawline, scratching his five-o'clock shadow.

I gave him a flat look, swallowing the fluttery feeling in my chest. His charm was way more dangerous now that we were close friends. I was more likely to fall for it instead of dreaming about egging his precious Porsche like I would have months ago.

I cleared my throat and clapped twice. "Alright, we need to narrow this down to one dress."

"Why?" Samuel asked.

"Because I can only wear one dress to the gala."

Samuel looked at the dresses next to him, the skirts cascading over the back of the sofa. "Why can't I buy them all for you?"

"Because I have no use for five cocktail dresses."

"Nonsense," Samuel said. "We'll just have to go on a lot of dressy evening dates. I'd prefer dinner dates, but if you are into the theater, I could be bribed into attending a performance." He grinned devilishly.

I turned away from Samuel and went back to peering at my reflection. "You're incorrigible."

"Aren't you going to ask what I could be bribed with?" Samuel asked with too much happiness for it to be an answer that wouldn't embarrass me.

"No."

"I'll give you a hint."

"I don't want a hint." I twirled, secretly enjoying the way the tea-length dress twirled around my legs.

Samuel held up three fingers, which I could see in his reflection in the mirror. "It involves you, and me, and making out—"

"*Sam!*"

The store clerk, who was hanging up a pale pink gown I had rejected a few minutes ago, laughed, reminding me we weren't alone. "You two are just the cutest."

Samuel put on his polite smile. "Why, thank you. I believe so too. But Nat can be so stingy with her affection."

The lady sighed. "You have quite the story too. A Warner and a Mann? Who would have guessed?"

"I've been planning it for years," Samuel said.

The clerk laughed.

I smiled thinly, reminding myself that Samuel was just putting on a show for the staff. It didn't mean anything. Not a thing.

Samuel stood up from the vintage sofa and sauntered toward me, a mischievous glint in his eyes. He stopped when he was just behind me and leaned in to kiss my temple, making my heart skip a beat.

"Say what you will," he started, "but why not just get them all? My mother is already planning multiple engagement parties for us anyway."

I stiffened up. "What do you mean?"

"We have to throw one at Warner Print to celebrate with the employees, then there'll be a party for our families, and probably one for Warner Print's top clients." Samuel shrugged casually, as if it was no big deal.

"Wait, wait." My hand shot up to interrupt this insanity as I switched to whispering urgently. "I knew what you meant by multiple parties, but you can't possibly mean they're actually happening!"

Samuel tilted his head, feigning confusion. "Why not?"

I started to squawk indignantly but stopped myself when I noticed the clerk watching us with curiosity.

We should have gone shopping in a mall in Milwaukee or Madison instead of this small dress boutique in Fox Creek. Then we wouldn't have had to act out our fake engagement like this. On the other hand, if we went to the mall, who knows what other stores Samuel would've dragged me into?

"Honey." I turned around and hugged Samuel so I could whisper in his ear without the clerk hearing. "The more we play into this engagement shtick, the harder it's going to be to break up."

"Nat, you worry too much. We have plenty of time to engineer our breakup," Samuel said, his voice low and soothing. My arms were still draped over his shoulders, so I felt it when he abruptly tensed up. "Unless ... you have someone else you want to date?"

"No!" I blurted, pulling back so I could look up at his face. "I never would have proposed *this* if that were true."

Samuel's shoulders immediately relaxed. "Then loosen up and have fun."

Unable to hold back my disgust at his breezy attitude, I once again leaned into him so I could rest my chin on his shoulder and grumble. "You're going to give me heartburn with your cavalier attitude."

My gaze was drawn to the boutique's small front window and bustling Main Street beyond it just in time to see Owen and Jenna stroll past the dress store, Jenna's bright pink winter coat drawing my eye like a neon sign. Despite the cold weather, they were all smiles and laughter.

Motivated by the core strength of all little sisters—nosiness—I pushed past Samuel and sprinted across the store. I planted myself against the glass front door and craned my neck so I had the right angle to watch my brother and Samuel's cousin disappear down the sidewalk.

"Sam!" I shouted.

Samuel rushed over, concern etched on his face. "What's wrong?"

"Look!" I pointed at Owen and Jenna, who had stopped to wait for the light at a street corner. My voice rose with outrage. "They're on a second date!"

Samuel curled an arm around my shoulders—he was a lot better at this performing aspect than I was. "Didn't you want Owen and Jenna to go on more dates?"

"Of course I did. But Owen never told me he'd asked Jenna out on a second date! I listened to him chatter about their first date for *hours*. How dare he arrange a second one and not tell me!" I fumed as I watched the pair cross the street.

Samuel's lips curled in a smile that used to spell trouble for me but which—with our fake relationship—I was coming to enjoy. "Do you want to follow them?" he asked.

"Absolutely!" I spun around, pointing myself in the direction of the changing room. "Just give me a minute to get changed."

"No time for that," Samuel declared. "We'll lose sight of them." He turned around and addressed the clerk, who had been eavesdropping on our conversation. "Could you scan the tag on her dress? She'll be wearing it out of the store."

"Of course," the clerk said, trying to hide her amusement as she headed to the register.

I darted to the counter, extending my arm so the clerk could scan the tag attached to the sleeve of the beautiful dress.

Samuel confidently strode to the vintage sofa, grabbing his coat with an air of authority. "Get your clothes and put on your jacket and boots."

"On it!" I rushed into the store's only changing room.

Hastily, I rolled up the clothes I'd arrived in before hurriedly zipping up my puffy parka and yanking on my boots. I topped off my ensemble with my pom-pom hat, then happened to glance at my reflection in the mirror. Suppressing a snort at my mismatched appearance, I burst out of the changing room to find Samuel standing by the register, putting his credit card back in his wallet as the store clerk folded up the other four dresses I'd liked and placed them in a couple of store bags.

"What are you doing?" I asked.

Samuel casually took my clothes from me, tossing them into one of the bags before collecting all his purchases. "I paid for everything."

"Everything? But I was going to buy my dress, and I just wanted one!"

"Too late now." Samuel shrugged. "I've paid for them all, and we'll just waste time returning the gowns when we could be following Jenna and Owen."

My scowl deepened as I realized how masterfully he had manipulated the situation.

"Are you seriously playing this game with me?" I growled, though my brother's date still held my curiosity hostage.

Samuel leaned into my personal space. "Is it working?"

"No," I said, then paused. "Yes!"

Samuel laughed as my desire to support Owen and discover what was happening between him and Jenna ultimately won out over my sense of monetary pride. I hurried to the store's front door, with Samuel following behind. Together, we opened the door and stepped onto the crowded sidewalk.

"There they are!" I pointed down the street where Owen and Jenna were strolling, oblivious to our presence.

Samuel followed my gaze as he stopped by his Porsche and its coveted streetside parking spot long enough to deposit the bags of dresses in the back seat. "Come on." Samuel grabbed my hand and led me down the sidewalk toward our unsuspecting quarry.

"Has Jenna mentioned anything to you about her dates with Owen?" I asked.

Samuel shook his head. "No, she hasn't."

"Really?" I frowned, disappointed on behalf of my brother. "Maybe that means she didn't have a great time."

"Nah. It's mostly a testament to the fact that I try to avoid discussing romantic entanglements with my family."

"Why? The Warners are so invested in our relationship. They were supportive of our romance from the start." We paused at a crosswalk, waiting for the sign to change.

"Trust me, their investment in our relationship is not by my choice," Samuel said.

The crosswalk sign lit up, so he hustled me across the street without further explanation.

Samuel, tall enough to peer over the tops of the heads of other Fox Creek residents who crowded the sidewalk, kept me briefed. "Jenna and Owen just went into Cherry's Dairy Bar."

Still hand in hand, we speed-walked down the sidewalk.

"That's promising, right? Getting together on a weekend, particularly in a place that's as popular with the locals as Cherry's is," I said.

We stopped under the dairy bar's red-and-white striped awning, and I pulled my hand free from Samuel's so I could cup my hands around my eyes and squint through the window, spotting Jenna and Owen selecting a table inside.

"Looks like they're getting settled in and plan to order something," I said.

"You want to keep spying on them?" Samuel asked.

"Yeah," I said.

Samuel nodded. "Very well. But how are we going to get inside without being noticed?"

I chuckled. "Leave that to me."

Chapter 23

Natalie

Tip #23: *Good disguises are a must-have for subterfuge.*

Feathers dropped behind me like a crumb trail as Samuel and I stepped out of the back room into the main dining area of Cherry's Dairy Bar. With each movement, my black feather boa dropped more feathers—it would be a miracle if the thing didn't fall apart before the subterfuge was discovered, and I was starting to suspect I resembled a half-plucked ostrich.

Samuel, on the other hand, looked like a mysterious but handsome stranger in his blue sunglasses, black scarf, and fedora.

"If I'd known your grand idea involved raiding the lost-and-found box and getting the cook to let us in through the back door, I might've had second thoughts about spying on Owen and Jenna." Samuel adjusted his hat.

"Quit being so fussy." I stood on my tiptoes as I tried to find Owen and Jenna in the crowded dairy bar. I had to hold in place the monstrosity of a borrowed trapper hat—which was red and black with fake fur lining the earflaps—I'd pulled down to cover the sides of my face. "No one will recognize us."

Samuel glanced back at the kitchen door we'd snuck through. "Who was that cook anyway?"

"Joe," I said. "He's dating my great aunt's boyfriend's daughter."

"Is there anyone in this town you're not related to or connected with?" Samuel asked.

"My family has no connections to you Warners."

"No connections yet," Samuel corrected. With his sunglasses on I couldn't read his eyes to tell if he was joking or serious.

"Right," I said, deciding he must be talking about Jenna and Owen, not us.

Spotting an open table, I gestured for Samuel to follow me, my boa shedding more feathers as we crossed the room.

The dairy bar was vintage-themed, complete with ice cream-parlor knickknacks and booths, a jukebox that actually worked, and a cranky woman named Cherry running the show. All the waitresses wore pink uniforms, adding to the nostalgic ambiance.

We slid into a cramped vinyl booth built into the wall, barely able to see Owen and Jenna at their cozy two-person table in the center of the restaurant.

I squinted, trying to catch glimpses of their expressions. "I can't see very well."

Samuel fiddled with the brim of his fedora. "And I can't decide if this is more or less hygienic than rented bowling shoes.

I'm thinking the overall look is worse, as fedoras can be cringey on men my age, whereas everyone was forced to wear the bowling shoes at Cosmic Bowl."

I glanced over at him, taking in his broad shoulders, the dreamy planes of his face, and his dark hair that showed on the sides of his head. The aviator sunglasses hid his gorgeous gray eyes, but he made them look like a conscious fashion choice. "You look great," I said, sighing. I used to not care that he was unbelievably genetically blessed with hotness because he irritated me. Now that we were friends, I had to ignore it because friends don't ogle each other!

"That sigh doesn't make it sound like I look all that great," Samuel said.

"No, you look better than great; you look handsome, which is why I was sighing, because it's unfair you can look so hot no matter what you're wearing."

Samuel immediately stopped fiddling with his hat. "You think I'm hot?"

"Isn't this a surprise?" The familiar voice startled me out of mooning over Samuel.

Leaning out of the booth, I saw my cousin Madison, dressed in the pink Cherry's Dairy Bar uniform, scoot around a table before she came to a stop next to our booth.

"Madison?" I gaped. "What are you doing here? You don't work at Cherry's!"

Madison snapped the gum she was chewing. "Nice to see you too, Nat."

"Ah, Madison, the cousin who gives her kids questionable sex-ed lessons. How are you?" Samuel gave my cousin a winning smile.

"Warner." Madison acknowledged him with a nod. "I'm doing fine, thanks for asking. I hope you two are having a great date?"

"We are," Samuel said.

I waved the tip of my boa like a flag. "I'm still lost. Why are you here, Madison? I repeat: You don't work here."

Madison waggled the dairy bar's paper menus at me. "I used to work here when I was in high school, remember?"

"Your youngest kid is six," I said. "High school was a long time ago."

Madison narrowed her eyes at me. "Are you looking to get your food sabotaged?"

I meekly took the stained paper menus from Madison and handed one to Samuel.

"To answer your question—even if the wording was rude," Madison began, "I still cover shifts here occasionally. My best friend is the shift manager, and two of her high schoolers called out sick tonight." Madison eyed our unusual attire. "So, what's with the wardrobe?"

"Natalie raided the lost and found to procure disguises for us," Samuel said.

"Disguises? Are you two spying on Owen and Jenna?" Madison asked.

"Yep," I said.

"Interesting." Madison took out a little notepad and pen from a pocket of her uniform. "Anyway, are you ready to order?"

"How can you be so calm about Owen and Jenna?" I asked. "Aren't you curious about their date?"

"After having you two, the OG mortal enemies–turned–star-crossed lovers, end up engaged, Owen and Jenna's going on a date is tame in comparison. Now, are you ready to order or not?"

"Mint sundae, two scoops, please," I automatically said.

"And I'll take a large chocolate shake." Samuel plucked my menu from my hands and handed them back to Madison.

"You got it." Madison disappeared into the kitchen to put in our order, leaving us to our spying mission.

I craned my neck to catch a glimpse of Owen and Jenna. "Can you even see them from here?"

"Sort of." Samuel leaned back against the cushioned bench seat. "I can see Owen's back, but that's about it. He must be nervous. He's visibly sweated through the back of his blue shirt."

"He's a nervous sweater—it runs in the family," I said. "We need a better vantage point."

I peered around the dairy bar and noticed a pair of high schoolers leaving a high-top table that was a little closer to Owen and Jenna. "Perfect! Let's move."

I hurried off, the feathers from my boa fluttering as I rushed to claim our new spot. Samuel trailed me, looking cool and stylish whereas my face was starting to turn red from the heat of my trapper hat.

I hopped up onto one of the stools, pleased that I could now see more of Jenna's face, though Owen's was still mostly obscured.

Samuel nudged his stool next to mine before he slid onto it and casually draped an arm around my shoulders, a gesture I'd grown so accustomed to that I barely noticed and instead automatically leaned into him.

"Jenna looks happy, right?" I asked.

Samuel briefly flicked his sunglasses down, observing his cousin. "Well, she's always bubbly, but yeah. She seems like she's having fun."

I bit my lip.

"Stop worrying." He squeezed my shoulder. "Jenna wouldn't have said yes to a second date if she didn't actually like Owen."

"You're right. Thanks."

"Sure. So how long has Owen been crushing on Jenna?"

"I first noticed it about two years ago," I said.

"Ah, so not that long then."

I turned to look up at Samuel as if he'd grown a second head. "What are you talking about? Two years is a really long time to like someone and not make a move on them!"

He shrugged. "I know a guy who carried a torch for a girl for about a decade before finally getting her."

"Wow," I marveled, shaking my head. "That is a seriously slow-moving romance."

"It's called loyalty."

"Or really bad communication. Otherwise, how else could the girl not realize the guy liked her?"

"Sometimes people are just annoyingly oblivious, alright?" Samuel's voice was low and growly.

"If you say so." I leaned even further into him to try and see if I could get a better look. I practically ended up in Samuel's lap as I strained to see Owen's expression.

Madison emerged from the back kitchen area carrying Samuel's shake. She paused at our empty booth, a puzzled expression on her face, before spotting us in our new location.

"Really? Playing musical chairs now?" Madison plunked the large glass down in front of Samuel. "Here's your large chocolate shake."

"Sorry," I said. "I just wanted a better view of Owen and Jenna."

"Uh-huh," Madison said skeptically. "Or maybe you just wanted to cuddle up with your fiancé."

I blushed. "That's not—"

"You're not wrong," Samuel peeled back one of the earflaps of my hat so he could kiss me on the cheek. "We have a highly developed style of flirting that mostly involves awkward situations."

Madison rolled her eyes and started to walk off. "Does your terrible flirting include fighting? Because that would explain a lot."

"Madison!" I hissed, but she was already too far away to hear.

I drummed my fingers on the table. The scent of Cherry's Dairy Bar—a mix of sweet ice cream and grease from the food—tempted my stomach.

"Are you thinking about how much you love me?" Samuel asked.

I paused, my fingers hovering over the table. "I can't decide if your unshakable confidence is admirable or annoying."

"We're making progress, honey," Samuel said. "Before we started dating, you would have called me a raving egomaniac."

His smile made me uncomfortable, but I couldn't quite put a finger on why, which made me even more annoyed.

This was why we needed to break up. It would be too easy to get used to this—not just Samuel's hotness, but the way he spoiled me with the dresses and his willingness to join whatever crazy scheme I was hatching. The longer we took to break up, the more I would miss him.

Feeling antsy, I scoped out the room again. "We should move."

"To where?" Samuel asked.

"There." I pointed to a table that had just cleared on the opposite side of the room, which would give me a better view of Owen's face.

"Fine, but you better appreciate the wad of cash I'm going to have to leave Madison as a tip after all of this."

As we scooted around the perimeter of the room to avoid being seen, a few Fox Creek residents greeted me, complimenting my unique sense of style.

I slid onto a chair pulled up to our new table, feeling victorious now that I could see both Owen's and Jenna's faces.

Samuel sat down next to me and casually offered me his chocolate shake. "Want a taste? It's good."

I hesitated, but ... friends shared drinks all the time, right? Not to mention we were still pretending to be engaged. He'd probably offered to keep our cover.

I took the large glass and sipped from his paper straw, savoring the shake's velvety texture and decadent chocolate taste. "That is really good. Thank you." I took another sip, then handed it back.

"Of course." Samuel smiled at me, but his eyes were still hidden by his sunglasses. He planted his straw in his mouth. He must have been bored or something, because he kept the straw in his mouth even though he very obviously wasn't drinking his shake.

"Madison's coming this way," Samuel said. "She doesn't look too happy."

I waved his concern off with a dismissive hand. "It's worth it to see Owen and Jenna closer."

At that moment, Owen said something that made Jenna laugh and she leaned across the table to show my brother something on her cell phone, which made Owen smile so deeply his dimples showed.

A small stab of jealousy pricked my heart as I studied their easy smiles and genuine connection. "They look happy."

"Half as happy as we are." Samuel finally stopped sucking on his straw and casually plucked off his aviators.

I was going to scoff at him, but when I looked his way, his expression was serious. The usual polish his charm gave him was gone—his lips didn't twitch into an easy smile, and there was something raw about the look in his gray eyes. Too many moments of silence passed between us, and Samuel still held my eyes. I couldn't look away from him. I couldn't even blink, and I didn't know why.

"Finally found you two!" Madison's voice broke through the spell, shattering the drawn-out moment.

Madison set a sundae in front of me. It was a ridiculous creation: a scoop of vanilla complete with candy eyes, an ice cream cone hat, and whipped cream detailing that formed the face of a clown.

"What's this?" I asked.

"It's a clown sundae," Madison said, her voice dripping with sarcasm. "Since you're acting like a clown, I figured it was fitting. Besides, I had to give your mint sundae away because I couldn't find you."

"Joke's on you, because this is adorable." I whipped out my cell phone to take a picture. "And I told you, we're here because I want to see Jenna and Owen."

"Trust me, Natalie," Madison said. "You don't need this cloak-and-dagger thing. Jenna is too nice to say anything even if she saw you, and Owen is so over the moon he's oblivious to his surroundings. He didn't even notice when I gave him the wrong kind of fries."

I glanced over at Owen, who was nodding at something Jenna had said, his eyes shining with happiness. Madison was right; my brother was lost in his own little world.

"I get that you're worried. Everyone knows you and Owen are practically best friends," Madison continued, her voice softer now. "But he'll be fine when you and Samuel marry. He won't be lonely."

That should have comforted me, but as I looked at Samuel, a new realization settled heavily on me. While Owen might not be lonely, I would be once Samuel and I broke up, even if I still had my brother by my side.

Sensing my unease, Madison patted my shoulder before leaving to attend to another table.

"Are you OK?" Samuel asked.

I smiled, shaking off the heavy feeling that had taken residence in my chest. "Yeah, I'm fine. Thank you for playing along today."

Samuel shrugged, his charming smile effortlessly disarming any lingering tension. "I'm always down for an adventure with you, Natalie."

Chapter 24

Samuel

Tip #24: *Bringing food to your fake fiancée is a power move. Sharing your latte? That's how you win hearts.*

I smiled like an idiot as I held open the glass door of city hall for a harried-looking dad wrangling two rambunctious toddlers while wearing a snoozing baby strapped to his chest.

"Thanks, man," he said as he herded the kids inside.

My grin widened. "No problem." I was in such a good mood, I probably would've offered to babysit if he'd asked. OK, maybe not, but still. I felt on top of the world.

The aroma of my Literum chocolate strawberry latte wafted up as I took a sip, savoring the rich coffee goodness. I shifted the paper takeout bag to my other hand, my steps echoing on the polished marble floor as I made my way through the lobby.

City hall was a testament to small-town pride and questionable budget priorities. Towering Corinthian columns flanked the corridors, their elaborate capitals probably costing more than Nat's car. Ornate crown molding traced the high ceilings, and I swear I caught a cherub with Grandma Mann's face winking at me from a gaudy ceiling fresco.

Just as I rounded the corner toward Natalie's office, my phone buzzed insistently in my pocket like an angry hornet. I set my latte and the takeout bag on a nearby wooden bench and fished my phone out of my pocket.

Three texts from Miguel, each progressively more angry than the last.

> **Miguel**
> Where ARE you?

> **Miguel**
> We have a client meeting in THIRTY MINUTES!

> **Miguel**
> IF YOU'RE NOT BACK SOON I'M TELLING YOUR MOTHER!

I snorted. As if my mother would be anything but thrilled. Right on cue, a text from her popped up.

> **Mother**
> Is it true?? My workaholic son is taking time off for love?? I'm so proud!! Give Natalie a big kiss!

Her text was accompanied by a glut of emojis to communicate her joy.

Mother had been pestering me for years to find some work-life balance, and now she thought I finally had it. All thanks to this fake engagement with Natalie.

Fake. Right. I pushed away the pang in my chest at that word. I was going to savor every moment of bliss that I could and figure out the details later.

I pocketed my phone, picked up the food and my latte, and headed toward Natalie's station. Time to see my fiancée.

I approached the administration service window—which separated the public from the employees' desks like the DMV. I immediately spotted Natalie, her ash-brown, wavy hair cascading over her shoulders. She was hunched over some paperwork, her brow furrowed in concentration.

She was so cute when she was focused.

"Well, if it isn't my beautiful bride-to-be." I leaned against the counter with what I hoped was a roguish grin. "I come bearing gifts of sustenance and caffeine."

Natalie's head snapped up, her green eyes widening in surprise before crinkling with a smile that made my heart stop.

"Samuel!" she said. "Hold on, I'll be right out."

As she disappeared from the window, a smug grin spread across my face.

She was happy to see me. Really happy. Fake engagement or not, that had to mean something, right?

The door swung open, and there she was again, all long legs and cute girl-next-door charm. "You're a lifesaver," Natalie said, reaching for the bag. "I was so grateful when you texted to ask if I needed lunch. Thank you!"

I held the bag just out of reach. "Not so fast, Mann. There's a delivery fee."

Natalie playfully scowled. "Oh? And what might that be?"

When I leaned in, her eyes widened in confusion and I seized my chance.

I pressed my lips to hers in a soft, sweet kiss. It was achingly brief, but I savored the warmth of her lips and the momentary sensation that everything was as it should be.

Eventually I pulled back, my heart racing, and hoped she couldn't tell how much that simple kiss affected me. How much she affected me.

"Payment received," I said, my voice a bit rougher than I intended. "Your lunch awaits."

A loud clap echoed through the office, making Natalie jump. Her coworker, a matronly woman with an embroidered vest, was practically pressed against the window.

Natalie's face turned an adorable shade of crimson. It was a far cry from the fiery glares she used to throw my way when we were at each other's throats. This embarrassed, flustered Natalie? I could get used to her.

Natalie shook her head at her coworker, then held out her hands and made a grabbing motion. "Food. Please."

I handed over the paper bag. "Don't worry, no surprise ring this time. I save those for more public venues."

She scoffed, but there was something shining in her

gorgeous green eyes that I couldn't quite place. "Thanks again, Samuel. Really."

The sincerity in her voice hit me like a punch to the gut—I was in deep. This whole fake engagement thing was simultaneously the best and worst idea ever. Best because I got to be close to her like this. Worst because it wasn't real. Not for her anyway.

"Anything for you, Natalie." Unable to help myself, I reached out and tucked a stray strand of her wavy hair behind her ear. Her skin was warm beneath my fingertips, and I let my hand linger for a moment. "I'm always happy to see to your every need."

Natalie's coworker let out another exuberant round of applause, her clapping echoing through the marble hallway. "You two are just adorable!"

I grinned. "Thank you." I took a bow, basking in the validation. This, with Natalie, was everything I'd ever wanted.

Natalie made a shooing motion at her coworker. "Ignore her, or we'll end up with half the office out here gawking at us."

I waggled my eyebrows. "Would that be so bad?"

She swatted my arm playfully. "Have you eaten? I feel bad keeping you from your lunch."

"I had a working lunch with Isaac earlier." I took a casual a sip of my latte and hoped. Come on, Natalie. Take the bait. "But I couldn't resist stopping by Literum for their limited-time chocolate strawberry latte. Have you tried it?"

Natalie's eyes lit up. "They brought it back? I love that flavor!"

I knew that, of course. It's why I'd gotten it in the first place. But I kept my face neutral as I held out the cup. "Yes, it's back for the rest of the winter season. Want a sip?"

She hesitated for a moment before taking the cup from my hand.

Natalie took a long sip, her eyes fluttering closed in pleasure. "Mmm," she hummed. "That's even better than I remembered. Wow, I need to get down there and get one of these, stat."

I watched her, drinking in the sight of her enjoyment far more than I had the actual latte. "Good?"

She nodded emphatically. "So good. Thanks for sharing."

I took the cup back and channeled every ounce of charm I had. "Of course. I'm always happy to share an indirect kiss with you, pookie." I took a deliberate sip from the exact spot her lips had just touched.

Natalie scrunched up her nose, but I could see the smile tugging at the corners of her mouth. "You're such a flirt, sweetie pie."

I winked. "Only with you, honey cakes."

Before Natalie could respond, her coworker's voice rang out from behind the service desk. "Shucks, Natalie, as much as I'm enjoying the performance, you ought to take ten minutes to sit down and eat and flirt with that fiancé of yours."

Natalie's eyebrows shot up. "What? But we're swamped with paperwork. No one's taking lunch away from their desk today."

Natalie's coworker waved her hand dismissively. "We're not about to keep Fox Creek's Romeo and Juliet apart. Just eat fast, OK?"

"Thanks," Natalie said, her brows furrowing into a puzzled V until she turned to me. "There's some seating in the lobby area. Shall we?"

I offered my hand to Natalie, and to my delight, she took it without hesitation. Her fingers intertwined with mine naturally, as if we'd been doing this for years instead of just a few weeks.

"I'm looking forward to the gala tomorrow night," Natalie said as we strolled toward the lobby. "I've got my makeup all planned out to match my dress."

"Should I coordinate my tie with your dress? That's what engaged couples do, right?" I pretended to innocently ask.

Natalie laughed. "Are you actually asking for fashion advice? Between the two of us, you're the way more fashionable one. I thought you came out of the womb wearing Armani."

I lifted our joint palms so I could kiss the top of Natalie's hand. "I'll have you know I was a Gucci baby, thank you very much."

Natalie laughed, and satisfaction brewed in my gut. I loved making her laugh. If I could spend the rest of my life doing just that, I'd die a happy man.

Unfortunately, I didn't think her laughter was a sign she was starting to see me as more than the annoying guy she'd grown up despising.

Maybe more hardcore flirting was in order?

I knew I should suck it up and just tell Natalie I loved her. But every time I thought about confessing, my courage deserted me. What if it ruined all of this? Could she even ever see me in a romantic light?

Natalie and the Mann clan had definitely toned down the town rivalry, and we were absolutely close friends. But I didn't want to lose these precious moments with her when they were all I'd dreamed about for the past decade.

No, I'd just keep at it and hope that maybe Natalie would catch on.

Chapter 25

Natalie

Tip #25: *Fake fiancés should always have your back. Bonus points if they shut down snooty guests on your behalf.*

As Samuel and I stepped into the opulent hotel ballroom, arm in arm, my breath caught at the beauty of the gala.

Music from a live string quartet set up near the back of the room wound around me like a friendly cat rubbing against my legs. Tables adorned with white linens and towering centerpieces made of roses, hydrangeas, and lilies filled the space, while well-dressed gala attendees mingled, their laughter and clinking glasses creating a lively atmosphere.

"Are you sure about this?" I nervously whispered.

"Sure about what?" Samuel glanced down at me with amusement.

"About me being here. I might screw up and affect Warner Print's reputation ..." I leaned in close so I could whisper, "and all for a fake engagement."

"Relax, Nat." Samuel gave my arm a comforting squeeze, and I caught a whiff of his cologne—a combination of woody cedar and cardamom that smelled so good it was distracting. "You'll do fine. Besides, I'm happy to have you here with me."

"It's your funeral," I said. "You can't say later I didn't warn you."

Samuel tenderly kissed me on the cheek. There was something in his gaze that I couldn't quite place except to say that he looked way too affectionate considering it was pretend.

"You look beautiful tonight," Samuel said.

"Thank you." I brushed the skirt of the emerald-green gown I'd chosen for the night, then glanced over Samuel's tailored suit that accentuated his athletic build, the crisp white shirt, and sleek black tie adding to his allure. "And you are really handsome."

"I will never tire of getting compliments from you." Samuel smirked like a cat that had finally cornered a mouse, and my mouselike senses started going off, warning me that his look was hunger, and not for food.

"Samuel!" someone called out.

We both turned to see Isaac approaching, a pretty woman on his arm. She exuded effortless elegance, her polished manners and constant, polite smile making her every bit the type of professional woman who belonged in this kind of place.

"Is that Isaac's girlfriend?" I asked as they approached.

Samuel barked with laughter. "Please. Isaac wouldn't know romance if it waited in the bushes to club him upside his thick head. That's his long-suffering executive assistant, who has been his de facto date and second set of hands since we started working at Warner Print."

"Ah." I nodded. "I'm not sure if I should admire her competency or her work ethic that makes her keep up with Isaac."

"Both," Samuel suggested. "You should also pity her. Lots and lots of pity."

Isaac and his date reached us, Isaac taking charge of the introductions.

"Sam, Nat, glad to see you made it." The warmth in his voice when he used my nickname surprised me. "Nat, this is Charlotte Fisher, my secretary. Charlotte, this is Natalie Mann, Sam's fiancée."

"It's a pleasure to finally meet you." Charlotte offered her hand.

I shook it. "Likewise. Do you happen to be Kathy Fisher's daughter?"

"Yes," Charlotte said. "She's told me a lot about you."

"And I've heard a lot about you too," I said.

"Let me guess," Samuel said. "You two are related?"

"Nope," I said. "But our mothers work together."

"Of course they do," Samuel said dryly.

"Charlotte, it's so nice to have a fellow Fox Creek resident at the gala," I said with genuine relief. "Please tell me if I make any faux pas tonight."

"Of course, but I'm sure it won't be necessary," Charlotte said. "You'll do just fine."

"Absolutely," Samuel agreed, adjusting his arm so he could take my hand in his and squeeze it. "And don't worry. You're too stunning for anyone to notice if you do happen to make a mistake." He winked playfully.

Ignoring Samuel's flirty remark, I turned my attention to Isaac. "Who else from your family is here tonight?"

"Mother and Grandfather are already making the rounds," Isaac said. "Logan's here as well, but don't be surprised if he slips away. He's never been one for parties, and he's infamous for skipping out early."

Samuel briefly consulted his cell phone. "Uncle Charles texted me on the drive over. He and Aunt Jamie will be late. Apparently, she decided to go ice fishing before the gala, and it took him quite a while to drag her away from her ice shack to get ready."

"Classic Aunt Jamie," Isaac said.

"Does that mean Jenna isn't here tonight?" I asked.

"No, she had a night shift at the hospital she couldn't get out of," Charlotte said.

"Got it. Then is there anyone at the party I should be wary of or be extra careful around?" I asked.

Samuel and Isaac exchanged twin expressions of confusion, their foreheads furrowing the exact same way.

"Why would you need to be careful around anyone?" Samuel asked, puzzled.

"I don't exactly have the Warner reputation and standing backing me up like you all do," I said.

"Of course you do. You have all the Warner money at your beck and call," Samuel said. "You're about to marry a Warner, remember?"

We all shared a laugh, mine bordering on maniacal, as Samuel had just figuratively scored one on me again.

I swung our joint hands. "Isn't he funny? His humor is one of his many charms." Internally, I was surprised to realize that I genuinely enjoyed our banter these days rather than letting it enrage me.

"Indeed," Charlotte agreed, briefly bowing her head. "You two are such a well-matched couple. And Samuel is correct. Soon, you'll be a Warner, and you'll receive the same respect—

and toadying up to—that the Warner family is afforded and annoyed by."

Isaac nodded in agreement. "If anyone dares treat you discourteously, find the nearest Warner and let them know. The problem will be resolved immediately."

I was touched by Isaac's offer. Isaac was the colder twin. It was obvious he was making an effort, which made me feel bad that Samuel and I were technically abusing his goodwill.

"Don't fret, pet," Samuel said. "This is a charity gala, remember? The proceeds are going to an after-school program, so it's theoretically a purely social event." He paused for a moment before conceding, "Of course, there's always gossip, social maneuvering, and petty squabbles at any party."

"Wow," I said sarcastically, "you're really selling it."

"Look on the bright side," Samuel said. "At least you're not wearing rented, potentially diseased bowling shoes."

"That really offended you, didn't it?" I laughed, remembering our bowling adventure.

"Yes." Samuel theatrically sniffed. "It did."

"I didn't realize you were such a germaphobe," I said. "I'll keep that in mind next time you want to try my drink."

"What?" Samuel straightened, all signs of playacting leaving his body. "No—that's not fair."

Isaac turned to Charlotte and gestured at his twin. "Didn't I tell you? Sam is completely under Natalie's thumb."

"It certainly seems like it," Charlotte agreed, her smile shifting from polite professionalism to something more personal and welcoming. "Congratulations, Natalie. All of us at Warner Print are very excited to have you join the Warner family."

"Thank you," I said, touched by her welcome and feeling increasingly guilty. Now it wasn't just Isaac's goodwill we were abusing, but Warner Print's employees' too.

Once this was all over, I was going to have to take serious inventory of just how far I was willing to go in pursuit of my goal, because this did not feel good.

Isaac glanced around the ballroom. "We should start mingling. I see a few clients we need to greet. Divide and conquer?"

"Yes," Samuel said. "Let's get it over with as fast as possible. Good luck, Isaac, Charlotte."

We parted ways. Isaac and Charlotte dove straight into the crowd, while Samuel and I picked our way around the ballroom's perimeter.

The stares from the other gala attendees were a weight on my back as Samuel raised my hand so he could kiss my fingers. His gesture likely seemed careless to those watching, but I was sure it was a calculated move.

"Are you sure you want me with you? Talking to clients is exactly the kind of thing I'm worried about." I scanned the sea of well-dressed strangers. "If I say or do something wrong, it could have repercussions on Warner Print."

"Relax, Nat." A hint of amusement lingered in Samuel's voice. "I've seen you interact with the public while you work. You're professional—better than if you'd been trained for this sort of thing."

I opened and closed my mouth a few times, positively speechless. That was ... unexpectedly personal.

"Besides"—Samuel mischievously swung our clasped hands—"I've had firsthand experience of how you handle people you hate, so I know you have nothing to fear."

"True. You used to bring out the worst in me." I laughed as my tension dissolved.

Samuel stopped our slow stroll around the ballroom. He stepped in front of me so we were face to face and clasped both of my hands in his. "What do you mean by 'used to'?" His gray eyes bore into mine, and I was suddenly aware of the space between us, which seemed both huge and too little at the same time.

I tried to swallow, but my mouth was bone dry. "Used to as in, it's in the past. Things have changed."

"They certainly have." Samuel breeched the gap between us, angling his head toward mine. My breath hitched as I realized he was going to kiss me, and I didn't want to block him or turn away. Samuel squeezed my hands as our lips nearly brushed, and my eyes started to flutter shut.

"Samuel Warner!" The interruption jolted us apart.

Samuel sighed, then reluctantly faced the man. When he saw who it was, he grinned. "Darius Carter! It's been a while."

I took in the older, well-dressed African American man, who had deep smile lines around his mouth and eyes. He seemed innately likable and a lot friendlier than I thought anyone at this gala would be.

Darius chuckled as he shook Samuel's hand. "I heard you got engaged, but I almost didn't believe it—you've never been romantically interested in anyone!"

"That would be because I was hiding my heart back in Fox Creek." Samuel, still holding one of my hands, tugged me forward so I was shoulder to shoulder with him. "Darius, this is Natalie, my fiancée. Natalie, this is Darius. He's a client of Warner Print—he owns several fine dining restaurants, and we handle all their graphic design and advertisement printing."

"Hello, Natalie!" Darius greeted me warmly, extending his hand.

"Hello, Darius," I replied, shaking his hand. If everyone else at this gala was as friendly as he was, maybe the evening wouldn't be so bad after all.

An hour passed, and I was starting to feel like we were

trapped in a never-ending game of meet and greet as Samuel and I circulated around the ballroom.

My mind was spinning with the names and faces of so many people I'd met. Most everyone was nice, like Darius, but it was a lot to face in a room that was getting increasingly hotter and with a stomach that was threatening to start growling.

I squeezed Samuel's hand, which he had been holding since we started our rounds. He glanced down at me, concern etching his handsome features.

"I need a break," I whispered. "I'll be back shortly."

"Sure thing." Samuel planted a sweet kiss on my forehead before turning to greet a trio of women who were about his mother's age.

As I slipped away, I had just enough time to hear one of the women ask, "Was that your famed fiancée?"

"Yes," Samuel said. "Isn't she gorgeous?"

I hustled through the crowd, anxious to flee before I heard Samuel say even more nice things about me for the sake of our lie.

My original plan was to head to a bathroom just to get out of the stuffy ballroom for a moment, but when I was making my way to one of the open doors, I spotted a server carrying a tray of hors d'oeuvres.

My stomach rumbled at the sight, and I knew if I didn't grab something it would likely growl at the most embarrassing moment possible.

So I turned away from the door and approached the server. "Pardon me, but what are you serving?"

The server lowered his tray for me. "Good evening. These are fig, pecan, and brie puff bites, and on this side we have mushroom-stuffed phyllo cups."

"Thank you, I'll take one of each, please." I gratefully took a napkin and the offered appetizers.

I nibbled on the fig, pecan, and brie puff bite, savoring the creamy, tangy cheese mingling with the sweetness of the figs and the crunchiness of the pecans as I spun in a slow circle, searching for the nearest door.

I found it when I finished the puff and was about to try the mushroom-stuffed phyllo cup when someone asked, "Are you Samuel Warner's fiancée?"

Crap. I'd taken too long to make my exit.

An older couple who looked like they were in their early sixties, impeccably dressed and oozing money, approached me.

"Yes. I'm Natalie Mann."

"Ah," the wife of the duo said, her narrowed eyes matching the pinched end of her nose.

"We are the Hurtzes," the husband said.

"It's a pleasure to meet you," I said.

The husband huffed, clearly miffed that I didn't recognize their name. (Didn't they seem fun?)

I nodded my head to the pair. "If you'll excuse me—"

The wife interrupted me, her voice dripping with disdain. "Is it true that you're a mere town clerk?"

I instantly swapped to my work mode, pasting on my customer service smile. "Yes, I'm the Fox Creek town clerk."

"I see. Congratulations on catching Samuel," the wife drawled. "He was such a sought-after bachelor. So many women had their eyes on him." She looked me over pointedly. "I suppose all their attempts were useless, seeing how Samuel appears to have ... interesting taste."

I gazed at the older woman in wonder. I wasn't surprised she was being snobby to me. I'd just assumed that in upper society, insults would be subtler and more condescending, or at least hurtful!

This woman, however, was about on par with an ornery Fox Creek resident who didn't want to pay property taxes.

"Well," I said sweetly, feigning innocence, "I'm grateful Samuel has such unusual tastes since I am admittedly selfish, and I enjoy having his eyes all to myself."

The wife's face turned a shade of red that matched her dress. "How-how crass!"

"Yes," I said. "Now, I must be going—"

"Do you plan on getting a real job?" the husband asked, apparently taking up the charge on behalf of his stammering wife. "Or will you simply live off Samuel since you don't have any skills or knowledge to contribute to Warner Print?"

Channeling my inner actress once more, I batted my eyelashes. "You know, I hadn't really thought about it. But now that you mention it, I suppose I'm grateful Samuel doesn't need my help. That way, I can just waste my time mingling at parties like tonight's gala. After all, if you two are any indication, it doesn't require any skill at all."

I internally cackled as the couple fumed. That's what you get when you act like rude toads!

The wife sputtered, so offended she was unable to form words. I idly wondered if maybe I'd pushed the boundaries too far for this type of party while the husband squared his shoulders and glared at me. "Look here, you ..." he started, but suddenly, his face turned an interesting mix of mottled purple, and he trailed off.

At first, I worried he might be having a health emergency, but then I heard a dark, angry voice behind me. "What were you about to call my fiancée?" Samuel demanded, his tone icy.

I peered behind me, surprised at this side of Samuel I'd never seen before.

His fine face was contorted into a mask of fury, his brow furrowed and his jaw clenched. His piercing gray eyes were stormy with anger as he glared at the couple. He was intimidating, almost like a force of nature.

And I, his supposed worst enemy, had never before seen him like this even though we'd spent our adult lives arguing.

The Hurtzes scrambled for words, trying to save face.

"We-we just wanted to greet the woman you're marrying, Samuel," the wife stammered. "But she's been downright rude to us. I must say, we're disappointed in your selection."

Samuel slipped his arm around my back, his voice sharp. "And why would you think I care about your opinions or feelings?"

The wife nudged her husband, who finally managed to speak up. "We knew your father, Samuel. He'd be disappointed with your choice of fiancée."

The blow was below the belt and completely uncalled for. How *dare* they bring up Samuel's father when losing him had been so difficult for the Warners? I balled my hands into fists and wished I could do something, *anything*, to set the awful couple straight.

Samuel was also angry, but not for the same reason. "Just because you knew my father doesn't mean I have to care what you think," he spat out, each word dripping with venom. "But in this case I will correct you. He knew exactly who Natalie was before he died, and he knew how amazing, loyal, empathetic, and lovely she is."

Uh ... was he sure about that? While I was moved over Samuel's passionate defense of me, if Samuel's dad knew who I was, it was probably because I ran my mouth off as a Mann and not because he found any trait of mine admirable. I fought with his son all the time, for cryin' out loud.

The gala attendees around us were starting to turn in our direction and whisper to one another as they watched the show.

Mrs. Hurtz sniffed. "Say what you will, I demand an apology from her."

"Apology?" Samuel scoffed. "You can demand all you want.

Natalie has nothing to apologize for. She treated you with more politeness than you deserve."

Mr. Hurtz narrowed his eyes, trying to regain some control. "Watch what you say, Samuel. I'm friends with several Warner Print clients, and I'll be sure to tell them about this interaction."

Samuel tilted his head back, a look of supreme satisfaction settling over his face. "Go ahead. Tell your friends. If they're anything like you, we don't want them as clients anyway."

Mrs. Hurtz leaned forward, her eyes beady in the low lights of the ballroom. "But the loss of business will hurt you!"

"Please." Samuel smirked, his confidence returning in full force. "We're Warners."

More people had gathered around us, whispering and watching the spectacle unfold.

I leaned into Samuel's side. "Sam, maybe we should leave. We're getting a lot of unnecessary attention."

"Leave? When they haven't even begun to regret their actions?" His gaze was still angry and cold as he scoffed at the couple. "I won't stand for anyone insulting you, Nat."

The genuine feeling behind his statement rattled my heart —he really was doing this because he was upset they'd insulted me, not because he was playacting.

I smiled up at him. "I'm fine, really. They're not worth wasting time arguing with. Besides, wouldn't you rather spend that time flirting with me?"

"When you put it that way ..." Samuel shifted all of his attention to me, and the tension in the air dissipated as he turned back into the charming Samuel I knew. "Fine. We can go."

As we turned to leave, the Hurtzes' anger still simmered.

The husband barked out to Samuel, "If your father could see you now, he'd be disappointed with how you turned out!"

Estelle Warner appeared behind the pair like a silent,

elegant social assassin. Her voice was dangerously polite as she asked, "What exactly did you just say about my son and my future daughter-in-law?"

The Hurtzes spun around to face Estelle and stammered, trying to find an explanation that would satisfy the ice queen before them. Estelle's frosty gaze remained unimpressed. "If you find the Warner family so revolting," she said, her words like steel, "I'm more than happy to break all business and social ties with you. We have standards, after all."

I stared at Estelle in awe, admiring how a woman so beautiful and poised could look so dark and intimidating. I made a mental note to memorize her mannerisms for future encounters with grumpy Fox Creek residents.

The crowd around us began to murmur, their whispers growing louder until Logan—tall, broad-shouldered, and shadowlike—stepped up behind Estelle. The moment they caught sight of him, most partygoers immediately looked away, too afraid of his imposing presence to continue watching the drama unfold. Under Logan's steely gaze, the Hurtzes gulped and finally fell silent.

"Family attack dog strikes again," Walter remarked as he joined Samuel and me, gesturing to Logan.

"He's good at his job," Samuel said.

Walter made a coughing harrumph of agreement, then turned to us and mashed his lips together. "Why were you two wasting time with those unpleasant snakes?"

"The snakes cornered Nat." Samuel squeezed the hand that he'd possessively settled on my waist. "And they discovered she has claws."

Walter chuckled and chucked me under the chin. "We Warner men do have a soft spot for firecrackers."

I pulled my attention away from watching Estelle and

Logan give the Hurtzes a dressing down. "Aww, thank you, Walter."

Samuel tapped a finger on my side to get me to look at him. "Are you really OK? You've been quiet, which concerns me."

"I was just thinking that when I grow up, I want to be like your mother," I joked.

Samuel made a pained expression. "Please never tell her that. If you do, you might replace Chuck as her favorite child—even if you are an in-law. And Isaac and I can't handle the additional competition when we're already losing to a dog."

I laughed and glanced again at the Warner matron and attack dog.

Logan's imposing figure towered over the Hurtzes as he spoke to them in a deep, rumbly tone that I couldn't quite make out. Estelle watched with an air of satisfaction, and the expressions on the Hurtzes' faces told me everything I needed to know: Logan was putting them in their place.

Samuel must have been feeling a lot better, because he nudged me. "What's that you've got there, Nat?" He pointedly stared at my slightly crumpled napkin that held the second hors d'oeuvre I didn't get a chance to try.

"According to the server, it's a mushroom-stuffed phyllo cup," I said.

Samuel studied the napkin. "Can I have it?"

"Sure." I held out the napkin to him, but instead of taking it, he gave me a sappy look that brimmed with dramatized adoration.

"Will you feed it to me?" he asked. "I don't want to let you go." He squeezed my waist again for emphasis.

It amazed me how this flirty guy could also be so intimidating when roused. But after his passionate defense of me earlier, I was inclined to give in to him instead of refusing like I normally would have. "Sure," I said. "Open up." I held the phyllo cup up to his lips.

"Really?" Walter rolled his eyes, amused. "If you two are going to get lost in your little world of love, I'm going to watch Logan figuratively tar and feather the Hurtzes." He gestured toward the ongoing confrontation.

"Have fun," I said.

"Thanks. And good luck getting any personal space tonight, Natalie." Walter snorted, then strode off, leaving us alone.

I once again held the phyllo cup up to Samuel's mouth. Instead of devouring it in one bite like I expected, he bit off half and chewed thoughtfully. When he took the second half, his tongue brushed against my fingertips in a way that made my toes curl in my strappy shoes.

"Samuel!" I scolded.

"Can't blame a guy for seizing every opportunity," Samuel said, unapologetic.

I shook my head as I wiped my fingers off on my napkin, my smile dying when I felt the eyes of more partygoers watching us.

"Want to step out for some fresh air?" Samuel asked.

"Absolutely," I agreed gratefully. He guided me toward the door with the gentle pressure of his arm around my waist, leaving behind the whispers and stares of the crowd.

The abrupt change in temperature from the stuffy ballroom to the much cooler hallway made me break out in goose bumps. I ventured a glance back toward Walter, Estelle, and Logan, their support still a pleasant surprise to me. They had come to my defense without hesitation, something that both warmed my heart and left me in awe. I felt a surge of gratitude and affection for them.

"Nat?" Samuel's voice snapped me out of my reverie. I looked up at him, even more handsome than usual with the extra shadows from the low lighting playing across the planes of his face, and smiled.

"Thank you, Sam." My voice was rough with emotion I didn't want to identify. "You didn't have to go as far as you did to defend me, but I appreciate that you did."

Samuel tugged me closer. "Any time."

I leaned my head against his shoulder as we strolled down the hallway together.

Chapter 26

Natalie

Tip #26: *It is totally possible to fake date and actually be friends. Friends who kiss in front of family, but still friends. Just. Friends.*

Snowflakes tipsily drifted down from clouds so low-hanging it felt like I could touch them if I had a ladder tall enough.

I simultaneously snorted and huffed, using my breath to flick a snowflake off the tip of my nose as I stood outside my parents' house and wondered if I was crazy. "Are you sure you want to do this, Sam?"

Samuel, holding a Tupperware container of my homemade beer dip and a bag of pretzels that he insisted on carrying for me, smiled. "Absolutely."

"This is your last chance. Mann family gatherings can be a lot."

Samuel bumped his arm against mine, which I barely felt due to all the thick padding from our coats. "I can handle it."

I bit my lip. "Not all of the Manns will be as nice to you as the Warners have been to me."

"I'm aware," Samuel said. "And I won't take it personally. My family had a very good reason to be so welcoming to you, after all."

I was about to ask him what he meant when the front door swung open, revealing my mom's smiling face.

"Hey, you two!" Mom waved us inside. "Why are you standing out here freezing? Everyone's been waiting for you!"

As we stepped into the house, I glanced at Samuel, who was busy smiling at Mom. "Thank you for inviting me," he said.

"Of course!" Mom said. "Everyone is so excited to meet you and congratulate you two!"

"I'm sure they are," I muttered as we removed our boots.

Mom plucked the dip and bag of pretzels from Samuel's grasp. "This is perfect, Natalie! Mike was just asking if you'd be bringing your famous homemade beer dip! I'll just go put it out with the rest of the appetizers."

"Thanks, Mom." I handed my coat to Samuel, who was already trying to figure out where to hang them on the ever-overloaded coat rack. "The coats go on the bed in the spare bedroom—"

"Nat!"

"Natalie!"

"Congratulations!"

I almost fell over when I was abruptly surrounded by a gaggle of my female cousins, who all talked at once.

"Nat, it's so romantic that you two are getting married!" one cousin gushed.

"Keely told me she was there when he proposed," another cousin chimed in. "He used a book! That's so sweet!"

"Congratulations!" came another voice, followed by, "Show us the ring! We need to see the ring!"

Feeling oddly shy, I held out my hand, displaying the beautiful ring with the leaflike emeralds framing the diamond. My cousins oohed and aahed over it, their eyes wide with admiration as they jostled to get a better view.

"It's Samuel's grandmother's ring," I said.

"How romantic!"

"Wow, he really went all out!"

As the questions and exclamations continued, I checked on Samuel. To my relief, I saw Owen handing him a can of beer and taking our coats from him. They said something to each other, but I couldn't hear what over my cousins' excited shrieks.

When Owen slipped off to store our coats, my Uncle Mike greeted Samuel, giving him a once-over before nodding in approval and offering his hand. Samuel shook it and looked comfortable, chatting casually with him.

Since Samuel was doing OK, I let my cousins steer me into the living room. Every seat in the room was taken, and more relatives flooded the living room as they came from the kitchen and the den that had the TV going with a sports game.

The house was filled with the mouthwatering smell of garlic and chili. The heat from all the people packed inside made me feel cozy, while the loud chatter and rowdy discussions reminded me just how much fun Mann family get-togethers could be.

"When's the wedding?" Madison asked.

"You should make Owen be the ring bearer," Keely said. "I would pay to see that."

"It's a little early to be thinking about the ceremony since we don't even have a date." I checked on Samuel again. He'd followed us into the living room and was keeping an eye on me as he continued his conversation with Uncle Mike.

"Quiet down, everyone!" Grandma Mann's voice cut through the cacophony of laughter and conversation like a knife.

A hush fell over the room, and Samuel edged his way through my cousins to stand shoulder to shoulder with me. He took my hand with his free one, intertwining our fingers.

I squeezed it for reassurance.

Grandma and Grandpa Mann shuffled forward, their gazes fixed on Samuel. My female cousins scattered like leaves in the wind, leaving us standing alone, the center of attention.

A knot of worry formed in my stomach. My fears were totally unnecessary since Samuel wasn't really my fiancé, but as close as we'd gotten since we started fake dating, I really wanted my family to like him.

Grandpa Mann folded his arms across his chest and looked back and forth between Samuel and me, the wrinkles on his forehead puckering as he studied us.

I gulped.

Grandma Mann raised her penciled-in eyebrows at me. "Paul." Grandma Mann turned to my father, who was leaning against the kitchen doorframe. "What do you think of this young man?"

Dad thoughtfully scratched his beard before slowly raising a thumb in approval. The room erupted in cheers as my relatives hooted and hollered.

"Alright, alright, hold on," Grandma Mann yelled, silencing the crowd once again.

Her eyes met Grandpa Mann's, and they exchanged knowing nods. With a wink at me, Grandpa turned his attention to Samuel.

"Samuel," he began, his voice warm but firm. "Will you take care of our Natalie? Will you make her your highest priority in life?"

Samuel, in an Oscar-worthy performance that was so good it felt real, smiled down at me with affection. "Of course I will, sir. Natalie is my everything. She means the world to me."

A collective *aww* echoed through the room, and I blushed. Grandpa Mann clasped Samuel's shoulder, then nodded to Grandma Mann.

"The verdict is in," she announced. "Sam is worthy of our Nat!"

Another round of cheers filled the air. It was so loud I swear I felt the vibrations in my gut.

Samuel gently squeezed my hand, dragging my attention to him. He kept his eyes on mine as he slowly lifted my hand to his lips. When he pressed his lips to the pads of my fingers it caused a chorus of cooing from my female relatives in the crowd.

I, oddly, found that I couldn't look away from Samuel's gray eyes, and a tiny voice in my brain whispered that even if he was a fake boyfriend, Samuel was definitely the best significant other I'd ever had.

"Alright, everyone!" Mom clapped her hands together in glee. "To celebrate my baby girl's engagement to Samuel, who is such a sweet boy, let's eat! There's food and drinks in the kitchen!"

The Manns cheered again, swarming the kitchen like bees to honey.

Samuel and I were carried along with the flow of traffic. As we entered the bustling kitchen, I marveled at the sheer amount of food covering every available surface.

Two crockpots of chili bubbled away on the counter, cast iron skillets of golden cornbread were lined up in a row on the stovetop, and the steaming baked potatoes in the tray next to the crockpots begged for toppings. The scents of garlic bread and homemade mac and cheese mingled with the fruity aroma of a fresh fruit salad.

"Does your family always celebrate with this much food?" Samuel asked.

I glanced at the folding table dedicated entirely to desserts. "How else would we celebrate?"

Samuel laughed. "Good point."

Keely appeared, handing us each a paper plate. "Food is a love language for the Manns, so you better get used to it!"

Samuel let go of my hand so he could take the plate. "Don't worry about me. I'm going to enjoy all future Mann family get-togethers."

My shoulders relaxed in relief that Samuel would get along fine during future family functions. Then I remembered that once our fake relationship ended, he wouldn't be attending these get-togethers anymore. We'd had so much fun the past few months. Although I knew we'd still be friends after all of this, I was going to miss his close presence.

Samuel bumped my shoulder with his. "Hey, sweet pea, are you OK?"

"I'm great." I forced a smile. "I was just figuring out my food strategy. I need to leave room for dessert, so I have to plan accordingly."

"Yes, dessert is serious business for you." Samuel leaned down and planted a tender kiss on my temple that I felt all the way down in my gut.

For the first time I wondered if I really was as unmoved by our unlikely chemistry as I'd thought.

We stuffed ourselves with glorious, delicious food until we couldn't eat a single bite more. The warmth of the house, combined with the delicious feast we'd just devoured, made me feel drowsy, and about two hours later I could barely keep up with the excited chatter of my mother and aunts in the garage, where electric space heaters hummed away and a few kiddos played card games.

Stifling a yawn, I extricated myself from the conversation with no problems—I'd sufficiently shown off both Samuel and my ring, so my family no longer crowded around us.

I slipped into the house and stumbled my way to the living room, which was momentarily unoccupied, as the family mostly filled the kitchen, den, and garage.

I sank into the worn plaid couch, its saggy but soft cushions sucking me down. A pillow found its way into my arms, and I snuggled into the corner of the couch, closing my eyes for a moment.

As I began to doze, the muffled sounds of conversation from the rest of the house seeped through me.

"... Why are you Warners so keen to renovate the old middle school into luxury condos?" Owen's voice floated into the room, accompanied by Samuel's distinctive baritone.

"Look, Owen." Samuel's voice grew louder—they must have entered the living room, but my eyelids were too heavy to double-check. "Even if the school is used for adult education courses some evenings, for the most part it sits empty, and it's falling apart. The city can't afford the necessary repairs or upgrades that would have to come with remodeling it, like fixing its lack of accessibility. Rather than let it crumble and rot, isn't it better to save it and put it to good use?"

Samuel had a point. The city didn't have the resources to spend on the aging building. I knew that firsthand. While I still felt it was a vital building considering the importance of the adult education classes it hosted, if repairs weren't made, it would likely be unusable in a decade.

My eyelids felt heavy, and despite trying I still couldn't manage to open them.

"Samuel?" I murmured drowsily.

"Sorry." Samuel's voice grew quieter, but I could tell he was close by. "Did we wake you?"

"Nah," I mumbled, my sleepy brain struggling to form coherent thoughts. "Just ... dozing."

"That's good." His voice held a smile. "Keep on resting, Nat."

The couch shuddered as Samuel settled down next to me, his warm presence immediately comforting.

He wrapped an arm around me, pulling my sleepy form out of the corner I'd wedged myself into and tipping me against his chest. My cheek found a comfortable spot on his shoulder, and my pillow fell from my arms.

As I leaned into Sam, it occurred to me we didn't need this level of cuddling to sell our relationship. My family was already sold on our engagement, and Owen was the only one here to see us anyway. But as Samuel spread a soft blanket over my lap, I realized that I wanted this closeness with him.

Giving in, I snuggled into his chest, wrapping my arms around his waist. A contented sigh escaped my lips as his hand rubbed my lower back, sending pleasant shivers up my spine.

Owen's voice cut through the cozy moment like a knife, his tone sour. "You two are something else."

Samuel chuckled—a deep, rich sound that vibrated pleasantly in his chest and that I felt, wrapped around him as I was. "You don't say? Then why don't you share why you didn't invite Jenna to this get-together, Owen?"

"You know what? On second thought, you deserve to get plagued by Natalie." Owen's words held a hint of annoyance, but I could tell it was a siblinglike playfulness and not malice in his voice.

My eyelids grew heavier as I listened to the distant murmurings of conversation.

"Going back to our original discussion about the school," Owen said. "I agree the school does need to get sold off since the city can't afford its upkeep. However, you Warners could fix it up and use it for something besides luxury condos."

"What would you suggest we do with it?" Samuel asked.

"You could turn it into a community center," Owen said.

"In order for it to be a city community center and not a privately owned events center, the city would have to own it," Samuel said.

That was the catch. Since Fox Creek couldn't afford the school, what could the Warners possibly do with the building that would be good for the community? Maybe a compromise was the best way to go.

"Apartments," I muttered, barely able to form a coherent sentence.

"What was that, babe?" Samuel stopped rubbing my lower back so he could smooth the blanket on my lap.

I stifled a yawn. "You could renovate the old school into housing."

Samuel's fingers brushed my cheek. "That's what my family is planning to do."

"No, not luxury condos," I murmured. "Regular apartments, with lower rent."

"That's not a bad idea," Owen said. "Fox Creek doesn't have a lot of apartment buildings, and most of the residents wouldn't be able to afford a luxury condo. Mind you, I think we need a community center more, but there you have it."

"I see," Samuel said.

I couldn't tell how he felt about the suggestion, but at least I knew firsthand his body hadn't stiffened up, so there was that.

"Owen!" Mom called from the kitchen, her voice cutting through the hum of conversation in the living room.

"I'll be right back—it's not wise to keep Mom waiting." Owen's voice grew fainter. "I enjoyed talking with you, Samuel."

"I enjoyed it too," Samuel said.

"Did Owen leave?" I drowsily asked, still unable to open my eyes.

"Yes," Samuel said.

I yawned as Samuel wrapped both of his arms around me and rested his chin on the top of my head. I relaxed, feeling safe and cozy in his arms.

"Are you comfortable?" Samuel asked.

"Very."

We listened to the hum of conversation and laughter that leaked into the quiet living room.

"Your family is a lot of fun," Samuel said.

"Thanks. I think so too. But I like your family a lot."

"Good." Samuel traced his fingers up and down my spine.

We were quiet for another few moments.

"Natalie."

"Hmm?"

Samuel sounded serious, so I managed to open my eyes and peel my head off his shoulder. I gazed into his gray eyes, which seemed darker in the dim light of the living room.

My heartbeat echoed in my ears, and the sounds of the family get-together faded.

We leaned closer together, and my eyes fluttered shut before we kissed.

It was different from any of the kisses we'd shared before, all of which had been in front of an audience specifically to sell our charade.

Not that those hadn't been unexpectedly enjoyable, but this ... this was on a totally different level.

Samuel started gentle, with a little pressure that built with each second that passed. We broke the kiss for a moment. Samuel immediately pulled me close again, and his lips were fire against mine. He cradled the back of my head with one hand, keeping our connection burning—as if I had the strength or will to end our kiss.

"Sorry, Sam. Mom needed me to empty more ice into a drinks cooler," Owen called out—thankfully before he entered the room.

I pulled back from Sam. I didn't get too far, though, as Samuel still had his arms locked around me.

I tried to tug myself free, but Samuel reeled me in and pressed my head to his shoulder, returning me to the position I'd been in while dozing. Which was very nice and all, except I was now very much awake and did *not* feel like dozing anymore!

"No worries," Samuel said. It was only because I was splayed against his chest that I heard the breathlessness in his voice.

I scrunched my eyes shut before Owen entered the living room and pressed my face into Samuel's neck in an effort to hide. Samuel held me closer than he had before, not giving me any wiggle room to slip away.

I heard Dad's recliner groan—Owen must have been sitting down.

"My dude," Owen said. "Do you really have to hold her like that when it's just us?"

"Absolutely," Samuel said.

I felt my cheeks heat at the certainty in Samuel's voice. My hand, hidden between his back and the couch, tapped on his spine.

Samuel, in return, kissed my temple.

"Gross," Owen said. "Anyway, what did you think of the Packers' season?"

With Samuel and Owen launching into a detailed discussion about football, my heart started to slow down, and my brain function picked up again.

That kiss. What had *that* been?

I was comfortable with Samuel. We were friends. Yes, friends who kissed in front of family, but weirdly it had worked in my brain.

That kiss though ... friends didn't kiss like that. And I'd been more than happy to participate in it.

I'd known forever that Samuel was unbearably attractive, and I'd known since I dubbed him a friend that I liked his sense of humor, appreciated his subtly caring nature, and enjoyed hanging out with him.

But.

That.

Kiss.

It had stripped me of all excuses and explanations I could give for my relationship with Samuel. The answer was obvious. I was in love with Samuel Warner. I'd fallen for him, probably sometime after his fake but incredibly sweet proposal, and I hadn't wanted to admit it.

But now I didn't have a choice. I had to face my feelings head-on and accept them.

I just didn't know what I was going to do about them.

Then again, I had some time. Samuel and I wouldn't even bother discussing ending our fake relationship-turned-engagement until Owen and Jenna were settled. I could figure this out —whether that meant stifling my feelings because Samuel didn't return them and I wasn't going to risk the truce we'd reached with a confession, or it meant talking it over with Samuel to see if there was a possibility of ... something.

As Sam and Owen continued their conversation about football, I reflexively grabbed Samuel's soft shirt.

I had time. I just needed to remember that or I'd be overwhelmed by the implications of all this.

Thank goodness for time and the fact that Owen rivaled a tortoise for speed when it came to love!

Chapter 27

Natalie

Tip #27: *If you're disappointed when you can finally end your fake engagement, perhaps you need to rethink your feelings.*

The rich scents of coffee and cocoa filled the air, and I heard the hissing whistle of a barista heating up milk. I took a sip of my chocolate strawberry latte and peeled off my vest, the comfy warmth of Literum heating me right up after my frosty walk from city hall to the quaint café/bookstore.

It was quiet in the back room, away from the hustle and bustle of customers perusing books and sipping on their own drinks. I couldn't help but think back to the last time I sat here in the back room, proposing my fake dating idea to Samuel. So much had changed since then.

"Hey, Nat." Owen smiled awkwardly as he slipped into the back room. He carried a ceramic cup and saucer, likely filled with a French vanilla cappuccino, his usual drink of choice.

"Hey, Owen."

Owen set his cup and saucer down on the coffee table before shrugging off his jacket.

I watched him impatiently. "Spill it. What's so important that you needed to meet up over my lunch break?" I asked. "I had to promise the mayor I'd bring her one of Literum's giant molasses cookies to get permission to come here."

Owen fussed over his cappuccino cup, rotating it so the handle faced him, and remained standing. "I was thinking ... Samuel fit right in at our family get-together last Sunday."

"Uh-huh." I raised an eyebrow, amused by his obvious stalling. "You don't say?"

Owen nervously rubbed his hands together. "Do you think the Manns have accepted your relationship?" He made air quotes after peering down the hallway to make sure no one was heading our way. "Based on how they treated him, I'd say so."

"I agree." I took another sip of my mocha, the rich chocolate and tangy strawberry flavors mingling together perfectly. "They seem less hostile toward the Warners too."

"Good." Relief washed over Owen's face. "That means introducing Jenna to the family as my girlfriend will be easier than I thought."

I stared at Owen with a mixture of shock and excitement. "Are you serious?" I set my latte down on the coffee table with a slight tremble in my hand.

"Dead serious." Owen's smile grew even wider. "I finally took the plunge and asked Jenna to be exclusive last night. She said yes!"

"Owen!" I squealed, unable to contain my excitement. I

leaped to my feet and threw my arms around him, hugging him tightly. "Congratulations! I'm so happy for you!"

"Thanks, Nat." Owen hugged me back, almost lifting me off the floor. "I can hardly believe it myself."

As we pulled apart, I grabbed his wrists and yanked his arms up and down in a cheer, my enthusiasm bubbling over. "You did it, Owen! I knew you two would make a great couple!"

"Thank you." Owen was all smiles when we both plopped down in chairs.

"Alright." I picked up my latte once more. "This definitely deserves a toast."

Owen raised his ceramic mug, and I tapped my paper to-go cup against it.

"To your new relationship!" I said.

"To happiness!"

We both took sips of our hot drinks.

I savored the velvety taste and barely noticed when Owen set his mug down and looked at me intently.

"Speaking of relationships," he began. "What are you going to do about you and Samuel?"

I choked on my latte, the liquid catching in my throat as I coughed and spluttered before setting my drink down on the coffee table. "What?" I croaked.

"Come on, Nat." Owen's voice was gentle but insistent. "I'm your brother. You can't fool me. There's something going on between you two."

Something felt like an understatement, but I couldn't bring myself to admit it.

I wiped my mouth with a napkin and tried to regain my composure. "Seriously, what do you mean?" I asked.

Owen leaned forward in his chair. "I've seen the way you two have been around each other lately. All the cuddling and touching? That's not just acting."

My heart clenched, and I felt a flicker of panic. How on earth did he pick up on my feelings for Samuel so quickly when I had only just realized them myself?

I gave him a dismissive wave. "Samuel and I are friends."

"Maybe I would've believed that before Sunday. But after seeing you two snuggled up on the couch together, there's no way that's all there is to it."

I swallowed hard and was incredibly grateful Owen hadn't caught us kissing. Also, was this how Owen felt every time I got nosy about him and Jenna? Because if so, I repented of my sins of nosiness.

"Nat," Owen's expression softened as he continued, "I just want you to be happy."

I shifted uncomfortably in my seat. "Samuel and I haven't really discussed the finer details of how to plan out the end of our relationship."

"I'm not asking about your playacting," Owen said. "I'm asking about your feelings."

I exhaled slowly as I realized Owen wasn't going to let me squirm out of this.

Admittedly, it was healthy to face my feelings for Samuel, but it didn't make it any less scary!

"Fine. I like him, and I wish dating him weren't an act," I said.

Owen just nodded in that obnoxious older-sibling way. "Alright, then what are you going to do about it?"

The question hung in the air, suffocating and impossible to ignore. "I don't know."

I'd assumed I had weeks before Owen would officially ask Jenna to date, but now my prep time was reduced to nothing. I had no idea how to proceed.

"Talk to Samuel about it," Owen said. "You two are friends

now, and with Jenna and I dating, you're free to do whatever you want."

The knot of anxiety tightened in my stomach. "Just because I like him doesn't mean he feels the same way."

"Look, I can't say for sure how much Samuel likes you, but the guy obviously feels something for you. His excuse that family pressure made him propose to you is laughably thin."

Could Owen be right? Was there a chance that Samuel felt the same way about me? The engagement thing was very sudden. Still, as much as I wanted to hope, I was afraid to let myself believe it.

"I don't know, but either way, thanks for encouraging me, Owen."

"Sure. I owe you for all the support you gave me with Jenna." Owen sipped his cappuccino. "You know, when you first told me about your crazy fake dating plan, I thought Samuel must be trying to pull one over on you."

"Really? Why?"

Owen grimaced. "Because it's insane that Samuel agreed so easily to such a harebrained plan that didn't benefit him much."

"Didn't benefit him? What are you talking about?" I asked. "Since our families are in a truce, way fewer people are hostile to the Warners."

"Yeah, but Samuel isn't the type to care what people think about him."

I paused, thinking back to the gala and how recklessly Samuel had confronted the Hurtzes. "You're right." I drummed my fingers on my thigh. "Do you have any guesses why he agreed so easily to my plan?"

"Nothing I feel certain about," Owen said cautiously. "But I think his easy compliance means something."

I stared at my latte, scared to ponder Owen's observation too much. I didn't want to give myself false hope. "Maybe you're right. Either way, I need to tell Samuel about all of this."

"Including your feelings?" Owen asked.

I rolled my eyes. "I would like to be more subtle than trumpeting that to him, but yes. I meant we'll have to talk about what we want the future to look like for us."

"And you won't wait to discuss it?"

I scowled at him. "I can't put it off since you and Jenna are official, so we have to discuss it regardless of how I feel." I tugged at the sleeves of my sweater. "I'll try visiting him at his office after work tonight."

"Good luck," Owen said, supremely self-satisfied.

I nodded and tried to ignore the nerves that were starting to shudder at the thought of my future conversation with Samuel.

Owen picked up his cappuccino cup and again raised it in a toast. "To a romance with a Warner!"

I laughed and picked up my latte to tap it against his cup. "Cheers."

Chapter 28

Natalie

Tip #28: *Be true to yourself and your fake fiancé about your feelings. Confessing is scary, but hopefully will be worth it.*

I cautiously stepped into the office building on the Warner Print campus. As it was after hours, it looked like almost everyone had already left. Thankfully, I spotted Charlotte, Isaac's executive assistant, bundled up in her winter coat and heading in my direction—probably to leave for the night.

When Charlotte saw me, she flashed me a warm smile. "Hello, Natalie. Are you here to see Samuel?"

"Yes! But he doesn't know I'm coming."

"A surprise visit? He'll love that," Charlotte said. "He's in a meeting room with Miguel and Isaac right now, but they should be finished with all official business."

"Thanks, Charlotte. Where's the meeting room?"

Charlotte gave me instructions, pointing to the hallway I'd need to take. "It'll be the only room with a light on in that hallway, since the rest of the staff headed home for the night."

"Thank you for the help. Have a nice evening."

Charlotte smiled. "Of course. Enjoy!" She waved, then stepped outside into the chilly night air.

Following Charlotte's directions, I took the hallway she'd pointed out and spotted the meeting room easily enough. Not only was the light inside the room on, the door was open, so I could hear Samuel's smooth laugh, mingling with Miguel's more reserved chuckle. I was about to call out to Samuel, but something Miguel said stopped me in my tracks.

"You wouldn't believe the conniption the board had over your sudden engagement," Miguel said, his voice tinged with amusement.

"Really?" Samuel asked. "Why haven't I heard about it from any of them personally?"

"I only found out because one of the board members accidentally cc'd me in the chain email in which they were lamenting the situation," Miguel said.

My heart skipped a beat. Was our fake relationship causing problems for Samuel? I leaned against the wall as I listened.

"How mature of them," Samuel said, his voice growing an edge to it.

"Don't worry about it," Miguel said. "The board members know that your romantic decisions are a personal matter and beyond the scope of their jurisdiction. It just surprised them."

Samuel laughed, and I heard the tenseness melt from his voice. "It's a shame I can't tell them how Natalie's plan to stop our feuding families has positively impacted Warner Print. They'd throw us a party."

Unbidden, a small smile tugged at my lips. It wasn't a bad

thing that Warner Print was benefiting from this—especially since I'd come to realize that both families frequently had valid arguments.

"Speaking of success," Miguel said. There was the sound of a chair scraping the ground before he continued. "You've certainly had a lot of wins lately. You've finally gotten some headway on some of your long-term plans, even if it wasn't entirely your own doing."

"What topic are you dancing around?" Samuel asked.

"Nothing, nothing," Miguel assured him innocently. "I just meant that you've worked hard to get here."

"Of course I have," Samuel said, sounding a bit defensive. "It hasn't been easy."

"True," Miguel said. "You did work hard to get the purchase of the old middle school pushed through. But it seems like your long-term plan, the one you came up with roughly a decade ago, has only seen any real forward movement because you lucked out when Natalie suggested the fake relationship idea."

I frowned, trying to make sense of their vague conversation. I wasn't thrilled it sounded like the Warners were continuing with their luxury condo idea, but what on earth was this long-term plan they were talking about? Was it something I should be worried about, or was I just overthinking things?

A decade ago Samuel would have been in college, just like me. What plan could he have possibly made back then that would be affected by us fake dating?

We'd fought like cats and dogs in high school. There was no way Samuel had any kind of positive feelings for me back then when he was planning out his life. I doubted he'd had the emotional maturity then to make mending the fence between our families a life goal of his, and if it had been, he'd done a terrible job of it with the way he'd plagued me.

"I admit that I lucked out when Natalie approached me,"

Samuel said, his voice low but determined. "But I've done my best to take full advantage of our agreement."

"Yes," Miguel said, a touch of skepticism in his tone. "You certainly strategized to make the arrangement as beneficial as possible. Although, in hindsight, I'm not sure if all of your moves were the wisest."

I cringed, a little pained by how businesslike they sounded discussing our relationship—or rather, our farce of a relationship. It was kind of cold considering we were close friends now.

"Are you referring to me asking Natalie to marry me?" Samuel asked Miguel, his voice tense.

"Exactly," Miguel replied. "That was quite the misstep, don't you think?"

I covered my mouth with my hand to hold in a gasp of surprise, and my heart sank.

"I did what I had to do," Samuel said. "And what's with this change in attitude? You supported the proposal."

"I did," Miguel agreed. "Because I thought you'd take action after it instead of dragging your feet!"

"What are you getting at?"

"I'm trying to point out that you need to tell Natalie the truth about everything!"

Truth? The truth about what? My heart already ached from the casual way Miguel and Samuel were discussing his proposal to me—which apparently was nothing more than a chess move instead of a family-inspired impulse as he'd told me.

Samuel sighed. "It's not that I haven't tried."

Miguel snorted. "Cut the crap—you have not! You'd be perfectly happy to continue the way things are because you don't want to risk something happening. I told you after the proposal that you needed to talk to her, and I meant it. I'm not willing to keep my silence on the issue much longer."

"I understand that you're mad."

"Then do something about it!"

The exchange was a dagger to my heart. Not that I thought Samuel was betraying me for some nefarious plot. Despite the overheard conversation, I knew Samuel well enough to believe that he wouldn't hurt me like that.

But the talk of risking things, hidden truths, and Samuel's willingness to propose to me for some kind of goal ... It was obvious I didn't matter to him as much as he mattered to me, and there was no way he had any romantic feelings for me.

Not a chance.

My vision blurred from the stinging tears pooling in my eyes. I pushed off the wall and staggered down the hallway.

I had to get out of here.

Owen had been right—it was odd that Samuel had so suddenly asked me to marry him. He was a genius when it came to handling people, after all.

"Owen and Jenna are getting serious." Miguel's voice drifted down the hall. "You're running out of time, Sam."

"I'll do whatever it takes to make this succeed," Samuel replied firmly. "There is no other option."

As I stumbled away from their conversation, my heart raced with questions. I didn't dare pick up my pace until I was out of hearing range. Then I fled to the office building's entrance.

I burst through the double doors, my heart pounding as I ran across the visitor parking lot to my car. The cold night air stung my face, but I hardly noticed as I fumbled with my keys and threw myself into the driver's seat.

"Get a grip, Natalie." My breath fogged up the windows and tears stung my eyes, making it hard to see. I tried to push down the torrent of emotions that threatened to consume me, but it was like holding back a tidal wave.

Numbly, I started the car and drove off, needing to put some distance between myself and Samuel—between myself and the conversation I'd just overheard.

I mindlessly drove. I had no idea where I was going until I pulled into Owen's driveway. I paused for a moment, teary-eyed, and tried to regain control of my emotions.

The one positive to all of this heartbreak was that I could keep my dignity since I never told Samuel how I felt. But I couldn't even be mad at him about it. It wasn't his fault I'd fallen in love with him, and he'd always been upfront about his drive to see Warner Print succeed. He'd lied about why he proposed to me, but ...

"Ugh, I can't even think straight!" I rummaged around in the car glove box for some old, tattered napkins to clean myself up.

In defense of my poor broken heart, Samuel hadn't been entirely professional in his dealings with me. There were several times when he'd acted in ways that could make someone question his intentions, but now that I thought about it, he'd always been careful to maintain boundaries between me and his family. Like when he'd freaked out about me being at his mother's house without him or when his grandfather had taken me out for dinner.

But why would he lie about why he'd asked me to be fake engaged when he'd been open about the Warners' plan for the middle school?

"Why is this so complicated?" I groaned, my voice loud in the quiet confines of my car.

The truth was, I was scared—scared of what I'd just discovered and terrified of what it meant.

I gripped the steering wheel so tightly my knuckles turned white. I didn't know what truth Miguel was hinting at. Maybe I was just blowing this whole thing out of proportion.

However, the mention of Samuel's decade-long life plan kept gnawing at me, like a puzzle piece that refused to fit.

But it would be OK. I'd confront Samuel when I was ready to find out the truth. At least now I knew he didn't feel the same way about me as I did him.

Taking a deep breath, I picked up my phone and typed out a text message to Samuel.

> Great news—Owen and Jenna are officially going out! This means we can plan our breakup. :)

As soon as I hit send, a strange mixture of relief and sadness washed over me. This was a heartbreak, but I was almost thirty and was no stranger to the feeling. It would go away eventually, even if it hurt like hell for the moment.

I exhaled, then opened my phone's contact list and dialed. As soon as the phone picked up, I spoke. "Hey, Owen. Are you home?" I tried to swallow the pain that strangled my throat, but my voice cracked. "I could use some help."

Chapter 29

Samuel

Tip #29: *Even the best laid plans can spiral out of control. Try not to get too possessive/obsessive when that happens. It's a red flag.*

I stood up, tossing my phone on the meeting room table, and started unrolling the sleeves of my now-wrinkled button-up.

Miguel checked his watch. "I can't wait to get home. It's been a long week." He smoothed his goatee. "Are you going to see Natalie tonight?"

"We don't have any plans." I stretched my arms over my head as I considered my oblivious fiancée and the game I was playing to win her over. "But I'm planning to call and see if she's free."

"It's such a shame," Miguel said. "She could have you wrapped completely around her little finger if she just knew you loved her."

Before we could continue our conversation, Isaac returned to the meeting room and looked around expectantly.

"What's up?" I asked.

Isaac slipped his hands into the pockets of his trousers. "Did you have a nice visit with Natalie?"

I frowned. "What are you talking about?"

"Charlotte texted me," Isaac said. "She ran into Natalie coming into the building as Charlotte was heading out. Charlotte gave her directions to the meeting room."

I shifted, my posture tensing—had something happened to Natalie? How could Charlotte have chatted with her and Natalie not appeared by this point?

"That's odd," Miguel said.

"Yeah, it is." I strode to the far end of the table to grab my suit coat and shrug it on. "She must have gotten lost somewhere in the building. I'd better call her."

My phone chimed with a new message. Isaac leaned over the table where'd I'd tossed it and read the screen. "You don't need to bother, Sam. Natalie just texted you."

Relief washed over me as I strode back to Isaac, my hand outstretched for my phone.

Isaac's expression shifted into a frown as he stared at the screen.

"What's wrong?" asked Miguel.

"This text ... she says: Great news—Owen and Jenna are officially going out," Isaac read aloud. "This means we can plan our breakup." He looked up at me, puzzled. "What is she talking about?"

A knot formed in my stomach.

No.

No, no. I was so close to winning her over, so close to getting the only thing I'd wanted in my adult life. I needed to talk to her and stall, to give me more time.

I snatched my phone from Isaac's hand. "I need to make a call."

As I stepped out of the meeting room and into the hallway, I hit Natalie's speed dial number.

"Come on, Nat," I muttered under my breath, my voice barely audible over the insistent ringtone echoing in my ear. After several rings, I was greeted by the chirpy sound of her voicemail message.

My concern was sidestepping closer to panic as I disconnected the call.

I tried her number again, hope and desperation warring within me. Once again, her voicemail was the only response. "Damn it."

I needed to talk to her and delay her idea of a breakup. But we were engaged, which meant she'd be motivated to do it delicately. Surely that would give me plenty of time. Right?

I ignored the nagging voice in the back of my mind that reminded me I'd had a decade already and had still failed. I paused to text her when I reached the entrance of the office building, taking pains to keep the text's tone light.

> Hey, just wanted to chat about Owen and Jenna. Also, Charlotte said you came by Warner Print, but I never saw you. Everything OK?

If I could get her talking, I could assess her feelings. Hopefully we could work things out and I could salvage this.

I gripped my phone tightly when I saw the message marked as read, but then nothing. No reply, no explanation. Just silence.

The feeling of dread that had been gnawing at the edges of my mind grew stronger. Something wasn't right.

"Think," I muttered to myself, trying to come up with a strategy. "What else can I do?"

The answer came to me in a flash. It was quite possibly overreacting, and at the very least pushy, but I could head to Natalie's apartment. I needed to see her—to look into her eyes and make sure she was OK. And if that meant showing up at her apartment unannounced, so be it.

"Great." I leaned against my Porsche, utterly defeated about half an hour later.

The howling wind and snow flicking my face hardly fazed me, and I barely noticed the cold despite only having my suit coat—I was too concerned about Natalie.

Her apartment was dark. Not a single light shone from what I knew were her two windows in the tiny brick building.

Still, I couldn't just stand there without trying. I walked up to the locked gate and buzzed her apartment.

Nothing happened, and the sinking feeling in my chest grew heavier.

"Come on, Nat." I glanced back at her dark windows as I returned to my car.

I grabbed my phone and dialed her number once more. This time, when her voicemail greeted me, I left a message, working hard to make sure my voice sounded natural. "Hello, Nat, I'm just trying to get ahold of you. I have some things I'd like to talk over with you. Sorry for bothering you, but could you please get back to me?"

I hung up as I climbed into my Porsche. I tossed my phone onto the passenger seat, ignoring the thin layer of snow that swept in with me.

What if I was blowing this out of proportion? What if my desperate attempts to reach her were only scaring her?

"Natalie said we could break up once Jenna and Owen were solid. But I proposed to her. The engagement means she can't break up with me very quickly, so I still have time to win her over," I said, trying to make myself feel better.

If that was true, why did it feel like I'd already lost her?

My phone rang, and I snatched it up, hoping to see Natalie's name on the screen. Instead, it was Isaac. Disappointment coursed through me, and I tossed the phone back onto the car seat, running my hand through my hair in frustration.

It seemed I needed to give her time. Coming on too strong might ruin things. I'd wait until tomorrow, which seemed like an eternity away.

The following morning, Saturday, I pulled up in front of Natalie's parents' ranch house, parking my Porsche at the curb. The sleepless night had taken its toll on me, leaving my eyes gritty from exhaustion. My worries about Natalie gnawed at my insides as I stepped out of the car and walked up the salted driveway and then across the freshly shoveled sidewalk.

Taking a deep breath, I rang the doorbell and waited.

After a moment, the door opened, revealing Patty, Natalie's mom. Her smile was welcoming, which I took as a good sign. "Hello, Samuel. Come on in."

"Actually, I'm here to see if you or Paul have heard from

Nat," I said. "She sent me a text last night, and I've been trying to get ahold of her ever since."

Patty looked confused, her brow furrowing in concern. "I haven't heard anything this morning. But when I called Owen last night, he texted back saying he and Natalie were out together so he couldn't pick up."

A wave of relief washed over me, only to be replaced by tension as I recalled that Owen was the only Mann family member who knew about our farce of a relationship.

What on earth was going on? It felt like I was missing something, but I didn't know how to fix it, as I didn't know what was going on!

"Are you OK, Samuel?" Worry etched a crease of concern between Patty's eyebrows.

"Thank you for asking, but I'm fine." I felt anything but. "I just really need to talk to Nat."

"Alright, Samuel. But take care of yourself, OK? Maybe take a nap, you look exhausted."

"Will do." I turned to leave.

"Drive safely—and look out for deer," Patty warned me with the old Wisconsin adage before she shut the door.

I started the short walk back to my car, feeling guilty that I hadn't recognized how amazing and kind the Manns were until I started dating Natalie.

As soon as I reached my car, my phone buzzed in my pocket. Pulling it out, I saw that it was my mother calling. With a resigned sigh, I answered the call as I opened the car door and got in. "Hello, Mother."

"Samuel, what on earth is going on?" Mother's voice was lined with worry. "Isaac and Miguel are at my house telling me you're not actually engaged to Natalie—"

"Everything's fine," I cut her off before she could really get going. "I just need to talk to Natalie. Have you or Isaac happened to hear from her?" I asked, fearing the answer.

"No, we haven't. What's wrong, Samuel? Why won't you tell me?"

"Nothing's wrong." I leaned my head back against the headrest. "I have to go. I'll talk to you later."

"Wait—" Mother started, but I hung up before she could say anything else.

Sitting there in my Porsche, I darkly wondered what I had done wrong. I must have done something, because Natalie wasn't the type to go radio silent. I racked my brain for any clue.

Yesterday I'd texted her good morning over breakfast, using the pretense of asking her what her schedule was for the weekend. Her reply had seemed happy, and she'd used multiple emojis. I'd been downright smug when she sent me a picture of the chocolate strawberry latte she got during her lunch break with Owen. It was only since my unexpected proposal that Natalie had started initiating friendly texts that had nothing to do with our relationship, so this had been a win.

I knew she'd gone back to work after lunch with Owen, and the next I'd heard of her was when Charlotte texted Isaac that she'd met Natalie when leaving Warner Print. Charlotte had stayed after hours to help Isaac with our meeting, so Natalie must have come after the meeting was already wrapped up, when everyone from the office was already gone.

All of that was logical—Natalie worked, too, so it would take her some time to get over to Warner Print. But I didn't see anything unusual, and how could—wait.

When Charlotte left, the meeting was officially over. Isaac had gone back to his office to fetch his coat, and Miguel and I had talked about a couple of different topics, one of which was Natalie.

Could she have overheard my conversation with Miguel?

But it wouldn't matter if she had. We hadn't said anything negative about her or the Manns.

Unless ... she'd heard the conversation, realized I was in love with her, and understandably freaked out. If she learned the personal enemy who'd been dogging her since high school was madly in love with her, that would be enough to make anyone nervous.

If that was the case, my multiple calls and texts, and visit to her apartment wouldn't have helped reassure her that I was an emotionally well-adapted individual.

"Great." I rubbed my temples. "Way to go. I've become the creepiest fake boyfriend ever."

Maybe I could talk to Owen. He knew about us, and he'd been with Natalie last night. But would contacting him be too much?

My phone rang. I grabbed it and stared at the screen as Jenna's name flashed across it.

Jenna wasn't Natalie, but she might have a clue what was going on with Natalie since apparently she and Owen were official based on the text Natalie had sent. With that hope in mind, I swiped to answer the call.

"Hello?"

"Samuel Warner, what the hell is going on?!" Jenna's normally bubbly tone was hot with rage.

"What?" I asked, confused.

"How could you not tell Natalie you're in love with her?" Jenna's voice was growly, like an angry tiger.

"Oh."

"When Owen told me this morning that you two were fake dating, I couldn't believe it. The entire Warner family knows you've been head over heels for Natalie since college! How could you go along with this crazy idea and not just tell Natalie you're in love with her?" Jenna's voice grew louder until she was practically yelling into the phone.

"I wanted to, but it was never the right time," I said.

"It was never the right time?" Jenna echoed me in a mocking tone. "Samuel. You are the CEO of Warner Print. You're supposed to be smart! So! Logically, you should know, then, that *any time since Natalie asked to fake date would have been the right time!*"

Jenna's biting words didn't bother me. Jenna was sweet until you crossed her, and then she came out swinging.

"I thought I could get around it if I tricked her into falling in love with me while we were fake dating."

"Tricking someone into love isn't a great start to a relationship," Jenna said. "Why would you do that instead of coming clean?"

"Because if I told Natalie, I could lose her forever," I growled.

"Yeah, well, it looks to me like you're still in danger of losing her, so it's not like your ploy was a great fix!"

"You don't get it. If I lost my chance with Natalie—"

"No, I completely get it," Jenna interrupted me. "Opening your yap and telling Natalie you love her and hearing her reject you is a lot more emotionally terrifying than hoping you could trap her into something. But here's the problem with your plan: They both depend on Natalie making a choice! It was always up to her whether she'd accept or reject you, and despite how much more terrifying it might be for you, she personally would have looked a lot more favorably at you if you'd grown a spine and told her instead of all this stupid subterfuge!" Jenna ranted.

I fell silent.

What could I say? Jenna was right.

Because of my cowardice, I'd royally messed up. Natalie's rejecting me was always going to be a risk I couldn't mitigate.

Talking to her about it seemed impossibly hard because of my feelings, but if I loved Natalie as much as I claimed to, I should have been willing to risk myself on her behalf.

I rubbed my gritty eyes with my thumb and pointer finger. "If you've talked to Owen, you must know how Natalie is doing?"

"Yes!" Jenna barked. "She cried her eyes out last night because she overheard you and Miguel chortling to each other, obviously about something stupid."

I frowned. "Is she that upset that I love her?"

"No! She still doesn't know how you feel because, *Samuel Warner*, you didn't tell her! Instead she's convinced you saw the fake relationship as a business transaction and you've been focused on how to use it for Warner Print's advantage."

"How that could have been her takeaway? I don't know what part of the conversation she overheard, but it was mostly Miguel reminding me that my progress with Natalie wasn't totally real since the entire relationship was a farce."

"I don't know either. But you better think about how you're going to fix it!"

"Sorry," I said. "I didn't mean to cause any strain on your relationship with Owen."

"You didn't, because Owen and I act like adults and talk things out!" Jenna snarled. She let out an aggravated sigh, and when she spoke again her voice was significantly softer. "I'm upset and informing you that you need to fix this because I care about *you*. You've been in love with Natalie for so long, and Natalie is such an amazing person. I want this to work out for you."

"Have you seen her?" I asked. "Do you think it's already beyond fixing?"

Jenna was quiet for a moment. "I chatted with her for a little bit. She's not angry with you, if that's what you're asking, but it's almost worse. She has no idea about your feelings but believes you've been hiding something from her. You'll have to do something to prove her trust in you was warranted."

It wasn't the answer I was hoping to hear, but at least now I knew what was happening. "Do you know where she is?"

"Not right this moment," Jenna said. "But I'll text you when I find out—if she is ready to face you."

"Got it. Thanks, Jenna."

"Yeah," Jenna said. "Consider this your payback for the work you and Natalie did to smooth things over between our families. Take care of yourself."

"Sure," I agreed without any feeling. "Bye."

"Bye."

I sagged in my driver's seat.

Natalie was OK.

She completely misunderstood everything about my feelings for her, but I couldn't blame her when I'd been a piss-poor communicator for a decade.

I'd do my best to make it up to her, though. I just didn't know how I'd convince her how I really felt ...

Chapter 30

Natalie

Tip #30: *Once your extensive relationship lies have been discovered, apologize to those you lied to.*

The scent of cocoa from my steaming mug tickled my nose as I sat in Owen's cozy living room, nestled into the plush cushions of his couch. I was supposed to be absorbed in the romance novel I had picked out, but my mind kept wandering back to Samuel.

I glanced at my cell phone on the coffee table and resisted the urge to check it again. He hadn't called or texted since this morning. I decided I'd wait until Monday to reach out to him, when I was sure I could keep my emotions in check. Since it was Saturday midafternoon, that meant I had quite a while before I'd be facing him.

I groaned. "Why do relationships have to suck?"

The empty room offered no solace; Owen had left right after lunch.

The doorbell abruptly rang, jolting me from my thoughts. "Owen didn't mention he was expecting anyone ... but that doesn't mean anything in nosy Fox Creek," I muttered.

Setting my cocoa down, I got up and padded to the front door. I swung it open and almost screamed at the sight of Logan's tall and imposing form standing on Owen's front stoop. Isaac stood next to him, his profile turned away from me. (I knew it was Isaac even before seeing his glasses because of his poker-straight posture; Samuel's stance was more relaxed.)

"Hello." My voice wavered with the greeting.

Isaac blinked in surprise and turned toward me. "Hello, Natalie. I apologize for our sudden intrusion. We didn't think you'd actually answer the door."

I eyed Isaac, then Logan. "Why are you here?"

"We want to talk," Isaac said.

I half shut the door, just in case. "Is Samuel with you?"

"No," Isaac said.

I clutched the door handle. "What would you like to talk about?"

Isaac adjusted his glasses and looked awkward before peering up at Logan.

As usual, Logan said nothing.

"Well," Isaac hesitantly started.

"I can't take it anymore!" Jenna popped out from behind Logan and squirmed her way between the two men. "It seems this youngest generation of Warner men is terrible at communicating. Hello, Natalie." Jenna smiled at me before wrapping me in a comforting hug.

"Hi, Jenna." I patted her back and relaxed into the hug. "What's going on?"

Jenna released me and backed up a step. "Owen told me you were holed up in his house, so we three came over here to ask if you'd be willing to talk to our family."

I started to shake my head, but Isaac was quick to add, "We'd like to talk to you *without* Samuel present."

I took a deep breath, my heart making a break for my throat as I tried to steady my voice. "What do you want to talk to me about?"

Isaac hesitated, his mouth opening and closing as if searching for the right words. Jenna, however, had no such issue. "We want to discuss your fake relationship with Samuel."

My stomach dropped, and I exhaled deeply.

I supposed it was inevitable they'd found out considering Owen had asked for my permission to tell Jenna everything. And who knew what Samuel was saying to them?

I glanced at Logan, recalling his intimidating reputation as the Warner family attack dog, and wondered if I was in for a legal battle.

"Are you pressing charges against me for misleading you all or something?" I asked.

Jenna shook her head. "No, not at all."

Isaac tugged on his leather driving gloves, his dark eyes meeting mine. "Quite the opposite, actually. Our mother wants to extend an invitation to come to her house, right now, to reassure you that we don't blame you."

A mixture of relief and confusion swirled inside me.

Part of me knew it wasn't very smart to go hang with Samuel's family when I was trying to avoid him, but another part reminded me they had been nothing but welcoming and kind.

What sold me, though, was the nagging thought that going with them would help me get some answers about whatever it was Samuel was working toward, and it might be easier to hear it from them instead of the guy I was in love with.

"Alright," I reluctantly agreed, nodding at Isaac. "I'll come."

"Thank you, Natalie," Isaac said, his usually reserved demeanor softening. "I can drive."

"I'll drive myself," I said. (I wanted a getaway car in case things went south.)

"Certainly. I'll ride with you," Isaac said in a tone that offered no room for arguments. Maybe he was afraid I'd give them the slip?

Isaac tossed his car keys to Jenna.

"Wait by my car, please. I just need a second to grab my things." I pointed to my hatchback parked on the curb. As Isaac headed for the car, I went back inside.

I took a deep breath and quickly sent a text to Owen, letting him know where I was going. Then I grabbed my coat and purse, locked the front door behind me, and joined Isaac by my car.

He seemed as tense as I felt. Yay. This car ride was going to be buckets of fun.

"Let's go." I unlocked the car and slid into the driver's seat. Isaac got in, his tall frame folding into the passenger side with practiced ease.

The silence between us was heavy. I drove for several blocks before Isaac finally spoke up.

"I promised my mother I wouldn't say anything without the rest of the family present," he began, glancing at me. "But as Samuel's twin, I feel like I need to tell you that whatever you overheard him saying ... well ..." He paused, his eyes glued on the road.

"Isaac, it's fine. I understand that Samuel was using our fake relationship to his advantage, and that's OK. That's how I sold him on the idea, after all."

He shook his head, his lips pressed together in irritation. "No, well, yes, but—" He stopped himself and sighed. "It's not my place to explain what Samuel is after. I just want to assure you that he would never, ever want to hurt you. Ever."

In a way, I knew he was right. Samuel wasn't cruel. But remembering the conversation about a plan Samuel had had for years and years ...

Perhaps it was more that I knew Samuel would never *mean* to hurt me. But he also probably never would have imagined I'd fall in love with him given our turbulent history, so I doubt he'd planned for such a circumstance.

We continued the drive in silence, the beauty of the snow-covered landscape soothing me as we made our way to Estelle's house. But the closer we got, the more nervous I grew.

After driving for what felt like too long and simultaneously not long enough, we arrived, and I pulled into the driveway.

I parked, and we hopped out. Isaac walked with me to the front door, opening it for me and then stepping back so I could enter first.

"Thanks," I said.

I slipped inside, and as I tugged my boots off, the sound of tippy-tappy paws greeted me. Looking down, I saw Chuck scurrying toward me. Today he wore a blue bandanna adorned with white snowflakes tied around his neck, which complemented his snaggletooth underbite.

"Hello, Chuck!" I bent down to pick him up.

The warmth of his little body in my arms melted my nerves, replacing them with a sense of comfort.

"Natalie, dear," Estelle called out, her voice as inviting as ever. She swept into the foyer like royalty, wearing a long, black wool skirt and a blue sweater that accentuated her elegance. Walter followed close behind her, his usual mischievous twinkle noticeably absent from his eyes.

"Hi, Estelle," I said.

I set Chuck down as Estelle closed in on me. The Warner matron pulled me into a sweeping hug that was as comforting as Chuck's greeting. "Thank you for coming today. Isaac, be a dear and take Natalie's coat."

"Yes, Mother." Isaac held out his hand for my coat. After I shrugged it off, I passed it over to him.

"Thanks, Isaac."

"Of course."

"Hello, Natalie," Walter greeted me, his voice soothing and devoid of its usual sass.

"Hi, Walter."

The front door opened again, causing my heart to clench at the chance it could be Samuel. Thankfully, only Jenna and Logan entered.

Jenna shut the door behind them. "It's chilly out there!"

She and Logan kicked off their shoes and shed their coats.

Estelle clapped her hands together. "Good, we're all here. Everyone, let's move to the sunroom for a more comfortable place to talk and enjoy some hot drinks."

Estelle scooped Chuck up into her arms and planted a loud kiss on the top of his head, leaving behind a red lipstick mark and making Chuck wag his stubby tail. She then swept off for the sunroom, leaving us to trail behind her.

The sunroom was, as I'd come to expect from the Warners, nothing short of breathtaking. It was a luxurious space filled with wicker furniture covered in plush cushions and pillows. Sunlight streamed through the glass walls, and vibrant plants were positioned in every corner.

We all settled into chairs, forming something of a circle.

Estelle took a moment to hand Chuck off to Walter, who performatively rolled his eyes but nonetheless scratched the dog behind his ears when Chuck settled on his lap. With that settled, Estelle turned her attention to the tea tray resting on the coffee table in the center of our circle.

"Tea, anyone?" Estelle gracefully tipped the porcelain teapot, pouring the steaming, amber liquid into delicate china cups adorned with intricate flower patterns.

"Yes, please," I said.

Estelle handed me a steaming teacup and saucer. "Jamie and Charles wanted to be here, but I thought that might be a bit overwhelming for you, dear."

"Thank you." I put my saucer on the coffee table but cradled the warm cup in my hands. I took a deep breath, gathering the courage to ask the question that had been nagging at me ever since the Warners arrived on Owen's doorstep. "So ... why did you all want to talk to me? Isaac said you weren't mad."

Estelle hesitated, glancing around at her assembled family.

Isaac leaned forward in his seat. "We learned about your arrangement with Samuel yesterday. And I believe that my twin made some choices that led you to think one thing when the reality is quite different."

"Isaac!" Estelle frowned. "You make it sound like Samuel was trying to swindle her!"

"I'd say that's about right." Despite Jenna's flat tone, she daintily sipped from her teacup. "He certainly swindled the rest of us."

"What I meant to say," Isaac continued, ignoring the interruption, "is that our feelings have nothing to do with you. We should have known better than to fall for this farce. Samuel hadn't made any forward progress before this point; it's laughable to think he'd managed to do it in secret. His absolute arrogance would have given him away if he'd really achieved what he said he did."

I tried not to cringe at Isaac's words. I couldn't totally follow what he was saying, but it made me suspect I was right and

Samuel and I weren't as close as I'd believed. There was obviously something else going on beneath the veneer of our fake relationship that he hadn't told me about.

"Isaac, don't make things worse," Estelle said. "Natalie, dear ..." She trailed off, a soft smile on her lips as she searched for the right words.

But they never came. Instead, we sat in tense silence, the weight of unspoken apologies and secrets pressing down on all of us.

The aroma of chocolate mint tea filled my senses as I took a careful sip, the warmth of the drink thawing out the icy feeling that had crawled up the back of my throat.

The silence was broken, unexpectedly, by Walter. "Look, Natalie, we wanted to talk to you because Samuel messed things up."

Estelle nodded in agreement.

"Samuel stuck to the terms of our agreement," I said, fighting to keep my voice steady. "I can't fault him for that."

All of the Warners—from Jenna to Walter—were suspiciously blank-faced at that statement, which didn't exactly raise happy tingles in me.

I pushed on. "But I'm grateful you invited me here. I want to apologize for the lies Samuel and I concocted. I was dishonest with all of you when you were nothing but welcoming to me despite the fact that our families don't get along at all. I regret that."

Their blank looks oddly seemed to intensify, and even Estelle lost some of her elegant glamour as she patted the bun her hair was pulled back in. "Uh-huh," she said.

Logan, who had been silent until now, finally spoke up. "We know you suggested the idea to Samuel to try and get the Manns and Warners to stop fighting so Owen and Jenna could connect. We respect your reasoning and recognize you had honorable intentions." His voice was deep and smooth like shadows on a quiet lake.

I set my teacup down on my saucer. "Thank you, but I still feel guilty. While I might have meant well, the ends don't justify the means. The more our relationship lie grew, the worse I felt about misleading you all."

"It's not that we endorse lying," Jenna said, backing her brother up. "But we recognize the Manns and Warners would have continued to fight if you hadn't acted."

Before I could protest, Walter—absentmindedly petting Chuck—cut me off. "Apology accepted," he said with great firmness. "With that out of the way, we want to assure you that we, as a family unit, are grateful for your efforts to end the feud and have no hard feelings toward you."

Estelle eagerly nodded in agreement, and Isaac gave me a rare smile.

"It's on Samuel," Walter continued, "to explain things to you and make things right with you as far as your relationship goes."

I bit my lip, internally debating whether or not to reiterate that I wasn't angry with Samuel. Judging by the earnest expression on each Warner's face, doing so would only drag out the conversation. It didn't sit quite right with me, as Walter's acceptance of my apology seemed to be just to pacify me, but I guess I'd have to take it. "Thank you for your kindness. It means more to me than you know."

Chapter 31

Samuel

Tip #31: *If the family who was once your bitter enemy offers help in winning back your fake fiancée, take it.*

I sat in my office at Warner Print, staring blankly at my cell phone. The screen displayed a picture of Natalie and me, smiling with our faces smashed together so we could take a selfie. I'd snapped it during our visit to McBride Farm & Greenhouse.

My heart felt like a lead weight in my chest, and my mind seemed to be stuck in an endless loop of confusion. What should I do? What could I do?

"Wow, you really *are* here," a voice interrupted my thoughts.

I looked up to see Owen poking his head through the open door. "What are you doing here? You look like hell, man."

"Thanks." I leaned my head back against my chair. "Are you here to pummel me on behalf of your sister?"

"Believe it or not, no." Owen walked up to my desk and stuffed his hands into his jacket pockets. "You already look terrible enough. I don't think you need any more punishment." He studied my face. "So, what happened?"

"I don't know. I guess Natalie found out I'm in love with her?"

Owen coughed, then shook his head. "No, dude, that's definitely not why she's upset." His expression was a mix of concern and embarrassment.

"Then what made her cut me off?"

"She overheard you and Miguel talking about some long-term plan of yours. She thought dating her was just part of some bigger scheme for you to accomplish that goal, and she was hurt."

"Right, the long-term plan of dating and marrying Natalie that I settled on in college," I said, deadpan.

"Dude!" Owen groaned and bent over, embarrassed on my behalf since I wasn't. "Please say that kind of thing to her and not me!"

"What's the big deal about telling you I'm interested in Natalie?" I rested my hands on my desk. "Everyone must know by now."

"Not everyone," Owen said.

"You knew about it."

"Well. Jenna told me. She said you'd been mooning over Nat for years. Uh, although to your point, I had to fill my mom in when she called this morning saying you showed up at her house looking like death warmed up twice in the microwave. So it's safe to assume most of the Mann clan knows too."

"Great," I muttered.

"However, Natalie still doesn't know."

I snapped to my feet, sending my chair rolling behind me. "She doesn't know?"

"Nope."

"But she must suspect something."

Owen shook his head. "She doesn't have a clue. That's why she's so upset. She had no idea what your long-term plan was. She thought you were using her for some other purpose."

I nodded, unsure if Natalie's obliviousness was good or bad. "How angry do you think she'll be when she finds out?"

Owen made a strange noise. "I don't know, but you will get to find out since you should be the one to tell her."

I thought I was too numb to feel anything by this point, but I discovered there was a corner of my mind that was still operational as apprehension flooded my system. I wasn't stoked at the idea of facing Natalie's anger—or worse, her total indifference.

"Sam." Owen's voice took on a harder edge as he swapped into big brother mode. "You're going to tell Natalie. You owe it to her. Yes, her idea to fake date was crazy and started a lie, but in lying through omission you've really hurt her feelings. She's not crying because she's mad."

I stared at the patterned carpet of my office. "I'm sorry for hurting her."

Owen's expression softened. "Stop punishing yourself. Nobody in our family is mad at you. We all know you're helplessly in love with my sister. And as for Natalie, well," he hesitated, a wry smile tugging at the corners of his mouth, "your proposal should have raised a few warning bells, but she was too stubborn to let herself notice."

A weak chuckle that was more of a huff of air escaped me. "I didn't think she'd buy any excuse I came up with, to be honest. I was surprised when she accepted it."

"Yeah, you should have been," Owen said. "So, are you ready to face her?"

I clenched my jaw. "It could mean losing her forever if she doesn't take it well."

"Before this winter Nat hated your guts. So you wouldn't be much worse off."

"If that was supposed to be encouraging, it wasn't," I wryly said.

"Look, Samuel." Owen's expression was earnest as he met my gaze. "I love my sister, and honestly, I like you too. Just tell her the truth, OK?"

I turned my phone so the screen brightened, casting a blue glow across my face as I looked at the picture of Natalie and me one more time. I was just as sick as ever at the thought of losing her, but after Jenna's grilling, I knew both she and Owen were right. Natalie deserved to know.

"Do you know where she is?" I grabbed my wool coat from the coat hook, then slipped my car keys and phone into my coat pocket.

"Of course. Come on, I've even arranged a ride for you."

"It's fine. I can drive my Porsche."

Owen patted me on the back as we exited my office and walked down the hallway. "Samuel, you're practically an honorary Mann now. And being a Mann means you rarely get to do anything alone."

"What do you mean?"

"You'll see," Owen said cryptically.

A minute later, we stood outside facing the glorious ode-to-the-'90s full-size mouse-mobile van parked by the sidewalk. Grandma Mann yanked the side door open, hollering, "Time to move it or lose it, pretty boy!"

Owen shook my hand. "Don't worry, I'll give you the honor

of riding up front." He sprinted to the van and hurled himself into the seat next to Grandma Mann.

Slower to follow, I climbed into the front passenger seat and slammed the door shut.

"Keep your feet up!" Owen reminded me, buckling his seat belt. Memories of the furry mouse I'd evicted during my previous ride in this van were still fresh, so I hastily obeyed while securing my own seat belt.

"Good afternoon," Grandpa Mann said. "You look terrible."

"So I've been told."

"I bet Mike twenty-four hours' work at my table saw against twenty-four hours of labor with his chainsaw you'd look like this." Grandpa Mann cackled as he started the van and pulled onto the street. "Looks like little Mike will be removing some shrubs for me!"

"I'm glad to hear someone is profiting from my pain," I said.

"Spoken like a true Warner!" Grandma Mann laughed.

Grandpa Mann conspiratorially leaned in my direction. "I knew I'd get free labor. I've got the eye, so I know when a man is in love."

"Please. Even without her glasses Marjorie could see Samuel loves Natalie, and she's blind without her bifocals." Grandma Mann scoffed. "How could anyone miss it?"

Owen, his knuckles white as he clutched the edge of his seat, stared at the ground. "The majority of Fox Creek and I didn't know."

"Congratulations on having worse eyesight than Marjorie," Grandma Mann said.

I tried to muster a smile. "Thanks for your support."

"Don't thank us too early, kid." Grandpa Mann cleared his throat. "You made our precious pumpkin cry her eyes out."

Owen groaned. "I told Mom not to tell anyone about that! Natalie's gonna kill me."

Just then, a furry mouse hopped out from the space where the front dashboard console met the flooring.

I automatically grabbed the rolled-up newspaper from the dashboard, swatting at the tiny intruder. The mouse dodged each swing with impressive agility.

"I didn't mean to make Natalie cry," I said as I kept swinging at the mouse. "But I'm hoping she'll let me make it up to her."

"Good," said Grandpa Mann. "That's all we want."

The mouse finally turned tail and fled, disappearing back into the console. I tossed the newspaper back onto the dashboard.

"I don't know if I'm disappointed or happy that you adjust to the Mann brand of weirdness so easily," Owen groused.

As we drove farther from town, the sides of the road switched from bustling neighborhoods to snow-covered farm fields and then to thick forest.

"I'm quite surprised at your forgiving attitude, considering I've been told about the grudge you've held, sir, against my grandfather Warner for buying the last pint of a specific flavor of ice cream once at Cherry's Dairy Bar," I said.

"That was New Year Mint, and it's only in stock for two days out of the year!" Grandpa Mann grumbled. "Walter Warner doesn't even like that flavor! I tell ya."

"Anyway," Grandma Mann chimed in tartly, "don't give us too much credit. We're fixing to be merciful because we know you're about to run the gauntlet."

"Gauntlet?" I asked.

"You'll see," Grandma Mann said.

If she meant to be ominous, she was unsuccessful. I was already dreading Natalie's reaction when I talked to her. Whatever this gauntlet was couldn't be worse than that.

Grandpa Mann turned onto a familiar road. It took me a

moment before I realized this was the lakeside lane most of my family and I lived on. "Is Natalie at my house?"

Owen hooted. "Nope."

My dread started to build. If there was one thing worse than Natalie's reaction to my feelings, that would be Natalie's reaction to my feelings displayed in front of any of my family members. "Then ... is she with my mother?"

"Better," Grandpa Mann replied, a wicked grin on his face. "She's got your cousins, twin, and grandfather there as well. Lover boy back there rendezvoused with his ladylove and made all the arrangements." He jerked his thumb at Owen.

When I looked back at Owen, he winked at me. "Jenna and I owed you and Natalie one."

Grandpa Mann turned into the driveway of my mother's home, and for a moment I was confused.

The place looked like a parking lot, swarming with over a dozen cars and lots of people milling about. It took me a couple of moments to recognize them all as Natalie's relatives.

"Welcome to the gauntlet, Samuel," Grandma Mann said.

"Good luck." Owen leaned forward to pat me on the shoulder as Grandpa Mann parked the van.

I unbuckled my seat belt and got out. I was braced for anger—a justified reaction—but glancing at my mother's lake house made me more impatient than anything. Natalie was in there.

I made it around the front of the van before I was surrounded by Natalie's family.

Keely, skidding to a stop in front of me, gave me a thumbs-up. "Good luck—you better make her happy!"

I blinked in surprise, but before I could react, she stepped aside and Natalie's mother, Patty, was next.

Patty, misty-eyed, pulled me into a tight hug. "Don't you worry, Samuel. You just need to be honest with Nat, and everything will turn out right."

Patty pulled a tissue out of the sleeve of her jacket and turned to look behind her. "Paul? You coming?"

Paul, burly and stone-faced as usual, shouldered his way through the crowd of Manns. When he reached me, he stared for a long moment, his gaze unnervingly intense. Then, without a word, he offered his hand.

I took it. "I didn't mean to hurt Natalie," I said to Patty and Paul. "I'm sorry."

"You better be!" The next Mann relative to eye me up was Natalie's Uncle Mike. "Natalie's too good for you, kid."

"She is," I agreed.

Uncle Mike awkwardly scratched the back of his head. "Shoot. I didn't mean to kick you when you're down. Just treat her right, OK?"

I nodded and got a few steps closer to my mother's house before little Noah—wearing a bright orange snowsuit—threw himself at me, slamming into my gut.

"I don't care what Mom says about you, Samuel. You're nice!" Noah clung to me like a koala.

"Thanks, Noah," I smiled as Ryan peeled him off me.

"Lighten up, Samuel. You got this." Ryan grinned at me.

There were many more Manns around me, but Natalie's cousin Madison was the last one to stand between me and the front door. She narrowed her eyes as she studied me. "You'll do, Warner," she finally said. "You're weird enough to match Natalie's brand of chaos. Now go get her."

Despite the numbness and dread that had eaten me since Natalie had gone radio silent, I was finally able to smile. "Thanks."

I stepped onto the stoop and opened the front door. Just as I stepped inside I heard Keely shout, "Does anyone have an extra battery? My hearing aid just died."

"I got a new package in the van," Grandma Mann yelled. "Let me see if the mice got to 'em yet!"

With that exchange to cheer me up, I shut the front door.

Now, I just had to find Natalie and hope that I wasn't too late.

Chapter 32

Natalie

Tip #32: *Communicate, communicate, communicate!*

The luxurious sunroom was bathed in the soft glow of afternoon sunlight filtering through the floor-to-ceiling windows and casting intricate patterns on the plush carpet.

I sat comfortably on the well-cushioned wicker couch, sipping my delectable chocolate peppermint tea as I listened to Estelle.

"... It was Walter who insisted on taking me to the Paws and Claws rescue in person. He said I needed a companion after the loss of my husband." Estelle pursed her lips without smudging her flawless lipstick.

"And of course, you came with me most agreeably, without

complaining or arguing the *entire drive* there," Walter grumbled.

Estelle chuckled. "I admittedly wasn't sold on the idea. When we got there, I requested to see their ugliest dog out of sheer spite. They brought out Chuck, and how could I *not* fall in love with such a handsome fellow?" Estelle beamed at her pampered pooch, who was still sitting on Walter's lap but wildly wagged his stubby tail when he realized Estelle was talking to him.

"It could have been worse," Walter summarized as he petted Chuck. "She could have ended up with several dogs before the day was over."

A phone chimed with an incoming message. Jenna glanced at her phone and abruptly stood up. "The delivery's here. Come on, Isaac. You too, Logan."

Jenna bumped Logan's leg until the intimidating man stood, and Isaac was just a moment behind him.

Estelle gracefully stood. "I suppose I should make another pot of tea as this one has cooled, so I'll come with."

Estelle picked up her porcelain teapot as Jenna, Isaac, and Logan all slipped through the sunroom entrance into the dim mansion innards.

"Come along, Walter," Estelle called over her shoulder.

Walter looked up from scratching Chuck's belly. "What? Why?"

Estelle smiled guilelessly. "Because you need the walk. Now, let's go."

"I'd be happy to help," I offered.

"Nonsense," Estelle said. "You are our guest. You should relax and enjoy the pretty view. Come along, Walter!"

Walter grumbled as he stood up, Chuck still nestled in his arms, and followed his daughter-in-law out of the sunroom.

I was a little confused by the abrupt exit of all the Warners, but maybe they wanted to chat privately or—more likely—they were trying to give me some space.

I hunkered down deeper in the plush seat cushion and watched the wind kick up snow, which glittered in the sunshine.

A minute or two passed before I heard footsteps approaching the sunroom.

I set my teacup and saucer down on the coffee table and, assuming it was Estelle and/or Walter, called out, "Are you sure you don't need help with the tea after all? I can bring the tray."

The footsteps halted, but there was no reply.

My curiosity piqued, I twisted so I could better see the sunroom entrance and found myself staring at Samuel, his forearms braced on the doorframe.

He looked rough, as though he hadn't slept properly in days. His dark brown hair was tousled and unstyled, and he was wearing jeans and a black Henley that underlined the roughness he usually hid behind his suits and charm. Matching his image, his gray eyes held an intensity that burned right through me.

A sudden, inexplicable heat burned my chest. "Samuel," I managed to say, my voice barely above a whisper.

"Can we talk?" Samuel asked.

I wasn't sure I could handle whatever he wanted to talk about, but I cared too much about Samuel to ignore the urgency in his demeanor.

I sucked in a deep breath. "Sure."

With a slow, deliberate grace, Samuel sauntered into the sunroom and took a seat in a wicker chair next to my couch.

The silence stretched between us, thick and suffocating, unlike the easy, companionable silence we'd shared countless times before.

I glanced at my teacup, contemplating another sip of the

chocolate peppermint tea, but my hands trembled so much from my nerves I'd probably slosh it everywhere.

"I spoke with Owen," Samuel began.

Seeing the chance to potentially lighten the moment, I took it. "Did you talk to Owen, or did my nosy, bossy older brother find you and not give you any other choice except to talk to him?"

It was hypocritical of me given that I'd spent the past few months pushing Owen and Jenna together, but I'd do anything to break the tense strain between us.

Samuel didn't smile, but I was rewarded with a softening of his gaze. "It was possibly the latter."

"Fair enough," I said. "Jenna, Logan, and Isaac found me and brought me here to talk to your family, so I guess the same thing happened to me."

Samuel nodded slowly. "And what did they say?"

"Basically, they don't hold any grudges about our ... situation. They wanted me to know that they aren't mad about the fake relationship that they obviously found out about." I paused, afraid of the answer. "Do you know who else knows?"

Samuel ran a hand through his hair. "I'm pretty sure most of Fox Creek does by now. At least, everyone we know knows. I talked to a few of your relatives outside, and they expressed the same thing. They aren't mad at us for lying."

I sat up straighter, confused. "Wait, my family is outside?"

Samuel relaxed enough to crack a smile. "Yeah, the driveway is practically a parking lot with all the Mann cars out there."

"Why would they *do* that?" I covered my face with my hands. "Poor Estelle doesn't even know she's got the Mann clan on her front lawn!"

"Actually, I'm pretty sure she knows. Owen and Jenna have been texting back and forth."

"Yeah ... that was mentioned." It dawned on me that Jenna's incoming text message about a delivery must have been about Samuel.

Samuel cleared his throat. "I know we need to get on the same page about our relatives, but that's not what I actually want to discuss with you. We need to talk about us. I'm sorry—"

I cut him off before he could get any further. "There's nothing for you to apologize for. I'm just grateful that we were able to resolve the family feud, even if you had other goals in mind."

"You're right," Samuel ruefully said. "I had an additional goal I was working toward for the entire duration of our fake relationship. However, it isn't a goal you should be so understanding and quick to accept."

Samuel stared at the ground, gathering his thoughts as my heart sank all the way to my feet.

It looked like my worst fear was founded. If Samuel was warning me not to be so understanding, just what was his hidden agenda? I knew him well enough to know he wouldn't betray me and secretly be plotting against me, but what did this mean about our friendship?

I swallowed hard. "Then what's this other goal?"

Samuel finally looked up and met my gaze with a vulnerable intensity I'd never seen from him before. "The truth is, Nat ... I've been in love with you since college."

My heart, which was still figuratively down in my feet, flopped like a dying fish. Was I hearing this right?

I blinked, certain I must be having a stroke. "I'm sorry, I didn't understand that. Can you repeat it?"

"In college I made a long-term plan with the goal of marrying you ... because I'm in love with you," Samuel repeated.

"What?" was all I could manage, my ears ringing with disbelief.

"Remember when you worked as a waitress at the Fox Creek Country Club during winter break your college freshman year?"

"Yeah," I said, trying to wrap my head around where this was all leading.

"During that time, I came into the country club multiple times per week, whenever you had a shift. Sometimes it was with Isaac or Logan, sometimes with my parents, and occasionally with friends to get appetizers at the bar," Samuel continued, watching my face for any sign of recognition.

"Yeah, I remember. You were hands down the most obnoxious customer I ever had. You'd constantly stop me to ask for more ice, then less ice, then a lemon for your water, but then you didn't like the lemon so you wanted a new water, and on top of that you'd request updates on your food every five minutes."

A rueful smile twitched across Samuel's lips. "I never said I was any good at expressing my love for you. But it started then. I was desperate to be around you, as I hadn't seen you much since summer because we went to different colleges."

For a moment, I felt both guilt and amusement, as at the time, I had more than once considered spitting in Samuel's food as payback for all the extra stress he put me through at the country club. (His propensity to leave outrageous tips and my conscience were the only things that prevented that.)

"You're saying you've been trying to win me over since then. Did your grand strategy involve ticking me off and driving me crazy?"

Samuel started to reach for me, then seemed to think better of it and rested his hands on his knees. "I know it doesn't make much sense when you put it like that. But after I realized how important you were to me, I became a mess whenever I saw you."

I wrung my hands as I tried to make sense of it. My

emotions were in shambles, and I could barely think straight. Samuel *loved* me? But ... what?

I took a deep breath. "OK. Let's say I believe you. Why didn't you just tell me how you felt after college—when you *should* have known better? We're both almost thirty. We could have dealt with this like adults instead of playing mind games like bothering me at the country club."

"I tried to reach out to you," Samuel said.

"*When?*"

"The donations to the Fox Creek Friends of the Library—Warner Print didn't donate until I started working there and you joined the Friends of the Library as a member."

Samuel held my gaze and seemed to be waiting for some kind of confirmation, so I nodded.

"The donations started because I asked my dad to do it," Samuel said. "We sold the idea to the board as an attempt at community outreach, but I requested it because I figured it would be a way to meet you under positive circumstances, something I hadn't had the chance to do before."

"OK, except you were a pain in the butt over the donations," I said. "You always pretended you forgot the system for donating so it would take an excruciating amount of time to go over it with you."

"Yes, because I wanted to spend more time with you. You were so disdainful of us Warners I knew I didn't stand a chance of talking to you unless it was for a good reason."

I chewed the inside of my cheek as I thought. "Is that why you only visited city hall during my work hours, and you always asked for extra help and explanations for necessary paperwork that you very obviously understood?"

"Yes," Samuel said. "And I'm well aware I'd probably still be stuck at that stage if you hadn't pitched the fake relationship idea to me. You have no idea how grateful I am that Jenna caught Owen's attention."

"But how could you be *so bad* at flirting?" I asked, my pitch going higher as I felt my incredulousness build in my heart. "I'll give you that as adults you teased me and kept it to verbal banter, and you weren't childish or cruel, but that is a *low bar*. You're Samuel Warner! You've got it all—the looks, the charisma, the money, your family. There's nothing you lack!"

"There is, actually. I lack you—although I'm gratified to learn you do find me charming and handsome because you didn't react much whenever I kissed you, so I was starting to worry."

"*Samuel.*"

"Sorry." Samuel was quiet for a moment as he thought. "I only have myself to blame for my awkwardness—it's not your fault I couldn't hold a genuine conversation with you. I tried to fix it, but the more time passed, the more desperate I got, and I couldn't seem to overcome it because you mean so much to me. Still, I apologize—and I'll keep apologizing for the rest of our lives if you let me—for bungling my approaches with you."

I crossed my feet at the ankles as I studied him. Samuel met my gaze, unashamed. I could only hold the eye contact for a few moments before my nerves got to me and I looked away.

"If you want proof of my feelings, just think about our faked time together," Samuel said. "I dove straight into my role as your boyfriend, whereas you had to work hard to make yourself believable."

"You did immediately pull off the doting boyfriend act," I agreed, "or Grandma and Grandpa Mann never would have accepted you. I assumed it was just because you were a great boyfriend."

"I'm a great boyfriend to *you*. Because I got to do all the things I've always wanted to do with you, Nat."

"Then what was with your proposal?" I scooted forward so I sat on the edge of the couch cushion. "I'm assuming it wasn't actually you crumbling to family peer pressure?"

"I panicked when you mentioned that we might not have to pretend to be together much longer after Owen and Jenna went on their first date," Samuel said. "I knew you didn't hate me anymore, but I also knew you wouldn't hesitate to break things off once our fake relationship had served its purpose. I thought the proposal would force you to stay with me for longer because you wouldn't want to mess things up after all your work to fix our families."

"Walter said Isaac and your cousins all supported him giving you his wife's engagement ring because ..." I trailed off, the pieces of the puzzle finally falling into place.

"Because they all knew I'd been pining over you for years," Samuel confirmed. "That's also why I didn't want to leave you alone with any of my family members. I was afraid they would say something about the years I'd spent absolutely smitten with you."

I thought back to the night I had hung out with Walter and Estelle alone and how Samuel had rushed in, harried and concerned. I had assumed it was because he didn't trust me with his family, but now that I thought of it, he had frequently interrupted his family whenever they talked about *why* they were so happy for him.

"I broke probably half a dozen traffic laws trying to get to Mother's house that night we were supposed to have dinner here," Samuel admitted sheepishly, rubbing the back of his neck. "When I brought you around, there were multiple times my family almost gave me away."

I recalled the suspiciously blank expressions on the faces of Estelle, Walter, Isaac, Logan, and Jenna when I had insisted to them that Samuel didn't have feelings for me.

It all made sense now. Their knowing looks, their poorly masked surprise, and their determined attempts to bring us together were all because they knew the truth.

"Is that why Jenna was so mad today?" I asked, my voice barely above a whisper. "Because she knew you liked me and had just found out we were pretending?"

"Yes, except I don't just like you, Natalie." Samuel's eyes searched mine. "I love you."

The weight of his confession hung in the air between us, and I struggled to find the words to respond. "Why didn't you say something earlier? Wait, I can answer that myself. It was because I didn't hide how much I disliked you, right?"

Samuel shrugged. "If you want to give me an excuse, sure, but the truth is I didn't do a great job at doing anything to change your opinion of me. As you pointed out, my efforts were ... poorly done at best."

Samuel smiled hesitantly, then got off his chair and knelt in front of me, taking my hands in his. "But I want to change how you see me—not just my terrible bids for your attention, but who I really am. Which is why the Warners will be renovating the old middle school and turning it into apartments available at affordable rent levels and making a sizable donation to start a fund for a community center."

I stared at Samuel, shocked. "W-what?"

Samuel nodded. "I thought about what you and Owen said about luxury condos, and while there is a demand for them, I'm also aware there is a lack of good apartments at more affordable rates."

"And your family is OK with this?" I asked.

"Yes. We pride ourselves in taking care of our employees at Warner Print." Samuel squeezed my hands. "Housing costs affect them too. So the whole family was on board with the idea."

I closed my eyes, trying to sort through the whirlwind of emotions. "Thank you, Samuel. Your family is so much more amazing than I ever gave them credit for."

"Does that mean you think *I'm* amazing?" There was a teasing lilt to his voice that invited me to joke and banter with him. He was giving me an out, a way to end the conversation and move on instead of addressing the shock of a lifetime he'd delivered with it.

But I didn't want to banter and move on. No. I'd been hurt—unnecessarily, as it turned out—by the misunderstanding because I loved Samuel. And while Samuel might have been terrible at communicating his attraction, I wasn't going to accept that same low standard for myself.

I finally opened my eyes.

"Sam," I started, then stopped. There was a lump in my throat that made it hard to speak.

Samuel, still crouched in front of me and holding my hands, watched me with an intensity that made my palms clammy.

I sucked in a deep breath. "I came to your office on Friday as a surprise because I wanted to talk to you."

Samuel leaned back, and I saw some of the heat in his eyes extinguished. "So you *don't* think I'm amazing," he said, his voice neutral.

I could tell he was mentally heading in the opposite direction I wanted this conversation to go. Desperate to cut him off, I blurted out, "I was going to tell you I was in love with you."

Samuel froze, his expression unreadable.

"I mean, I'm still in love with you," I corrected. "When Owen and I met for lunch he said he and Jenna were official and I didn't want to end things with you, so I showed up at your office with the plan to talk to you and ..." I struggled to continue and found myself suddenly a lot more empathetic to Samuel's fumbled attempts at communication with me.

This was incredibly awkward—and I *knew* he loved me!

"The point is," I said, reining in my ramble, "I love you too. And I would like it if we could be together," I finished, my voice barely above a whisper. My heart pounded in my chest, and I held my breath, waiting for his response.

In the blink of an eye, Samuel's expression transformed from shock to unbridled joy. He moved to sit on the couch with me, then scooped me into his arms and pulled me into a passionate kiss.

Our lips met with an electric charge that made my fingers twitch. The kiss was sweet and intoxicating, filling my senses and making my head spin. Every fiber of my being felt alive, consumed by the realization that we both loved each other deeply, and this was just the beginning of our story together.

"I love you, Nat." Samuel pulled back from the kiss just long enough to speak, his voice filled with awe and devotion, before he kissed me again—this time more playfully.

I laughed into his mouth as he threaded his right hand through my hair and cradled the back of my head as if I was the most precious thing in the world.

"I love you," he repeated when we paused to catch our breath.

Before I could answer he kissed me again, this one long and lingering, filling me with a deliriously delicious warmth.

Everything was so perfect I would have thought I was dreaming except, with my arms wrapped around him, I could feel the tense muscles in his back and the movement in his shoulder when he braced me so I could lean into him instead of falling over.

We paused to catch our breath again and savor the moment, wrapped in each other's arms. I pressed my cheek against his chest, listening to the fast beat of his heart.

"I love you too, Samuel," I whispered, tears pricking the corners of my eyes.

A loud bang echoed from inside the house.

I startled, but Samuel seemed more preoccupied with me than whatever caused the noise.

"Should we check on that?" I asked.

Samuel pulled his hand from my hair so he could tilt my chin up toward him. "Don't worry, it's probably just one of our family members."

He kissed me again, momentarily distracting me, until I remembered that my family was wandering around Estelle's front lawn.

I pulled back from the kiss. "We should go assure them we've made up," I said, assuming I'd have to persuade him. To my surprise, he leaned back and studied me intently.

"Does this mean you're saying yes to my proposal?" he asked, his voice cautious.

"Huh?"

"You shouldn't feel any pressure." Samuel tapped the family engagement ring, which I hadn't taken off despite everything. "I'm happy to date you as long as you need, and I'm perfectly willing to propose again when you're ready. But I want to know where we are in our relationship."

"Samuel, you don't need to propose again." I chuckled. "Your first proposal couldn't have been any more perfect."

He smiled radiantly and swooped in for another kiss, but I stopped him with a finger over his lips. "Just so you know, though, we're going to have a *long* engagement."

He laughed, his eyes sparkling with love. "Natalie, I've waited a decade for you. Now that I know you're going to be mine, I'm fine waiting for you as long as you want."

We shared another short, sweet kiss.

"Since we're officially engaged now, shall we go tell our families?" I asked.

Samuel nodded, and we stood up from the couch. Samuel tucked a strand of hair behind my ear while I smoothed out his Henley. Then, together we walked hand in hand, leaving the bright sunroom.

We followed the faint hum of talking all the way to the formal dining room. Samuel's Aunt Jamie and Uncle Charles must have arrived at some point, as they were both there, handing out bottles of champagne, while Mom and Dad chatted animatedly with Estelle. The once-bitter enemies, the Manns and Warners, were now laughing together like old friends.

"Look who's here!" Keely shouted, drawing the attention of the entire room.

The laughter died down, and all eyes were on us. I glanced at Samuel, who smiled down at me and squeezed my hand.

"Well?" Grandma Mann demanded. "What's the status?"

Grinning, Samuel held up my left hand, the diamond-and-emerald engagement ring sparkling under the soft light.

"Who wants to help plan a wedding?" I asked.

The room erupted in cheers and excited chatter. Mom screamed in glee, grabbing Estelle's hands and yanking them up and down. Estelle's initial surprise quickly turned into pure happiness as she joined my mother, her usual reserve melting away.

Jenna, tears streaming down her face, snuggled into Owen, who playfully winked at me. Walter, ever the showman, popped a cork on a champagne bottle, sending foam spraying everywhere. Grandpa Mann, cradling a happy Chuck in his arms, shouted, "Congratulations, Nat and Sam!"

Isaac, standing closest to us, handed Samuel and me each a glass of champagne, his usually stoic face softening into a rare smile. "Congratulations on your transformation from enemies to engaged couple," he said.

"Thanks," Samuel said.

"Yeah, thank you for coming to get me, Isaac," I said.

"Of course. Anything for the town Romeo and Juliet." Isaac turned to face the room. "To our families!" he shouted.

"Hear! Hear!" Madison yelled.

Even Logan's ever-stony expression cracked into the tiniest of smiles.

As we all basked in the warmth of our newfound family unity, Samuel caught me off guard by pulling me into his arms and planting a surprise kiss on my lips.

The room erupted with whistles and laughter, but I barely noticed, too lost in the moment with him.

Epilogue

Natalie

Tip #33: *Remember to return to where it all started.*

"Before we move on to our next agenda item," I began, "once again I'd like to extend our sincerest thanks to Samuel Warner for Warner Print's generous donation to our organization this spring quarter."

I shuffled my papers, then rested my hands on top of the table before looking around at the handful of members of the Friends of the Library who had come to this month's meeting. My fellow members looked from me down the table to Samuel.

"Thank you, Natalie." Samuel leaned forward in his chair and gave me a smoldering smile. "As always, Warner Print is happy to support Fox Creek's public library."

I nodded and waited for Samuel to continue on and share where Warner Print wanted the money spent.

Samuel said nothing. He just kept smiling at me.

I shifted uneasily in my seat. "Samuel?"

"Yes, darling?"

I mashed my lips together and refrained from telling Samuel not to use pet names, because that was exactly what he wanted me to do. "Don't you remember?"

"Remember what?" Samuel asked.

"Warner Print is welcome to specify how they'd like us to use the funds," I said.

Samuel's eyebrows rose and he feigned surprise. "Right! I completely forgot about that part. Silly me!" His gray eyes twinkled as his flirty smile morphed into a smirk.

I yanked a stapled packet from a file folder I'd brought with me. "I am going to kill you."

"But baby doll, honey, light of my life, don't you want to spend extra time advising me how to spend the money?" Samuel asked.

I flung the packet of papers in his direction, and Samuel let them hit him in the face.

"Ow," he said.

"Sam." I stood up and planted my hands on the scratched table. "I swear on Warner Print that if you make this meeting go *any later*, I'm going to tell Estelle you asked to do the next round of wedding venue tours with her!"

One of the members whistled in admiration, and I heard more than one murmur about my dirty fighting tactics.

"You really want this meeting to end, huh?" Samuel said.

I stared at him. "Don't you?"

"No," Samuel said. "Because I'm not all that interested in sharing you for the rest of the evening."

"For cryin' out loud." Marjorie rolled her eyes. "I know

you're terrible with romance, Warner, but this takes the cake. If this is how you're going to proceed with your flirting, I suggest you wait until *after* you marry her, or she might rethink your engagement!"

Samuel idly tapped the packet of papers I'd flung at him. "Are you saying that to give me genuine advice, or are you saying that because you're also going to our engagement party after this meeting and you know Grandma Mann is running a bingo tournament?"

"Both," Marjorie said.

I massaged my forehead. "I'm a sucker for punishment. That's the only explanation."

Samuel stood up and made his way down to my end of the table. "Sorry, Nat. I couldn't help razzing you one last time." He kissed me on the right temple. "Warner Print would like the money to go to the roof replacement fund. Hopefully by the time of the next meeting, you'll be a Warner so *you* can represent Warner Print." He took my left hand and held it out so the Friends of the Library members could admire his grandmother's diamond-and-emerald ring on my finger.

"That's not happening," I dryly said. "Not only would it be a conflict of interest, but we have monthly meetings, and we aren't getting married until fall!"

Samuel sighed. "I can always hope that you'll fall victim to my pleading, can't I?" He leaned over and kissed me full on the lips in a heart-pounding moment that felt so good it made my toes curl in my shoes.

Propriety said I should pull back and end the kiss as we were in public, so it was a good thing I was a Mann, as we have no shame!

Samuel started to pull back, and I found myself chasing his lips, reluctant to let the moment end. The meeting room faded away, and all I could focus on were the feelings of his hand on my waist and his lips against mine.

Just months ago, the idea of Samuel Warner kissing me in public would have been laughable. Now, it felt as natural as breathing. We'd changed from enemies—well, *I* had thought we were enemies—to reluctant coconspirators in a fake relationship, to being in love and engaged.

"Natalie Mann," Marjorie said, her voice dripping with disgust. "I demand you stop making out with your fiancé and end this meeting now! Rumor has it Estelle Warner is providing some wine for the bingo tournament, and I won't miss it just because you two have a decade of PDAs to get caught up on!"

I laughed against Samuel's mouth before I finally pushed him away. "OK, OK. We'll save it for the party."

Samuel sighed. "I suppose I can wait that long," he announced to the room before again leaning into my space and whispering in my ear. "I love you, Natalie Mann."

When he started to pull away I grabbed him by the lapels of his suit coat. "And I love you, Samuel Warner."

Samuel stared at me with smoldering eyes, and I awkwardly cleared my throat before reluctantly turning my attention back to the meeting. "OK. The last item on our agenda: picking a date for the summer book sale!"

Epilogue

Samuel

Tip #34: *Live happily ever after!*

The soft glow of fairy lights illuminated Warner Print's campus cafeteria, turning it from a modern but tastefully elegant lobby into a romantic oasis. Long tables draped in white linens were adorned with vibrant floral arrangements from McBride Farm & Greenhouse, and fanciful balloon arches lined the walls, bringing spots of color to our engagement party. My heart swelled with happiness as I watched my beautiful fiancée mingle with my family.

Natalie had changed into a stunning black cocktail gown after the Friends of the Library meeting, showcasing her slender figure. She laughed, her expressive green eyes sparkling as she chatted with my grandfather, Jenna, and Owen.

"Congratulations on the engagement, Sam." Isaac raised his beer bottle in salute as he approached me. "For real this time, huh?"

"Thanks. I couldn't have done it without your help in making up with Natalie." I paused, then added, "I'm grateful to both our families for forgiving us for the lies and supporting our real relationship."

"Of course, I'd support you. We're twins." Isaac took a sip of his beer, then added, "I'm happy for both you and Natalie, but especially for you since you've been hopelessly in love for so long."

I sheepishly chuckled. "Yeah. I sometimes worry this is all a dream. Despite all my plans and hopes, I was losing faith I'd ever win Nat over."

"Let's be real. You never stood a chance," Isaac informed me with all the emotion of a rock. "It was Natalie who you fell in love with, so you needed her cooperation to get anywhere, particularly since you were indescribably bad at flirting with her."

"That's probably true."

Our conversation fell silent, and we turned our attention to the bingo tournament unfolding on the far side of the room. Grandma Mann and Mother had taken charge. Grandma Mann called out numbers with the gusto of a TV host and had somehow convinced Mother to act as a model of sorts and run the bingo machine. Mother pulled a selected bingo ball from the hopper and placed it on the ball tray with fancy flourishes while Grandma Mann barked at Uncle Mike that he couldn't play on his card and his children's abandoned cards at the same time.

I watched for a few moments before my gaze wandered from the chaotic bingo game to Natalie. She had parted with Grandfather, Jenna, and Owen and now was chatting with some of her coworkers.

Isaac took another sip of his beer. "You know, I'm surprised Connor and Max managed to clear their schedules and fly in for the party." He gestured in the direction of our cousins. (Connor was playing bingo with great determination. He made for an amusing picture, as he was seated between Marjorie and Natalie's Great Aunt Irma. Max was in the karaoke corner, belting out a Disney song that had the kids jumping around.)

"Really? You're surprised, even though you've been nothing but nosy since Natalie and I first announced we were dating?" I wryly asked.

Isaac shrugged. "I'm your twin. And I was shocked you'd managed to keep the biggest win of your life silent—which is why I wasn't *that* surprised when I found out the whole thing was originally fake."

"Connor and Max feel similarly. Connor told me they wanted to see for themselves that Natalie actually loved me and that I wasn't paying her or blackmailing her."

Isaac nodded. "That sounds like them. They're coming to Mother's for brunch tomorrow, correct?"

"Yeah. Natalie insisted." I sighed.

Isaac raised his beer bottle in a toast. "Good luck."

My attention strayed back to Natalie. "Thanks."

Isaac shifted. "And with my well wishes communicated, I think I'm going to call it a night."

"Really?" I asked, surprised. "Why?"

"I've had my fill of people for the day," Isaac dryly said. "Besides, there's no point in hanging around you when all you're going to do is gawk at your fiancée."

I laughed. "Fair enough."

Charlotte, Isaac's brilliant assistant, must have read Isaac's mood, because she headed our way with a businesslike smile. "Good evening, Samuel. Congratulations again on your happy engagement."

"Thanks, Charlotte."

"Of course." Charlotte pivoted to Isaac. "Is it time to leave?"

"Yes," Isaac said. "You're coming," he stated more than asked.

"Yes, but we need to say goodbye to Natalie first," Charlotte said.

"Why?" Isaac asked. "She's not going to notice I'm gone with most of the town here."

"You need to be polite to your future sister-in-law," Charlotte said, cementing her role as Isaac's unofficial social director.

"I suppose you're right. Let's go say our goodbyes." Isaac affectionately squeezed my shoulder. "Good night, Sam. Enjoy your night."

"Good night, Isaac." I slapped his back. "And thanks. Don't go back to work, OK?"

"Right, right."

Isaac offered his arm to Charlotte, and the duo strolled off in Natalie's direction.

A screech of a microphone followed by a yelp and then a chorus of giggles snapped me out of my reverie. Turning toward the source of the commotion, I got to see Ryan—who'd been purposely singing a Christmas carol off-key, crouched on the ground by the microphone and theatrically crying while Keely, Anna, and Noah threw balloons at him.

"Such harsh critics! I am wounded!" Ryan shouted.

Chuck barked and ran back and forth between Ryan and the kids, jumping and snapping at the balloons and occasionally crashing into Ryan in the process.

Watching the chaos unfold, I felt like the luckiest man alive. Everything that had led to this moment with Natalie seemed almost too good to be true.

"Are you having fun?" Natalie asked as she approached me, her eyes sparkling with mischief.

"Of course." I snuck an arm around Natalie's waist and pulled her flush against my chest. "How could I not be when I'm engaged to the most amazing woman in the world?"

Natalie blushed, her cheeks turning an adorable shade of pink. I gave in to my desire and slowly and reverently kissed Natalie. Having her in my arms, her lips molding to mine as she stood on tiptoe to twine her arms around my neck, I felt more content than I'd ever been in my life.

Madison gave a wolf whistle as she sauntered past us. "Aww, seeing you two kiss almost makes me forget about Nat's once dearly held annual tradition of smashing a pie in your face during the Fox Creek summer fair!"

Natalie pulled back from our kiss. "Thank you, peanut gallery, for your unwanted comments."

Madison winked. "Oh, I'm just getting started! Wait until the toasts start, then I'm going to bust out the story about that time Samuel bid on the mayor-for-a-day experience the city auctioned off for the playground fundraiser and he made you follow him around for the whole day." Madison thoughtfully tapped her chin. "You know, in hindsight it's really obvious Samuel had a thing for you, Nat, once you understand just how poor his communication skills are."

"Thanks, Madison," I dryly said. "I do so look forward to becoming related to you once Nat and I are married."

Natalie chuckled as she rested her head on my chest.

The room buzzed with conversation and laughter, creating a festive atmosphere as we took in the sights and sounds of our friends, family, and the residents of Fox Creek enjoying our engagement party.

"I love you, Samuel," Natalie whispered as she leaned back just enough to look up at me, her smile warm with affection.

"I love you too, Natalie," I murmured back, my heart swelling with love.

A Guide to Fake Dating Your Enemy

"I've got it!" Madison announced—she apparently hadn't felt like she'd been obnoxious enough already. "You two should write a book: *A Guide to Fake Dating Your Enemy*!"

The End

Natalie and Samuel's story might be over, but I wrote a special bonus epilogue just for you! To read it, all you need to do is signup for my newsletter using this form:
https://nikkibright.kit.com/bonus

Afterword

The next book in this series will tell the story of Samuel's twin brother, Isaac, and it will be available in April of 2025. I can't wait to share it with you!